Juniors

Also by Kaui Hart Hemmings

House of Thieves

The Descendants

The Possibilities

KAUI HART HEMMINGS

G. P. Putnam's Sons

An Imprint of Penguin Group (USA)

G. P. Putnam's Sons
Published by the Penguin Group
Penguin Group (USA) LLC
375 Hudson Street
New York, NY 10014

USA | Canada | UK | Ireland | Australia
New Zealand | India | South Africa | China
penguin.com
A Penguin Random House Company

Library of Congress Cataloging-in-Publication Data
Hemmings, Kaui Hart.
Juniors / Kaui Hart Hemmings.
pages cm
Summary: Seventeen-year-old Lea Lane must navigate a complex web of friendships and relationships after she and her mother move into the guest cottage of the fabulously wealthy West family in Honolulu.
[1. Interpersonal relations—Fiction. 2. Friendship—Fiction. 3. Wealth—Fiction. 4. High schools—Fiction. 5. Schools—Fiction. 6. Hawaii—Fiction.] I. Title.
PZ7.1.H46Ju 2015 [Fic]—dc23 2014040377

Printed in the United States of America.
ISBN 978-0-399-17360-8
1 3 5 7 9 10 8 6 4 2

Design by Marikka Tamura.
Text set in Minion Pro.

For Leo and Eleanor

1

THE PUNAHOU PEER COUNSELORS ARE TRYING TO LEAD a gym full of juniors on a "truth walk." Our ethics classes merged, so about fifty of us are against the wall of the gym, waiting to do whatever our peers have planned so we can be on our way to fulfilling our Spiritual, Ethical, Community Responsibility requirement for our spring semester. Sheri Ho stands before us in jean shorts that barely pass dress code. She's a senior, cute and well-liked, but not cool. I think to be cool at Punahou, you have to drink (but not too much) and hook up (but not too much). As a peer counselor who wears a platinum promise ring, she does neither. But maybe I'm wrong about what "cool" is. There are so many variations here. It's like looking at a menu for shave ice. Countless flavors and colors; even weird-sounding things like pickled mango or green tea can be really good and popular.

My mom and I moved here in December, and I started mid-junior year, which I think is totally rare. So, two months at this place, but it may as well be my first day. I've adjusted to some things—the academics, how much harder it is than my last school—the offerings and choices, the campus itself, which is the size of a university. It's the biggest private school in the US.

I've been playing catch-up socially too, scoping things out, getting the lay of the humid Hawaiian land. I feel like a surveyor or a pioneer, trying to know the ground I'm standing on and figure out where to stake my flag and settle. My mother grew up here, so we've visited a lot, but being a visitor is very different from living in Hawaii, especially when you're going to high school.

Sheri whistles, then speaks in a loud, cheerleader-like voice. "Okay, gang. Settle in, settle down." Four other counselors stand by her, moving to some kind of imaginary music, but now that the group has quieted down I realize music really is playing. *My milkshake brings all the boys to the yard.*

"Get all the way against the wall," she yells. "I'm talking to you, Cici; you, Jim; you, Shasha—up against the wall!"

I scan my classmates, the many flavors of them, waiting to begin. I guess in some way this is like any high school in America, little sects in a big congregation—the football players, the drama kids, the ROTCs, the mushers (what skaters and stoners are called here). In Hawaii there are surfers, paddlers, water polo players. At Storey, my school in San Francisco, there were only a few surfers and other groups that were more defined and permanent, like, "we're the sailor yacht club kids!" People here seem to venture out of their groups.

Pete Weiner (pronounced *Whiner* not *Weener,* though I'm not sure what I'd choose between the two) is standing to my right, and I can tell he's looking at me, waiting for me to acknowledge him. He has a football-shaped head and an expression that makes him look constantly on the verge of a sneeze. He's in my ethics class, and for some reason he's always sharing his asides. I figure I'm sort of like a test dummy. If I laugh, great, he'll shop his joke around. If I don't laugh, then at least he doesn't embarrass himself because who cares what Lea Lane thinks? Who's Lea Lane anyhow? Random-ass transfer student. At least in Hawaii people pronounce my name right—Lea like *Lei-a.* Not *Lee-a.*

"This song is so lame," he says. "'Her milkshake brings all the boys to the yard'? Sounds like she has a yeast infection."

"I don't get it," I say, hating that this guy feels so comfortable with me.

"Yeah, neither do I," he says.

I kick the toe of my shoe into the glassy floor, then stop when I remember we aren't supposed to wear black-soled shoes in the gym. I've been hyperalert to the rules, not wanting to draw attention to myself, which is pretty easy in a junior class of four hundred and four, and a school of almost four thousand students. It's hard to insert yourself so late in the game. I've planned to lay low—Lea low—head down, graduate, move on. But these past few weeks, I don't know, I'm lonely. I want to look around. I want to step more into the radar, get pulled over. Something, anything. In situations like this, or in chapel surrounded by so many students, I feel like if I vanished, if I melted into the floor, no one would notice I was gone. I'm getting bored being so quiet. I was quiet at my last school. Maybe I could reinvent myself, or at least remodel? Take the blank slate and mark it up.

"Okay, let's do this!" Sheri yells, and I laugh to myself at her crazed enthusiasm. "Remember. This is a safe zone. Nothing you do or say leaves this room. There are no teachers here, no parents. This is our time to *get real.*"

"I want to have sex with you, Sheri!" Jim yells. "Honestly. For real!"

All of Jim's "boys" erupt into laughter, except Mike Matson, who looks like he's being tethered by his girlfriend, Maile Beaucage. Her name always makes me think of a flower in a handsome jail, and whenever they hold hands, he seems to look at his group of friends longingly, like they're leaving on a booze cruise without him. Those boys are all dressed in T-shirts with surf logos, baggy shorts, caps worn low or backwards. They make the boys from my old school look like they're dressed to clock in at Google. I want to be over there, not over here. I want them to see me laughing.

"Okay, boys," Sheri says. "Settle down 'cause we're about to get internally rowdy. We're going to find out what's inside of us."

Our regular teacher isn't here, since we're about to get internally rowdy, but I wonder if Ms. Wood is hiding under the bleachers, trying to get glimpses into the real lives of teenagers. The peer counselors are giving us a sneak preview of things they do during Camp Paumalu, a four-day lovefest of trust falls and cathartic crying. I hear you do things like write a problem on a slab of wood, then punch through it karate-style while listening to "Eye of the Tiger."

"There are no winners in this race," Sheri says. "I'll be asking questions, and some of you will walk, and some of you won't. Everyone will get to the other side in the place that matters." She thumps her chest with a closed fist.

"Now. I want you to take five steps if, within this past month, you've made someone feel good!"

I immediately look to the pack of guys, and they're all smiling as if they've done something sexual. Poor Sheri. The land of innuendos is boundless. I'd say mostly the entire group walks—it's a pretty open-ended question.

"Now. Boo." Sheri makes an exaggerated sad face with a duck-lipped pout. "Walk if you've done something that made someone feel bad. Awesome," she says, as the bulk of the group takes a timid stroll. "It's okay. Own those steps. No judgment."

I walk, only because everyone else is and I don't want to be left behind.

"Walk if you've done something you're ashamed of."

"I just sharted," Jim says. "I'll take a walk."

Everyone laughs. I can't imagine a girl saying that, but if one did, I'm sure I'd like her. I walk, ashamed that girl can't be me, that I can only be funny on the inside.

"Now walk if you've recently said something behind someone's back," Sheri says.

Almost everyone walks again—with a collective sensation of relief, I think. This is easy and not too deep, like a trailer for a drama. I stay where I am. I haven't spoken behind anyone's back recently, not because I'm above such things, but because I don't have people to air my gripes to. Besides Danny, I don't really socialize with anyone. I like girls from my classes, but feel like I have a kind of guest membership with them, and honestly, I like them just because they're there. They're the ones I've seen so far, but I keep looking for more. My old friends were into debate club, cross-country, and pizza parties. On this campus, I overhear girls walking to classes or at paddling practice—*shut up, omg shut up. I know, right?* and admit I've stood before my bathroom mirror, imitating not just their words, but their inflections. *Shawt up, oh ma huw, shawt up. I knew, righta?* and not knowing if I'm making fun of them or wanting to be them.

I guess I'm not being very honest with this exercise. While I don't talk badly about people, I think badly about them. I take five steps.

"Walk if you've smoked a cigarette," one of the other counselors says.

Ross Shetland laughs and runs his five steps. A few others follow suit, but not many. We're a pot generation. Cigarettes are bad for you.

"Walk if you've lied to a friend."

I walk.

I've lied to friends. In second grade, I told Crystal Watanabe I had a monkey, and to every friend I had in San Francisco I said I was excited to move to Hawaii. I'm sure there have been countless fibs and exaggerations, but too harmless to remember here.

Innocent questions like these keep coming, and then we move to more difficult terrain.

"Walk if your parents are divorced," Sheri says. She looks like she's going to break into a sad song.

I walk, then stop myself. My dad left before I was born. My parents were never married, and my mother hardly knew him. I've never met him and probably never will. His name is Ray Piston aka Stranger Dad. The story I've been told is that he was handsome, arrogant, entitled. This part of my life has become like a fairy tale, something I know by heart and that seems like a fantasy.

My mom was taken with his swagger and young enough to

overlook the rest. He was visiting from New York, where he had a job in the hotel industry. He seemingly had very little to do, but made a lot of money doing it. Before him she had been in a quiet relationship—stable, sweet, good, but after she graduated from UCLA and came home to Hawaii, they broke up. She and Ray dated that summer, exclusively on her part, and not so exclusively on his, which she found out later. He did all the things she never thought she wanted or needed—gifts, dinners, trips, jewelry—and his reaction to her getting pregnant?

"Fabulous," he had said. "Now this is getting fun."

And then he left when my mom was six months pregnant, and she hasn't seen him since. What a guy.

He lives in Paris now. Done. For a long time I wanted to know him, to know my roots, but the more my mom told me, the less interested I became. At the Outrigger Canoe Club, where they hung out, he made the waitresses bring his meals over to him on the beach where he sunbathed by a canoe. Now when I think of him, I imagine a man dallying about Paris, making waitresses schlep up the Eiffel Tower to serve him croissants.

I've Googled him, of course, read his business profile, articles about legal battles with his properties. I've seen pictures of him at various charity events, posing with the same expression—like he's about to call out across the room to a pal. He looks handsome, smart, both careful and careless. His connection to me seems unreal, like I'm looking at a celebrity. I'm not his, and he's not mine. I kind of hate him.

"Walk if you've been cruel to someone you love," Sheri says.

Everyone walks; most heads are down. Pete Weiner has a little psycho smirk on his face. Mike Matson looks contemplative.

I walk too. I've been mean to my mom and to Lo, my best friend in San Francisco. Sometimes you're just mean to the people you love the most. You know you'll get a pass.

"Walk if someone you love has been cruel to you."

I walk. My San Francisco friends left my good-bye sushi dinner after an hour so they could go to Fletcher Ronson Jr.'s party. I saw the Instagram posts the next day in Honolulu. Girls are the cruelest.

"Walk if you've ever felt neglected," Sheri says in a solemn voice.

I walk into the pity party. I've been neglected my whole life, even though my dad never seemed real enough to be able to neglect me. Oddly, I feel more neglected by my mother, who is always there. I can't pinpoint why I feel this way. Sometimes I interpret it not as neglect, but as too much trust in me, which I've come to dislike.

We moved because my mom got a part in a TV drama being shot here. *No Borders*, it's called, and the pilot airs in three weeks, right after spring break. She plays a surgeon, Samantha Lovejoy, who has come with a group of doctors whose mission is to help people on a remote island. They fight, fall in love, doctor, and have lots of downtime to do montaged activities and enact overly complicated methods of revenge. My mom has a leading role, which is many steps up from her prior gigs, mainly nonrecurring parts in sitcoms and minor roles in movies—very minor—not even the best friend, but the acquaintance or the quirky secretary or a shop owner. She's done tons of commercials, both as an actor and a voice (chicken wings, deodorant, car insurance, Quilted Northern). I know I'm lucky. She could be insecure and envious, tormented, egotistical, like so many people in her business. Instead she's just happy for work.

Yes, I feel neglect, I feel it by looking around the room. I'm neglected by people who don't know they're wanted in the first place, by people who don't know my name, who possibly never will, even though I know all of theirs—first and last. But whose fault is that? It's my own. I'm getting closer to the middle now, to Sheri and the other counselors.

This question of neglect and the tougher ones that follow are making people look straight ahead, their faces dulling a bit. *Walk if you are afraid. Walk if you think people don't really know who you are. Walk if you love someone who doesn't love you back. Walk if you've been used or humiliated.* Everyone looks at Mia and Pua, two of the many girls whose Snapchat nude pictures were traded by boys who called themselves the Pokemon Trading Club. The boys were all expelled the second week I got here.

Walk if you feel that you'll never have enough. Walk if you do things to feel good that aren't good for you. Walk if these things make you feel worse. These questions resonate inside us, triggering our brains to remember things specific or vague, which can be harder—not having a thing to stick a pin into.

Ross and Jim aren't making jokes after every question anymore, and the cluster of girls has been separated by their differing answers. The majority of the group is well ahead of me, which makes me feel boring. I need to steal, cheat, gossip, do drugs, text someone pictures of my boobs. Beside and behind me are the people I expect to see: Mark Lam, Mark Lum, Geoff Davenport, Sylvia Moncrief, the ballerinas, but then I see someone only a few steps ahead whose presence surprises me: Whitney. Beautiful, blessed Whitney West, daughter of a hotelier; she's like Hawaii's Paris Hilton. I make eye contact with her. She has never spoken to me before, even though our mothers are friends and my mom and her dad both went to Punahou.

Mom and the Wests have kept in touch, though it seems that Melanie's fondness for my mom is proportionate to my mom's success. A stint in a sitcom: Melanie West calls. A commercial for Crest Whitening Strips: not so much.

Now, for example, with a show set in Hawaii on the brink of its debut, Melanie is a close, close, super-close friend.

When my mom and I visited my grandparents—who passed away four and seven years ago—Melanie would have her come to dinner parties. She was Melanie's actress friend. I was never invited (rich people seem to have a no-kids rule), and my mom would come home feeling slightly proud and slightly degraded.

"I'm kind of like a circus monkey," she once said, having had to perform one-liners all night about the famous people she has come across in her career.

Whitney looks back and smiles at me, just slightly. I can't tell if it's a smile recognizing our family connection or if it's a kind of sly grin, telling me she's lying and she shouldn't be so far behind. Why is she so far behind? Is she not as experienced as I'd imagine her to be? Or maybe she's back here because nothing bad can touch her.

Her brother, Will, is a senior. He's her male equivalent, looks-wise, yet even more large and magnetic, pristine. My first week of school, I happened to pass him, thinking that he'd know who I was because of my mom. "Hey," I managed to say. He looked at me as though he wasn't sure if I'd spoken or burped, and he kept on walking.

"Walk if you feel like you're living your life to its fullest potential," Sheri says in a soft voice.

I don't move. Whitney doesn't either. Of course we don't. We're seventeen. I hope to God this isn't my fullest potential.

On the other side of the partition, I hear the dribbling of basketballs and feel like our little world is being intruded upon. Sheri turns the music up.

"Now," Sheri says, "walk if you've ever done anything illegal."

An easy one. Mostly everyone walks. I'm sure we've all had a drink, even the peer counselors.

"This week," Sheri says. "Walk if you've done something illegal this week."

It's Tuesday. I rack my brain for something, anything. Jaywalking perhaps, not using my blinker. Other people walk, and they all happen to be good-looking, as if only beautiful people can have such bad fun. They're looking around with smirks on their faces. What have they done? I have always known that my life was a little predictable, but for the first time, I see it as totally disappointing. Whitney walks. I'm farther behind her now. What has she done in just two days? Mike turns around and gives her a knowing look that I don't think anyone else was supposed to see. I want to walk too. I want to seem interesting. No—I want to *be* interesting. This *is* a race, and I am far behind. And then I remember something. I guess it's not technically illegal, but whatever—it's against the rules. I proudly take five steps. I'm in the gym, and I'm wearing black-soled shoes.

• • •

When I get home my mom tells me something that brings me back to today's exercise, our crossing. I think of what I had felt during the truth walk—wanting a change, wanting something, anything, wanting to belong here, to just speak up. For me, it wasn't about getting real and confessing, it was seeing what little there was to be said.

When my mom tells me what's about to happen I experience a rush and then a kind of crushing. I'm stunned into silence—the what, why, when, whaaaat???? of it all stuck to my dumb tongue.

My mom tells me we're moving to 4461 Kahala Avenue. The home of Whitney West.

2

I IMMEDIATELY HAD TO GET ON MY BIKE AND RIDE OUT of Enchanted Lakes to clear my head. I rode through the other sections of Kailua, a town I know and love. I can't say that I love our house, though. I ride back into our neighborhood and park my cruiser in the carport and look at our dark town house, which sits alongside a canal that I believe to be a source of diseased tilapia and staph infections. According to my mom, we will move to a three-bedroom cottage on a thirty-thousand-square-foot lot right on the ocean. White sand, palm trees, disease-free fish.

Our current neighbors are a single mom with a red-faced toddler who is always screaming and beating his chest and, on the left, Dr. Rocker, a sex therapist for paraplegics. Our new neighbors will be less visible. I've already looked them up. On the right: Stanton Ichinose, founder of a hospital supply company and a recent addition to the Forbes list of world billionaires. To the left: Stavros Angelopoulos, a money manager known as "the Greek," who just purchased the home (his third) for a bargain at twenty-one million.

Moving into a new home bought with my mom's hard-earned money would sound awesome to me, but the thought of living in Whitney's cottage? I may as well go the cafeteria, put on a hairnet, and serve her two scoops of rice.

I walk in. My mom's in the kitchen, packing up a box. Her phone is docked and playing music—the poor sound quality is something she doesn't mind, but it drives me bonkers.

"You're packing already?" I ask. "You just told me two hours ago. I went for a ride, remember? To clear my head before getting more details. Now I need to reclear!"

"You don't need to reclear," she says, looking at me as if I'm joking around and not being completely heartfelt. Her smile is wide and filled with nice square teeth. She has a face that's calming. I don't know how she isn't some megastar. She's beautiful in this effortless and blooming way that makes me stare sometimes as if I don't know her at all.

"I just got inspired to organize," she says. She flips her hair back and rolls her head from side to side.

I look around at the stained carpet and worn armchairs that were here before we moved in. The chairs are covered with our things.

"There are *boxes*," I say. "I see boxes."

"May as well get started," she says. "The cottage is open, and we pay month-to-month here. Plus, it's kind of hard to know you're going somewhere but not heading there, right?" She ponders a spatula, the slightly melted plastic, and puts it aside. "This is crazy," she says, but in a way where "crazy" means exciting and not insane. She looks at me for confirmation, but I don't give her any, so she looks away, still smiling to herself.

I get a glass of water, wishing I had those poetry magnets to try to describe what I'm feeling with a limited choice of words.

I look at the small TV as if someone on it could help me out. The redheaded woman on the screen says she's going to stick it to cancer.

"How was school?" my mom asks. Her innocent everyday question has no place here, and how does one ever answer that question in ways other than "good" or "okay" or by shrugging?

"It was somewhat taxing," I say. "I was nervous walking by this group of guys. They just sit in this spot, looking really bored, and I have to walk by them every day to get to biology."

My mom keeps sorting through utensils and cookware.

"Biology was kind of fun," I say. "We dissected a frog—I thought it would come shrink-wrapped like bacon the way they did at Storey, but Punahou doesn't use real frogs. They use a frog app, so we dissected on our laptops."

"Cool," she says, though I could have said "I have herpes" and elicited the same response.

"Creative writing was creative," I continue. "Our teacher is kind of lame. I think he wants to be like a movie teacher—you know, all irreverent and inspiring—but it just makes him look like a tool. I ate a papaya and a Dove bar and some sushi at the snack bar. And in ethical responsibility, we did an exercise that had the ironic effect of making me want to be more unethical."

My mom sifts through a drawer. I'm always super detailed as punishment for her asking me how school was, but she keeps asking and, as far as I can tell, she listens here and there. I try to catch her tuning out.

I walk around to get air in my shirt—it's so hot in here, and I'm sweaty from the bike ride. I can't help but feel thrilled that we're leaving. We've always known we wouldn't stay in this condo, so we never bothered to make it our own. My mom's been keeping an eye out for rentals in Maunawili, or something in town. I'm not sure how we could have made this our own, anyway. It seems designed for anonymity.

"I jumped off the roof of the gym into the pool," I say. "Herpes."

She throws some plastic spoons into the trash. "Are you swimming for PE?"

Caught her.

"How was *your* day?" I ask. "Any other news? Or just that we're moving in with strangers."

"They're not strangers," she says and runs her hand through her hair. "The Wests are longtime friends."

It's funny how my mom's voice takes on a Hawaiian lilt at times. I sit on a bar stool and drum my fingers against the counter. "I'm not understanding how all this happened. Melanie just asked if you wanted to live in their cottage, and you said yes?" I'm hoping the repeated verbalization will make it seem less bizarre.

"Yes," my mom says. "That's what happened." She looks like she's holding back laughter.

"Why would she ask? How did it even come up?"

Since we got here, it seems like my mom is constantly taking calls from or going to events with Melanie. With dogs, you multiply their ages by seven to get the human equivalent. It seems like for minor celebrities, when they come to Hawaii, their celebrity also multiplies by seven. San Francisco society couldn't care less about my mom, but here she's on what I call the charity circuit—going to fashion shows and dinners that benefit the arts or kids with diseases. She chaired some kind of Oscar party, which even she found to be ridiculous. Dentists and lawyers came out and walked a red carpet in their finery, all styled for the grand occasion of watching the Oscars on TV.

"It just . . . came up," my mom says. I spin on my stool, and she goes through the cabinet with the pots and pans. "She knew we wanted a new place. She was telling me to look in town, that everything was happening on her side. Then she kind of lit up and said we may as well use her cottage, because it's just sitting there. And I guess it made sense. We've been wanting to get out of here, and you know her—you can't mention anything without her texting solutions and offers, I swear."

She places the cookie sheets on the counter.

"No, I *don't* know her," I say. "I don't know her at all. How much is rent?"

"Do you think we'll need all of these pots?" she asks.

I don't care about the pots. Kahala is like the equivalent of the Presidio or Nob Hill. I remember a sixth-grade sleepover at my friend Ashley's in the Presidio. Her house was supposedly inspired by a castle in France. Her mother told me to make myself at home. I stood on the cold marble floors, looked up at the grand staircase and the chandelier, and thought, *I don't know how to do that.*

My mom tucks her hair behind her ear. "So, she won't let me pay rent."

"What?" I automatically think of the charity circuit.

"I know, it's crazy," she says off my look. "But I'll try anyway. I offered to cook for them—"

"What? That's ridiculous—like an employee?"

She resumes her packing, gathering kitchenware and putting it into a box, her hair falling back in front of her eyes. "No, no, not like that. Just as a friend. A friendly neighbor. You know I love cooking."

"Is this some kind of pity party? Should I wear ripped clothes and hold out a tin cup?"

She stops packing, finally stops moving and avoiding the sight of me—my slumped shoulders and questioning face.

"It saves money and gives us a place before I decide if we can make living in Hawaii permanent. Who knows if the show will get renewed, and if it doesn't, then we'll be staying anyway so you can finish school." She blows out a puff of air. "Plus, it will be fun." She holds out her fists in a kind of cheering move. "It's beautiful, there's a pool, surf, it's closer to school, closer to everything, and you know the kids, right? They're nice kids, aren't they? It will be a good thing. Really great."

I don't say anything to her or her happy little fists, but my first feeling is of anger toward her versus empathy when she said it would save money. I don't expect a lot, but sometimes all I want is an unawareness of money matters. I feel that I know too much.

I know that this week, Times has zucchini for $1.49 a pound, which is less than the farmers' market on Thursday. I know that this week Foodland has the cheapest cabbage, and Safeway has blueberries that are buy one get one free.

I know tuition at Punahou is expensive and renting is outrageous, and I know that my mom does pretty much everything on her own. I've never been denied anything. Gymnastics, ballet, tap, musical theater, piano, ukulele, a brief stint on the bass guitar, ski trips, after-school care, art, private school, car. I've done and still do it all, but am always aware of her working for it and working alone. Maybe this is how all kids with single parents feel.

And so I don't say that this arrangement, especially if she cooks, makes her seem like a live-in maid, because I'm sure this has already crossed her mind. I think when people see my mom on TV, they figure we're super wealthy. She has access, she looks the part, but she's in—not *of*—a certain world.

"Just have Stranger Dad send some money," I say.

When I asked once how she affords private school, she said he's helped a bit with tuition when needed. She ignores my suggestion.

"Melanie's excited. She says Whitney adores you."

"I've never spoken to Whitney in my life." I open the freezer and grab a Popsicle, which makes me feel like a little kid.

"Well, she thinks you and Whitney will really get along. It'll be fun. I promise. And Melanie says to use the pool, come over for barbecues, dinner. She says whenever we want we can sit with the family."

For some reason, this makes me tear up a bit, and I'm not sure why. Is it because I could sit with my mother and the family and I'm happy, or is it because I'd be allowed to sit with my mother and the family and this is tin-cup humiliating?

"We'll have our own space though, right?" I say. "So we won't be sitting with them anyway." I take the wrapper off the grape Popsicle and sit back down.

She doesn't answer me, knowing I'm getting worked up. I'm chewing my Popsicle like a rabbit.

"I'm not going," I say, but she doesn't stop packing, which makes my heart beat fast, like I'm fighting with someone who won't hit back. We both know it's a pitiful threat.

"When are we going?" I mumble.

"We can move in now," she says. "This week. Tomorrow."

She won't look at me. *Look at me,* I want to say.

I don't understand my anger completely. I'm angry that what we have isn't good enough. I'm angry that I have so much and don't have a thing.

"It will be a good change for you," my mom says. "Something different from Enchanted Lakes."

I know she's implying I have nothing to lose. She knows my daily routine and knows I won't be leaving or giving up very much. Plucking me out of what's familiar could only be for the best. I have no attachments here. My mom's life is the one that matters.

I look out at the canal through the living room window. Across the water is the shirtless man smoking a cigarette and rubbing his hard, round stomach. There is nothing enchanted about this lake, but I'll miss the town, Kailua, the way I feel at ease here. It's a place I could see myself growing into, tailoring it to fit.

I like my routines, even though they're pretty solo—biking on the path by the marsh, the sounds of the birds and my tires on the gravel, the light shooting through the clouds and spilling over the Ko'olaus down onto the expanse of the Kawainui grass. Walking up to the Lanikai pillboxes, looking out at the windward coast and down at Waimanalo, which from that distance looks vacant and wild. Some days I walk with Danny up to the Pali Lookout, and we're often the only ones on the trail until we get to the top and are joined by the people who come on tour buses. The wind is so strong at the top you can't hear anything but the sound of it, and you feel you'll be swept away. When I'm up there, I always think of my grandmother, who lived here all her life, driving to town on the old highway. I think of the battles fought in that very spot, battles to unite the island chain.

"My routines," I say. *I have a life here. Kind of.*

My mom looks up and sighs. "Be grateful. You can still do everything you ever did. We'll be half an hour away."

Then I'll be visiting someone else's backyard.

"You'll find other routines," she says. "Whitney will show you around, I'm sure."

"What a carrot," I say. "She'll show me around Kahala Mall? Or the Outrigger? Great."

"She's a nice girl," my mom says. "And what a beauty."

There's nothing that makes me feel worse than my mom complimenting another girl: it's less about her praising someone else than that she's suggesting I change or try harder. Whitney, hair the color of burnt butter, golden skin that's slightly freckled. If you described us, it would sound as though we looked alike, but the results of our similar traits are different. I feel like I don't wear my brown hair and brown eyes and petite frame as well as she does. I straighten, throw my shoulders back.

"She could help you meet people," my mom says. "You can't just tag along after Danny."

"I don't need to meet more people," I say. "And I don't tag along."

Danny's a childhood friend, and I don't tag along after him, no way. Do I? No. He wants me with him. He asks me to do stuff with him all the time.

"Anyway," she says, closing a box and giving it a tap. "That's the plan. That's what we're doing, so—"

"So we'll all be friends now? I'll meet tons of people and have tons of fun?" I'm embarrassed that my voice betrays me. It sounds hopeful and not sardonic, as I intended. That is her aspiration for me, and yes, fine, maybe it's mine too, but her desiring it makes me feel I'm lacking something I didn't know I needed. "Whatever," I say and throw out my wrapper, then walk to my room where I look in the mirror and see all the things I'm missing. I stick out my purple tongue.

3

ONE WEEK LATER, AND WE'VE PACKED UP OUR LITTLE lives just like that. On Saturday we take our first load over in my mom's car, going the long way through Waimanalo so we can stop by Danny's. It would have been more efficient to have brought my car too, but I didn't want to make the first trip alone.

The day is so clean and clear. The ocean glimmers along the coast. We get to see things here that people pay to see on their honeymoons. I automatically hear "Waimanalo Blues" in my head, a song Danny's dad, Toby, taught me on the ukulele. He's an attorney, but he performs sometimes at the resorts with his band.

"Do you see Danny at school?" my mom asks.

"Not that much," I say. "Sometimes we have lunch."

Since he's a childhood/summer-break/family friend, it's weird existing with him at school and in the real world. I'm seeing him in a new light and sometimes have an odd sensation of pride, as if seeing my kid all grown up. He's like a man now, this boy. Our mothers went to Punahou together and were close a long time ago, but not so much anymore. Auntie Stephanie. She moved to Maui after the divorce from Uncle Toby. When I visited in the summers, she'd take us to the crack seed store, and Danny and I would load up on li hing mui, kakimochi, tamarind wafers, and candy wrapped in rice paper that would dissolve in our mouths. I always remember this and also the summer we were twelve and would practice kissing on each other. We both pretend this has never happened, or maybe he has truly forgotten.

"I can't believe he's going to Berkeley," she says. "You're going to miss him."

Her smile is teasing and maddeningly infectious.

"What? Stop it." I hold down my grin.

"So cute," she says and looks at me like I'm heading off to prom.

"Oh my God, calm down."

We trail a truck with a bunch of shirtless kids in back. The truck is stenciled with a sexy woman and a tribute to a dead musician. The bulk of the land in Waimanalo belongs to Hawaiian homeland, so most of the residents are Hawaiian. It is definitely not the same here as it is in Kahala, though the landscape—its vibrant colors and defiant mountains—make it so much more beautiful and complex. That ocean is the most beautiful blue, like jewels underwater.

"Does he have a girlfriend?" my mom asks.

The thought makes me a little ill. It's like discussing a sibling or someone you don't really want to imagine being intimate with anyone. Danny and I have similar coloring, though I'm not as Hawaiian as he is, since my mom's only a quarter. I always imagine a nickel and a dime's worth of blood pinging through my body like a pinball. Danny's hapa—a bit of everything. His skin is the color of monkey pod tree bark. He has cheeks like mountain apples and brows that look almost penciled on. His body is something my mainland friends would freak out about. He's tan and sculpted but not in a gym-fit way. He looks like he could swim across a great channel.

"Ask him yourself," I say. I want to hear him answer no. I don't think we'd hang out if he had a girlfriend and wonder what this says about our friendship.

We stop in front of their house, which is always cheery, the yard in bloom with tiare and puakenikeni, and Toby's garden is loaded with vegetables.

"Look at that eggplant," my mom says.

"Look at that eyesore," I say.

Their next-door neighbors fly a Hawaiian flag and a sign that says DEFEND HAWAII. There's a skeleton of a Toyota in their yard that's been there for as long as I can remember, as well as a pop-up tent and rusted baby toys.

Danny comes out the kitchen door with my ukulele.

"Hey, Danny boy," my mom says when he leans down and rests his arms on my windowsill. He smells like salt water and BO.

"Hi, Auntie Ali. You leaving the windward side? Town bound? Lame."

"Moving on out," she says.

"Hey, Little Donkey," he says.

"Seriously, stop calling me that. Especially in public." I take a glance at myself in the side mirror. There's nothing worse than feeling like you look pretty good and being called an ass.

He passes my uke through the window.

"I'll see you Thursday?" he says. "I'm still tripped out you're moving in with Whitney West."

"Yeah, tell me about it," I say.

"I haven't cooked with you in a while," my mom says. "Bring me some of that eggplant, and we'll Iron Chef it up."

I cringe.

"Sounds good," Danny says. He puts his hand out for our farewell shake, which is more like a slap than a grip, then he walks out to the busy road and puts his hand out to stop traffic so my mom can back out. Only Danny could stop traffic so quickly.

We wave good-bye and get back on the road.

"You guys are so cute," my mom says.

"Stop it," I say. I force down a smile. I'll always be a little donkey in his eyes.

We drive in silence to Kahala, listening to music turned up loud. We have the same tastes: Gillian Welch, the Roots, Gabby and Cyril Pahinui, Graham Nash, plus random pop songs on the radio. She's okay like that.

She turns on Hunakai, the beginning of our new neighborhood, and I pretend not to look, but I see everything. The landscaping, the mailboxes, the lack of people walking their dogs or doing their own lawns or washing their cars. Some homes are laughably hideous, gold gates with blue metal dolphin fixtures, block-long driveway entrances; they make statements I can't quite decipher, yet they all seem to say, *Look at me, but don't come close.* I don't have an angry, simplistic distaste for people with money—I like it, want it, need it—but some people sure spend it in weird ways.

"Grandigross," I say.

"No kidding," she says.

We move into a nicer section. Some of the large homes sit next to old and small ones that haven't been torn down and resurrected. While these little ones are perfectly nice, in comparison to their fellow remodels, they look neglected. I guess it's like those shots showing the before and after, the after automatically making the before a failure.

It's not as though I haven't been to Kahala, even though I'm looking around like a total gaper. I surf at Diamond Head with Danny, but it's different this time. I'm nervous, and this nervousness is tinged with excitement and undue pride, like I'm a better person for living here.

"You're a good sport," my mom says.

"Yeah, yeah," I say. "I'll live."

She turns on Aukai, which is wide and quiet, hushed—it's almost like no one is here. Where is everyone?

"I'm serious," she says. "You've always been ready to go." She pats my leg.

It's true. The house in Topanga Canyon for her dystopian thriller, the apartment on Stanyan for the utopian (never released) comedy. I was happy to leave both times. Even moving here, she gave me a choice. I could finish up school while she flew back and forth, or we could move together. I chose the adventure, chose to leave the comforts of Storey, of the neighborhood, friends, and routines. I'm realizing that at some point, I should try to make a life I'm not so eager to leave.

"Tennis courts down that way," my mom says, nodding to the left, where I see a little kid straddling a bike, zoned out and picking his nose. "They're members of Waialae. Melanie said she could sign you up for lessons if you wanted."

"Why would I want tennis lessons? That's the stupidest thing I've ever heard."

My mom clears her throat. I hate when she pushes things on me or tries to guide me to something I may have done on my own. It's annoying—like when she sees someone she knows, and before I get the words out, she tells me to say hello.

"Grandpa used to say Waialae Country Club had no haoles," I say. "And the Outrigger has no Asians. Keeping it even, I guess."

"That's not true," my mom says. "Well, maybe. Anyway, you're welcome to use Waialae and the Outrigger."

I put my window down and let my arm hang out and surf the breeze. "I can't just go in there anytime," I say. "And it's not like I want to."

"You could go with Whitney."

"Why are you pushing her on me? You're like a friend dealer."

"I'm not pushing her," my mom says. "Never mind. Everything I say you argue against."

She turns the air up.

"Not everything," I say.

"You just did it again."

"That doesn't count. I'm just saying, not everything."

"You're still doing it."

I throw my hands up. "God!"

She puts my window back up. There's nothing worse than fighting in a car, trapped and on display, and I hate when a good moment turns in an instant and my mood is squashed. Maybe I *should* take tennis lessons—right now I would love to whack a ball across a court. *Whop!* I love that sound.

My mom turns on Koloa and then onto Kahala Avenue, which is loud, not with traffic, but with leaf blowers and weed whackers. She turns on her blinker, and I sit up straighter, trying to get a glimpse of what we're heading into. A long rock wall, a sleek wooden gate.

"This is it?" I ask, stating the obvious.

"This is it." She waits for an underfed woman jogger, slick with sweat, who is looking incredibly focused and unhappy.

"Eat a chicken," I say, then my mom makes the left into the Wests' driveway and stops before the gate.

"Do they know we're coming?" I ask.

"I told Melanie we'd be in and out all weekend. Who knows if we'll see anyone." She reaches up to a gate opener on the visor.

"Where'd you get that?"

"Melanie gave me one," she says and points it at the gate.

"When?"

"When I saw her yesterday."

"You were working."

She looks over at me. "Jeez, Lea, attack much? I had lunch with her yesterday. She came on set."

"First of all, gross that she came on set. Second of all, do not say 'attack much.' That is so lame."

She smiles and presses the button on the clicker again. "And here we are," she says in her cheerleader voice.

The gate hums and opens slowly. I realize I'm holding my breath. My mom drives in at a crawl, and I look at the long driveway that extends across the lot. I can see a rectangle of glimmering ocean through the glass doors in the middle of the home.

Soaring coconut trees are scattered around the grounds. Everything is perfectly manicured. Yardmen are clipping, mowing, blowing, weeding.

"This is us over here," my mom says. She veers off to the right, to the front edge of the lot where our new home, our cottage, sits above its own garage. The garage has a shiny wood door with black hardware.

"You must be happy," my mom says to me, referring to the garage. I've always wanted a garage, an odd wish, but I like having a place to put things, and after living in San Francisco, I cherish and deeply appreciate parking spots. When I worked at American Apparel on Haight I swear I spent more money on gas trying to find parking than I actually made at the store. I shrug, hiding my happiness.

She turns off the engine outside of the garage. "It's a stint. An adventure." I look over at the main house, and she follows my gaze. "Beautiful, isn't it?"

"I feel like Sabrina," I say.

"Who's Sabrina?"

"You know—the movie," I say.

"Oh," she says. "That Sabrina." She looks serene, recalling the movie. Audrey Hepburn, living in the servants' quarters with her dad, the chauffeur for the rich family.

"Remember, she falls in love with one of the sons," I say, reaching down for my backpack. "He treats her like shit. And the other brother treats her like shit too, but he's more responsible and good in the end. I forget what happens. I just remember she'd watch their lavish parties from a tree." I look at the coconut trees. Too tall and nowhere to hide.

My mom laughs. She has the widest smile—it spans her face, practically to her ears. She looks like she should be splashing in the surf for a J.Crew ad.

"What?" I say and open the door, but stay seated.

"Nothing, it's just . . . you're so articulate. So when you talk like a teenager—or swear—it makes me happy."

"That's funny," I say. "What a lark."

She pats me on the head, then keeps her hand there. "This, too, shall surpass."

"I don't like that saying either," I say, moving away. "You need new sayings."

"It's from the script," she says.

"Oh God," I say, getting out. "No wonder we're here."

"Come on," she says. "Let's look around!"

I don't mimic her optimism. Expressing acceptance seems risky somehow. Naive. I know there will be a cost to this. Still, I'm infected and am trying to tamp my enthusiasm down.

My mom pops the trunk and takes out her rolling suitcase. I take my backpack and bags of groceries from our emptied-out fridge and follow her up the stone steps and into our new home.

4

I HAVE A STRANGE RESPONSE WHEN I FIRST WALK IN. The place feels affectionate. Like it welcomes and wants me there. Maybe it's the flowers that someone left on the dining table, but it's other things too. The light, the view, the colors, even the bright material of the furniture. The walls are a soft yellow, like butter pecan ice cream; the air is crisp and quiet. It's air-conditioning, I realize, which we didn't have in the condo. At our Kailua place, I was always on the verge of a sneeze—the mildew, the mold, the humidity. Everything here is pure. It makes me feel like I've done something right.

"Nice," I say, relenting. I run my hand over the back of the sofa just beyond the dining table. The kitchen, eating area, and living room are all one great room.

"Oh my God," my mom says, taking it in. "Isn't this awesome?"

"Yeah," I say. "It is."

The furnishings are all unique. Nothing matches—there's a light green couch and bold, floral-printed love seats, and the dark wood dining table and the glass coffee table aren't from the same set. Still, everything goes together. This makes each thing seem valuable, like it's been collected over the years, or mulled over and chosen just for this room. It feels like our San Francisco apartment. I eye the flat-screen and the stereo. Music! My mom is inspecting the appliances in the kitchen. This doesn't feel like a place where the leftovers are stored. It also doesn't feel like something out of a catalogue, though it's beautiful enough that it could be. It's a home.

"Look at all this fruit," my mom says. I bring the groceries to the kitchen, where there's an array of fruit in a basket. I wash an apple and bite into it.

"Melanie's so thoughtful," my mom says. "Isn't this amazing?"

"The fruit basket?"

"Everything." She spreads one arm out like a model on a game show.

"Amazing," I say.

"God, Lea." Her face falls.

"What?" I take another bite. "Whenever I don't match your pep levels, you freak out. It's great! It's insane, okay? It surpasses. Oh ma haw, catchphrase."

"I'll go unload some more," she says.

She walks out like a disappointed puppy. What an actress. I'm quite the actress too, because as soon as she leaves, I practically run through our new place as if I'm on a timed shopping spree. I open every drawer and cupboard in the kitchen to find that we're fully equipped with matching pots and pans, coffeemaker, and utensils, all better versions of what we have. The kitchen has a bay window that overlooks some of the lawn and the driveway. I look down at my mom unloading a box, and my heart breaks for her a bit.

I rummage through the kitchen box she brought up, locating our magnets, one for each home we've lived in—a Harley-Davidson, an orange tabby cat, a banana, a Buddha, and from Kailua: Da Kine Plumbing and Heating. Now we'll need another. I put them on our new fridge. There. Home. I've marked my territory.

I open more kitchen drawers. There's even cleaning supplies and paper towels and napkins—it's like going to a vacation house, which is exactly what this is, I guess. I notice a bottle of red wine and another bouquet of flowers by the microwave, along with a note—*Everyone could use some Flowers! Welcome home. xoxo Mels.* The bottle says Flowers Pinot Noir.

My mom comes back in, and I show her the bottle.

"Yum," she says. "That's a good one."

I read something else in her expression, something like weariness, like she's about to go to work. She puts a box marked *kitchen* on the counter, and I tell her about all the things already here.

"Should we bother unpacking our kitchen stuff?" I ask.

"I guess we could leave our things in the garage." She follows my path, opening drawers, then looks around with her hands on her hips, surveying the place.

"Have you looked in the rooms yet?" she asks.

"Was just about to," I say.

"Take a look. I'll leave some stuff in the garage and bring up the rest. There's probably towels and sheets here. I didn't think about that."

"Maybe we'll get full wardrobes too," I say, but she doesn't register my joke. She never does—says I'm always getting stuck in Joke Town.

She takes the box she just brought up, and when she leaves, I open every closet I see around the main room before looking into each of the three bedrooms. The two bedrooms on the beach side share a bathroom, and each has a walk-in closet. The bedroom nearest the avenue is clearly the master because of its size, yet the smaller rooms have the best views of the ocean. I guess the arrangement is so the master bedroom doesn't overlook the main house, which would lessen its mastery.

My liking of the whole package—the decorations, the layout, the possibility of a life here—soon turns into entitlement, like of course I should have all this. I deserve no less. For a moment, I even inwardly balk at the fact that the laundry room is all the way downstairs in the garage. I guess it's pretty easy to adapt to better surroundings.

I wheel my suitcase into the doorway of the small room that sits away from the driveway. I could have both rooms if I wanted. Or one could be my art room or yoga room or ballet studio or meditation room! I do none of these things, but suddenly want to. It's like getting something for free, for a limited time, and you feel a certain pressure to wring out every last drop. A ukulele room!

My mom walks into the room I've decided to take with another one of my suitcases.

"This one yours?" she asks.

"Yeah," I say, as if not really sure.

"Nice," she says. "Everything is so lovely."

"Did you see yours?" I ask.

She puts her arm around me. "I did. The bed is like a hotel bed."

"Your favorite," I say.

The room has the same dark wood floors as the rest of the house. There's a high bed with a puffy white comforter and big, full pillows. I throw myself onto it, and it does feel like a hotel bed. My mom explores, opening the doors to the armoire where a big television is stored.

"Awesome!" I say.

"Told you this would be fun."

"I guess," I say. It's still confusing, unreal, though I put my questions/complaints/reservations aside for now, remembering the bedroom I just came from. Green carpets, brown wood walls, low ceilings, heat.

This looks like a room that belongs to me. This one offers me something. Like the living room, nothing matches, yet everything seems to be getting along. I walk up to the window and look at the main house.

"We should probably go over, let Melanie know we're here," my mom says.

"You can," I say, not turning around. The house looks like a hotel.

"It would be nice if you came along. She hasn't seen you since you were a little kid."

"It would be nice," I say and glance quickly at my mom to show her I'm not moving.

I know that she wants me to do these things to learn manners or something, but sometimes it feels like she just wants company, or that I'm a kind of shield for her. She doesn't have a husband, so I'm the one she brings along, and I'm the excuse she has when she wants to leave.

"Lea, they're doing a big thing here."

"Yeah," I say. "And I didn't ask them to."

"Please have some gratitude," she says.

"I will when I see them." I hate when she makes me feel this way. I'm shy and embarrassed, and so I show her anger instead. I start unpacking my suitcase for something to do.

"Just come with me to say hello. I don't even know if anyone's here. You can meet Whitney."

I don't answer. I refold my clothes like a maniac, as if this were the most important task in the world. I don't want to be shoved to their front door like a shy child forced to say "trick or treat."

"Not now, okay?" I say. "We just got here."

"I hope you're not going to have an attitude."

I throw the clothes down on the bed. "I don't have an attitude! I'm just getting adjusted—trying to enjoy myself a little. Explore the surroundings, relax."

She shakes her head, disappointed, giving me that wounded look. "I just thought some basic, decent manners wouldn't hurt." She takes her exit. And scene.

Decent manners wouldn't hurt. But it does hurt. And it hurts me to think that she has to be nice, that they're doing a "big thing here" and we have to pay them back. How? What will we owe them, exactly? Their part will always look bigger: free house, parking, grounds, water. Flowers in a vase, Flowers in a bottle, apples, oranges, bananas, oh my! Thank you, thank you, thank you!

I just want to stay put. For a second, I had a feeling of excitement to be home, but by going to say thank you, she's reminded me that we're just houseguests. None of this is ours.

5

I OPEN BOXES IN MY NEW ROOM, LOOKING AT MY things as if they're old friends. The built-in bookshelves are empty, and the first thing I do is arrange my books. I put the kid books I can't bear to get rid of into the closet—Ping, Eloise, Ferdinand, Beatrix Potters, Roald Dahls—and arrange the others on the shelf—Dickens, Austen, my young adults I get from the library whose titles I can never remember. *The Wonderful Awful. No Time Like Forever.* I line them up neatly, starting anew.

I like the comforter that's on the bed already, so I keep mine in its bag and put it in the pile of things to take downstairs, which is becoming huge. I don't need my old pillows, hangers, linens, towels. Everything here is better.

"Lea?" my mom calls from the living room. She's playing music. After I discovered Sonos and the home-filling speaker system, we can't stop playing music.

"Yeah!" I yell.

She walks to my doorway and whispers, "Whitney's here." She looks giddy, like some celebrity is right behind her, but she's trying to play it cool.

"Oh," I say. "Okay."

"I went over to see if Melanie was home, and Whitney was there. She wanted to say hi."

"Okay," I say, shooing her away, knowing she's covering for whatever she's done—probably told Whitney I was dying to say hello and that I have no friends. My mom moves away to make room for Whitney, giving me a supportive look like I'm about to sing a song or jump hurdles or something.

"Hey," Whitney says, from the doorway. She's barefoot, and her hair is wet, which tells me something about her—most girls don't like to get their hair wet. They just cook poolside like rotisserie chickens, taking intermittent dips up to their chins if they need to cool off. Her legs are muscled and long, even though she's not very tall.

"Hi," I say.

Her two front teeth are notably big, but in this weird way that makes you want your front teeth to be notably big too. She has a dark mole perched on top of her right cheekbone that I keep focusing on, so with that and the teeth, it takes me a while to register her entire face, but when I do, I see cruelty. It's not that she's scowling or smirking or anything. She just has that teen-movie-girl face, the popular one who gets one-upped at the end by the less pretty girl with the big, big heart. Maybe that's not fair, though. Maybe she's not cruel at all—maybe she's just pretty. Her eyes are large and a bit slanted, with thick lashes.

"My mom told me you were here," she says.

Yes, she clearly wanted to drop in and say hi. I want to tell her it's okay to go.

"I'm going to finish up out there," my mom says. "Can I get you guys a snack?"

Oh God. A snack. I imagine saying to Whitney, "Can I offer you some fruit your mom brought?" and serving it to her on one of her plates.

"No," I say.

"I'm good, thank you," Whitney says.

"Okay, I'll let you girls chat."

Whitney smiles at my mom, I don't, and then we're by ourselves. What are we supposed to chat about? She walks in, then takes slow steps around the room. I wonder if I should resume my task or follow her around like a realtor. She wears just a large T-shirt that has wet spots where her breasts are.

"Getting settled?" she asks, looking at the mess on the floor, my boxes and clothes.

"Yeah," I say. "Unpacking some things." Obviously.

She walks toward the window that faces the sea and her house.

"I've never been in here," she says. I look at the backs of her thin and strong legs.

"Really?" That seems weird to me. I'm someone who leaves no drawer unopened. I can't imagine not going into a house I owned.

"I mean, when it was finished, I peeked in," she says, "but I never looked at the bedrooms."

I guess not. Why would she? It would be like checking out the maid's quarters or the handyman's tool shed.

She looks at my books, and I remain quiet, as if someone's looking at my art right in front of me. I wish I had some of my pictures up—ones of my friends or of my mom and me in LA, dressed up for a premiere. She hops over a pile of my hats, then peeks into the bathroom. I hold myself back from saying anything, not because it would be something rude, but because it would be something nice. Apologetic, careful, false. Or it would just be plain lame, like "how's school?"

"You should come swim or lay out sometime," she says. She walks back to the window and sits down on the built-in bench with the beachy, blue cushion. "I have magazines. I'm done with them. So and so did this. So and so wore that. Those kind."

I laugh, needlessly, then stand up because I can't just stay crouched down by my boxes, but when I stand, I have nowhere to go. I feel my stupid clothes, my ratty nondesigner jeans, my sweatshirt with the stain that runs along the zipper like a sewage canal. I suck in my stomach and hold my hands together, cross my arms, then uncross them and say, "We were in the same ethics group, right?" as if I don't know.

"Oh yeah," she says.

She has no problem with the silence. She stays still. I walk over to the bed and sit down.

I think back to the peer-counselor-led session, the things we had done, and more important for me, the things we've never done and always wanted to do. I remember noticing she wasn't too far ahead of me and thinking she must be lying.

"That was a weird exercise," I say. "Walking across the room."

She looks like she's remembering something that happened ages ago. "Yeah. I kind of liked it. Made you think."

"Totally," I say.

"Did you see Laura Fujimoto?" She laughs. "Oh my God,

she got, like, all the way across. I always thought she was some goody-goody."

I laugh, or make a sound that approximates laughter.

"But who knows why she walked," Whitney says. "Hopefully 'cause she did bad shit and not because bad shit happened to her. Like what if she took her steps 'cause she was molested or something? And by the way, how the fuck is walking across the gym supposed to help her with that—or with any of our problems?"

"Yeah," I say again, ineptly. Where is my funny self? Where does it go when I'm intimidated? I fold shirts that I've already folded.

"Why'd you walk?" she asks.

"I don't know," I say. "I don't really remember."

She looks at me like I'm hiding something scandalous. Black-soled shoes in the gym. That's why I walked. Thug life.

"What about you?" I ask.

"I don't really remember," she says, and now she looks like she's the one hiding something scandalous.

Water drips from her hair onto my hardwood floor. Her hardwood floor. This is all hers. While it's easy to adapt to better things, it's probably hard to come back down.

"So do you like it?" she asks, and looks up at the ceiling.

I look around, as if considering. "Yeah, it works. My mom's going to be shooting more in town now, so . . ." I usually find that when I mention my mom, the attention turns immediately to her and sheds a more attractive light on me as well, but Whitney doesn't seem to care.

"Yeah, my mom's all amped on your mom's show." She gets

up and walks by me. Her hair smells like expensive perfume. She picks up the few things on my shelves—an old pencil box, a glass vase I made—then puts them down again. She's in charge, and I feel like I'm losing an invisible race. Even my posture is pathetic. It's like I've become suddenly infected with clumsiness and I'm afraid to move and spill my dignity.

"You going out tonight?" she asks.

"Not sure yet," I lie.

"You're friends with Danny, right?" Her smile is coy.

"Yeah," I say.

"He's kind of a dreamboat," she says.

I laugh, and a little spit darts out. I think she cringes.

She taps her nails against my ukulele on the shelf, and now she looks bored, like she's enduring a class in school. I wonder if she feels forced to stay and hang out with me. I don't know what to say to her and hate that I'm nervously trying to think of something.

I'm about to say something about the cottage, how it's nice, how everything's so great, so much better than our last place, thereby firmly establishing my rank notches below her, like I'm some kind of lady-in-waiting, but then a clear little bubble of snot comes out of Whitney's nostril, and I stop and stare at it. It's perfectly developed, a round and jolly little thing. She stands there, ignorant, and I can't help myself.

"Oh my God." I laugh.

"What?" she says, and I tell her to look in the mirror. She walks to the chest of drawers and looks into the large rectangular mirror that hangs above it.

"Whoa," she says. She tilts her head to the right, then left.

She doesn't sniffle or wipe it away. I watch her looking at herself.

"You may have set a record," I say.

"Now that is g money right there." She turns slowly and strikes a funny pose with her hands on her hips, her face in profile, proud like a conqueror. Then she breaks the pose and looks around, maybe for something to wipe her nose with. She ends up using her T-shirt. "Well, that was awesome. A nice welcoming. I'm such a spaz," she says, in a way that's the opposite of spazziness. Her way of speaking is languid, like her words have been out in the sun for too long.

We talk a little more, small talk, miniature talk, but it's comfortable now. It's because of the snot. If that hadn't happened I would have been nervous and resentful, and she would have forgotten me or treated me like some kind of ghetto foster child.

"I'm heading back out before the sun goes down," she says.

"Just going to finish unpacking," I say. I refrain from saying thank you—*Thank you for the house.*

Before she leaves, she returns with some paper towels and cleans up the water she dripped on the floor.

6

MY MOM AND I HAVE DINNER TOGETHER IN OUR NEW house, at our new table. She has given me a section of the shooting script for tomorrow.

```
EXT. HUT—DAY
EXTREME CLOSE-UP ON Samantha, deep in concentra-
tion. A mosquito lands on her cheek. She flinches,
tries to peer down at it, then slaps her face.

                    RICK
    If I could be a bug on that face.

                  SAMANTHA
    Then you'd be dead, idiot.

                    RICK
    Oh. Right.

PAN OUT to the arid land. A Jeep is seen in the
distance, driving closer to them, and very reck-
lessly.
```

RICK

Are we supposed to get in that thing?

SAMANTHA

If you're afraid of a Jeep, then we're in for a long ride.

RICK looks her over, unabashedly. She's wearing a loose, white tank top, damp with sweat. Her legs are golden and glistening.

SAMANTHA

Can I help you with something?

RICK

Actually, I was going to offer to help you with something.

Her eyebrows arch, intrigued.

RICK

Your breasts.

SAMANTHA

Excuse me?

RICK

I'm the breast in the west. I can give you a discount when we get back to the States.

She is disgusted, but he doesn't notice. He's serious, and really looking at them now, as if presented with a medical problem.

SAMANTHA

(mumbles)

You've got to be kidding me.

RICK

(using hand gestures)

A strong C would suit your frame. I like 'em a little spaced apart, not so uptight, you know, and with the nipples

(more hand gestures to illustrate his thoughts)

pointed diagonally.

SAMANTHA

Just shut up right now.

The Jeep is almost to them.

RICK

What?

SAMANTHA

Just be a bug on my face.

The Jeep pulls up in front of them. They stand and dust themselves off. They are stunned when they see their driver, a GIRL who looks to be about twelve. She is sitting on pillows.

GIRL

Howzit! Welcome to Molokana.

She smiles, revealing a few gold teeth.

GIRL (CONT'D)

Come on already, slowpokes. I got work to do, people to see, eel to eat.

RICK

Did she just say eel?

SAMANTHA

She just said eel.

I give the script back to my mom. "Can you say 'nipples' on TV?"

"I guess we'll see," she says. "It's bad, isn't it?" She takes a sip of wine. A soft light descends through the trees.

I eat the zucchini that's fallen out of my burrito. "It's fun. I like Samantha, and Rick is so awful that he's kind of awesome. And your legs are golden and glistening."

"Remember my friend on *Lost*?" she says.

"Of course. Can you pass the sour cream?"

She passes me the little white bowl. Even when it's just us, she always plates things in serving dishes.

"She got twenty thousand an episode when it first aired, and then when it became a hit, two hundred and fifty an episode."

"That's so cool."

"This isn't *Lost*," she says, tapping the script. "But here's to hoping for a back nine for twenty-two episodes!" She raises her glass, then leans in for a messy bite. Back nine is an order from the studios if they like the series, bringing it from thirteen episodes to twenty-two. I raise my glass of water. Here's to hoping. I look down at the script.

"Of course they made the local girl silly," I say.

"I know," she says, with a full mouth. "Just wait—later, Jenkins—the main guy—gets in a fight with the local doctor because the local wants to cure a patient by chanting."

"That's so loathsome. But this is so good," I say, chewing. "Spicy."

"It's the chorizo," she says. "And do you like the sweet potato in it?"

"Love," I say.

"So," she says, and I immediately know she's going to ask about Whitney. She finishes her bite. "How was this afternoon?" She says it casually, as if she hasn't been dying to ask me this question for hours. "What did Whitney have to say?"

She has a hopeful glimmer in her eye, and this time I know it's a real question, unlike "How was school?" She wants to know everything.

"Nothing, really," I say.

"She had to have said something."

I take my time with my next bite. I shrug my answer. "Not really," I say.

"Nothing?" She takes a sip of her wine. "God, this wine is good."

"Nothing that stands out," I say.

"Well, do you like her?"

"Jeez, Mom, relax."

"I'm relaxed. Very relaxed. Pass the cream back. My mouth is on fire."

We continue to eat, bluegrass playing, the sun gone.

"Did you guys make plans to—"

I let my fork clang against my plate. "No, we didn't make plans!" I yell.

She laughs. She loves riling me up, and I like pretending I'm riled—it's our little rhythm.

"I think it's fun, that's all," she says. "We both have friends who live by us. Maybe you guys can carpool."

"Oh my God, Mom, she's not my friend, and I'm sure she carpools with her actual friends or her brother."

Some of her friends I can't believe are in high school. They look like supermodels and act like twenty-year-olds. It's strange to feel so much younger than people your own age, something I never felt at Storey. I'm in classes with a few of Whitney's friends, and what surprises me is that some are really quiet and some are really smart. Brooke Breene, for instance. When we sit down in history, she whips on her glasses and takes notes in a plain Moleskine notebook. It made me rearrange my thoughts when I got here. The pretty girls can be the smart girls too.

Mom doesn't push the carpooling question any further, maybe not wanting to bring attention to the obvious: Whitney has her own friends and doesn't need any more. No one needs more friends at the end of her junior year.

"Okay," she says, holding up her hands. "Anyway, Friday they've invited us over for dinner. So we can all get to know one another."

"Fine," I say.

"Think you'll be happy here?" she asks. "So far, so good?"

"So far, so okay." I wonder if life will always be this way—the weight of good things sinking in, creating space that needs to be filled with more. Will I always feel guilty for having enough yet still wanting to tag on additions? Or is it good to keep wanting, because that means you feel worthy of more?

"This is our house, you know," she says. "You need to feel at home."

But I can't. Our house feels like the staff house.

"Give me a chance, then," I say. "Are you happy? Is this what you want?"

She looks me in the eye while she chews. She makes to speak, then wipes her mouth with her napkin.

"You need some roadside assistance?" I ask.

"What?"

"For your stall."

She laughs. "I'll always be happy with you around."

"I could make maple syrup out of that sap."

"That wasn't as funny," she says.

"Yes it was." I lightly bang my fist on the table for emphasis.

"I'm just trying to make this work," she says. "Make our time here work."

"But we can't stay at this house the whole time, can we?"

"Until you graduate?" She looks toward the kitchen window, then around at the room. "No, I doubt we would."

"Good," I say. "Because it's weird."

"It will be less weird," she says. "We'll get used to it, and you may really like Whitney, and Will seems like a nice boy."

Will West does not seem like a nice boy. He's even more intimidating than his sister. He seems surrounded by a velvet rope—like you'd have to have a certain look to join him. He wears polo shirts and probably hashtags everything with *#winning*. Still, he is pretty fine. If he talked to me, I'd talk back.

"Yeah, a nice kid who probably guffaws instead of laughs," I say.

"Oh, come on," my mom says. "You don't even know him. Give them a chance."

"Stop pushing," I say.

I remember when I was younger, I'd eat quickly, then get up to play piano while my mom finished the rest of her meal, serenading her. I stopped when she started dating a man who'd give me advice after each piece I played. He was the manager of a suit store and acted as if that were the epitome of success. He had a daughter—I was ten and she was thirteen at the time. She talked like a Latina gang member and told poorly constructed lies.

I enjoyed ripping the seams out of them, but hated the way she stood by the lies for so long, blinking her eyes rapidly and moving her head from side to side like the pit bull bobblehead in her father's leased Hummer. Once, she actually had the gall to think I'd believe that her dad was so rich that for her thirteenth birthday they flew to the Congo on a private jet to party "jungle-style."

I don't know what brought me to this memory, maybe the way my mom seems to be forcing the Wests on me, just as they had forced the daughter and me together, two people from incompatible habitats. Except in this case, I feel like the other girl, the lamer, the lesser.

"It's just that . . . I know you can be abrupt and grumpy, and I just want you to be nice and positive—"

"Oh my God, Mom, stop."

"Punahou's a very hard school to get into." She looks down at her plate, moving her fork around.

"I know, but I got in."

"They helped us, okay? Eddie helped us. He helped you. Even with a record like yours, it's almost impossible to transfer this late. He made it happen. And now we're here, and this is helping too. It's a good place to be until we know what the show will do."

"I see," I say, sitting back. A messy picture gets cleaned up. "So we need them," I state.

"Fine, Lei, yes." She puts her fork down and sits back, her face set with confidence. "Yes, we do. We need them."

Does a short name like Lea really need a nickname? It's never bothered me until this second. Don't be lazy! Say my name! A flush travels from my face, then down through my arms.

"So are you saying I wouldn't have gotten in on my own?" I ask.

"Sweetie," she says, "I don't think anyone could get in this late on their own."

I take a bite of the coleslaw, which was once delicious, and now I can barely taste it. I hear a light knock on our door. My mom and I exchange glances. I take a sip of water to wash my anger down. "Come in," she says.

Before either of us gets up, the door opens slightly and Melanie West steps in or, rather, sticks her head in.

"Hi!" Melanie says, and my mom squeals back, "Hi!"

"I didn't want to intrude, but—"

"No, no, come in!" my mom says, getting up. I follow, grinning and nodding like a geisha.

"Lea, this is Mrs. West. Melanie." She gives me that Mom look. The be-well-mannered-so-I-look-good look, and I keep my end of the bargain—I won't be abrupt or gloomy—though I refuse to squeal.

"Hello," I say. "Nice to meet you."

"Oh, I've met you before," she says. "You were just a little girl. Look at you!"

I can't.

"I've heard so much about you!" she says, and her smile reminds me of mine when I'm waiting for someone to hurry up and take the picture. "God, Ali, she looks just like you." People have said this so many times before, but I just don't see it. Melanie has on a floor-length, silky dress. Her hair is long, sleek, and thick like a pelt. I keep a smile plastered on my face, even though I know it's as fake as hers.

"I don't want to intrude—"

"You're not intruding at all!" my mom says.

"I just wanted to make sure everything was okay here."

"Oh my gosh," my mom says. "Are you kidding me? We feel like we're on vacation." My mom gives me another prodding look.

"It's great," I say.

"That is so nice of you to say," she says, as if we're politely accepting the conditions of an old cabin.

"It's a funky place, so I just wanted to make sure you knew the ins and outs." She looks around like she's checking things off. There's something intense and searching in her eyes. "I don't know if you've run the dishwasher yet, but there's a switch under the sink, and if the washer isn't working, then just flip the switch."

"Got it," my mom says. "Thank you so much for everything. The fruit, the wine, the house," she says laughing. I cringe.

"It's nothing," Melanie says and looks up. "The ceiling fans are silly, aren't they?"

I look up at the fans. They're like revolving banana leaves.

"They were sort of the trend back in the day." She gives "back in the day" little air quotes, and I can tell she's one of those people who probably air quote a lot, and in all the wrong places.

"They're beautiful," my mom says.

Melanie's eyes dart around the room and I wonder if she's going to comment on every object, every appliance, every cushion.

"Would you like a glass of wine?" my mom says.

Not a second goes by before Melanie says, "I'd love one!" She walks expertly to the kitchen and retrieves a glass from the cupboard over the microwave. "That's so nice of you."

"I love this kitchen," my mom says, walking to the counter with the bottle of wine and filling Melanie's glass.

"Oh, thanks." She looks around her kitchen. "Basic, really. I'm so sorry all these things are still in here. We use it as a guest cottage, so whatever you don't want, just let me know. Robbie's coming this week to fix the light outside your garage. If you want him to box up anything that you don't—"

"We're fine," my mom says. "Unless we shouldn't use them—"

"No! Please use everything. I just didn't want it to get in your way, or if it's not to your taste."

"No, it's all lovely."

This is so tedious. I look back and forth, back and forth. Can't they just drink their wine and be quiet?

"We actually ended up keeping a lot of our boxes packed," my mom says. "We're leaving them in the garage if that's okay."

"If you want, I can have them moved to our storage," Melanie says.

"Oh no," my mom says. "Don't bother. Everything is perfect. Cheers."

"Cheers!" Melanie says, and they clink glasses and take a sip. "I'm so happy you guys are here!"

"We're so happy we're here," my mom says.

Is this what friendships are like when you're grown up? Is this what I have to look forward to? My beautiful, fun mother seems like a different person. She's standing awkwardly too, with her hand holding her elbow.

"I'm going to go do my homework," I say, even though it's Saturday.

"I wish Whitney would do the same," Melanie says, then touches my mom's arm and launches into a conversation about how her housecleaner can come to the cottage unless my mom has her own. We do not have our own. We are the housecleaner. My mom gives me a look, a kind of good-night nod. I know she'd prefer to be with just me, how we were at the table, making our home.

I walk to my room, running my hand along the white wall. Do Whitney and Will know their dad helped get me into Punahou? Should I care? It's the way the world works, I guess. No one can do things on their own when it comes to stuff like this. The Wests are probably used to giving favors. They're probably used to determining someone's good fortune.

7

WHENEVER I PUT THE BLINKER ON TO PULL INTO THE Wests' driveway, I have a feeling of pride, like the person behind me or heading toward me must be wondering who I am. I wonder if my mom feels this way too—if she becomes the woman who lives here.

Today, Wednesday, I do the same thing I've done all week after school—open the gate, drive right up to our cottage, click the garage open, then seal myself in. No exploring, no meandering. I don't want to run into anyone, but today I stop on the first step and look at the yard between our houses—a vast divide I haven't yet crossed. I don't feel like I can. Since Saturday, I've heard and seen cars coming in and out, lights going on and off. Mainly, I see the yardmen. I have yet to meet Eddie or Will.

"Hello, hello!" I hear. Melanie comes around from the back of the cottage. "Sorry!" she says. "We're in your space."

"Oh, no problem."

A man is by her side, a tool belt around his waist. His face is red and dusty. "This is Robbie. Handy Robbie." She touches his back delicately, as if he might be a germ.

"And Will—where are you? Will?" She leans back to look for him.

Oh God. Will walks out from behind the garage, looking at his phone, then ends a text or something, looks up, and smiles. I'm shocked by the way his whole face lights up. She touches his shoulder and, I think, sort of pushes him toward me. She waves me over, and I walk down the steps while they wait, feeling their eyes on me.

"Hi," I say, at the bottom.

"Hi." He scrunches his nose, which is super cute. It's kind of like he's telling me that this is a little awkward for him too.

"Do you know each other?" Melanie asks.

"We don't," he says. "Nice to meet you." He sticks out his hand, and I shake it. It's smooth on the outside, callused on the inside.

"You too," I say. "I think I've seen you around Punahou. I'm going to high school there." Why did I say *high school*? Why not just *school*? "I'm living in the cottage now. With my mom." He grins as though I'd said something far more interesting, or maybe he totally misheard me. *We're living in the cottage. I'm totally high and cool.*

"Welcome," he says, looking down, then back up at my eyes.

"Yes," I say, for some stupid reason.

"Will was just leaving for the golf course," Melanie says. "Hon, maybe show Lea the club and the neighborhood before you go?"

"Oh, that's okay," I say. "I'm fine. I don't want—"

"Can you do that, hon?"

Melanie doesn't have a job that I know of, yet she's wearing a nice dress, along with big earrings and thin gold bracelets. I feel like she's always either very dressed up or wearing exercise clothes. She's different from the other women here—the paddlers, loud and confident, the moms in their bikinis and caps. I can't imagine her in the ocean.

"Um, sure, I have some time," Will says, glancing again at his phone.

"Thanks, hon," she says, then goes back to talking with Robbie.

"Ready?" Will asks. He seems to scan me, toe to head.

"Yeah," I say, at once mortified that this is happening, yet inexplicably grateful to Melanie for making it seem as though I don't have a choice.

I feel self-conscious sitting next to Will, even though he's looking ahead. I lift my thighs so they don't splay out on the seat. We drive down Kahala Avenue, and the day has become even more beautiful. It hasn't gotten hotter. Just clear blue skies and a crisp air.

"So," Will says, "this is the 'hood." He looks quickly at me, then back at the road and smiles. "Waialae's down thataway. Great golf course and tennis program."

"When do you need to golf?" I ask.

"About an hour," he says.

"Sorry," I say. "You don't really need to show me around. I've been here before so—"

"It's fine," he says and looks over at me and down at my legs. "I don't mind."

He drives with one hand on the wheel, looking so much like a man, like someone who could take care of you your whole life. For some reason, I don't want to like him or think he's cute.

Maybe to set myself apart from everyone else. He looks like someone who's never been refused.

"You can drop me somewhere if you want," I say.

"You want me to drop you on the side of the road?"

I look at the mansions on the side of the road, some that put me in mind of Tuscany, others Greece, some . . . who knows? Beverly Hills in the eighties? What's up with the lion statues and the turquoise turtles on iron gates?

"I meant if you want to get to golf earlier, it's fine. I could just sneak back to the cottage."

"My mom would see the gate opening," he says. "She'll be doing yoga in about a minute on the lawn." He changes the station on the radio, landing on an R&B love song. I hope he's not leaving it here because he thinks I like this sort of thing.

"She got an idea for me to drive you around," he says. "It's best just to go with her ideas." I'm put at ease, comfortable with the fact that all mothers are so similar—friend pushers. Social curators.

"She does yoga at a certain time?" I ask.

"Yeah." He laughs. "She hires this girl from the studio to do it with her and her friends."

"Why don't they just go to the studio?"

"What? Now, that wouldn't be as special." He disarms me with his eyes green like ferns.

"I can always walk around for a while," I say.

"You really want to get rid of me, huh?" he asks. He glances over, coy and amused, and my first thought is, *No. Never.*

"I just don't want you to feel obligated to hang out with me," I say, hoping that doesn't sound too pathetic.

"Look, I'll just show you the neighborhood. We'll turn back, and I'll bring you to the club. I'll let you know when I can't take it anymore, okay? Now, be quiet about it already."

"Okay," I say, holding down a smile.

He turns at the end of the road that skirts the edge of the neighborhood.

"I can't take it anymore," he says, and I laugh, relaxing my legs.

"Sorry—my mom . . . ," he says. "She gets things in her head. When I was younger, all of my playdates were highly organized. Had to be with the right kids, doing the right activities. I'm used to it."

"So I'm a playdate?" I ask, and immediately a heat runs through my arms and chest from feeling bold and at ease.

"I guess so. But a much better one than Rodney Nash. That kid was torture."

We drive up toward Diamond Head lookout, and he turns left and heads down a narrow road, which leads to a circular driveway. We stop in front of what looks to be an entrance to a fortress on the ocean.

"Doris Duke's place," he says, circling the driveway before coming to a stop. "Shangri La. It's pretty awesome inside. There's all this Islamic art and furniture. Every detail of the house she worked on."

"Why Islamic?" I ask, feeling I need to say something.

"She traveled a lot, saw things she liked, picked them up, buying as she went."

"Must be nice."

He looks over at me, and I sense disappointment, like I'm not getting something.

"She was the daughter of this tycoon, and still she was this adventurous person, didn't want to be defined . . ." He trails off. Maybe he's trying to sell her to me, along with aspects of himself. He's more than the son of someone big.

"That's cool," I say.

"In back, there's this pool area—it was a dock made for her yacht," Will says. "People jump off the wall."

"Fun," I say, thinking of Danny and how he's shown me a place near Makapu'u to jump from. A wooden plank hovering above clear blue water. I feel like I know the island by the jumps—Point in Hawaii Kai, far off the coast, black hot rocks, deep sea. The Mokuluas, little islands off Lanikai, high cliffs into roiling ocean. Maunawili Falls, slippery hike, cold mountain water.

"I want to do that," I say.

He laughs. "I've only done it once a long time ago. It's kind of a local thing, if you know what I mean."

Funny how people use that word here—*local.* It doesn't always refer to the people who live here, because then we'd all be locals. Sometimes it means people who talk pidgin. People who don't go to private schools, people who live in Waimanalo.

He drives back to the wide expanse of Diamond Head Road, and I wonder if Shangri La was just a part of the show-her-around tour. We follow a trolley filled with people holding their phones toward the ocean, catching shots of the surfers and people at the lookout holding their phones out too. The thing with tourists—you can't blame them. This view is beautiful, and no matter how long you've been here—the ocean and sunsets, the light at six A.M., the light at six P.M.—it never gets old. The thought gives me patience as we trail the trolley down the hill past the lighthouse.

"So how long are you living in the cottage for?" he asks.

It's like he's asking me how long I'm going to be using something of his.

"This sort of got sprung on me," I say, wanting to apologize.

"Oh, I'm sure it got sprung on your mom too." He smiles in a way that feels like pity. We drive past the fountain, then loop around and drive into the Outrigger, its *O* sign with the paddle across it, like a heart pierced by an arrow. He stops in the roundabout.

"Did you want to check things out in there?"

"Um, okay," I say, nervous and somewhat excited to be seen with him.

"Yeah, grab something to eat, get some sun, hang for a while? Or I can take you back."

"I'll hang out," I say.

"Cool. I need to get going, but my number's seven, eight, one, two—feel free to order whatever and put it on my tab."

"Okay, thanks." I get out, because what else can I do but show him I didn't think he was going to come in with me? I won't let him think that I was looking forward to walking in there with him, getting something to eat with him. That would be crazy.

"Thanks for the tour," I say, making my voice sound joyful and carefree.

"You're welcome," he says. "See you around."

He drives off, and I wave, mumbling to myself, "What the shitshow was that?"

• • •

I don't know where to go. I've been to the Outrigger a few times, but always with my mom. I walk down a set of stairs. Some women are in the basement of the parking garage, paddling in a stationary canoe—a two-seater hull placed in a vat of water that the paddlers use to focus on technique or something. It's a treadmill version of a canoe; they paddle furiously, but don't go anywhere. I look down at myself as if my non-belonging is something detectable, though it's probably the only exclusive club in the world where you look misplaced if you're overdressed versus underdressed. The women here, maybe around sixty years old, are barefoot and in bathing suits, practical, sporty ones, though one wears a bikini. She has wild frizzy curls and a plumeria tucked behind her ear. She gives me a friendly look, and I pretend I should be here.

In the hallway that leads out to the club, a group of guys walk from the other end. I recognize them from school and, without thinking, duck into the locker room so I don't have to pass them in the narrow hall. I can't just stand in front of the room attendant, a Filipino woman whose eyes light up as though she recognized me, so I go into the girls' locker room, hoping no one from my school will be there, but it's pretty empty—just a few six- or seven-year-old kids. They stand in front of the mirrors, striking funny poses. Their bikinis are so cute, just like the ones teenagers wear, but smaller. On the mainland people would probably freak out, think them too sexy, but here, it's just how it goes.

Where are their mothers? Kids are so free here. It makes them seem older, more capable, coordinated, but wild.

The little girl in the magenta bikini and trucker hat tells the other girl to put the shampoo back where it belongs. The friend obliges, and when she walks past me, I catch a scent of something familiar. It's the smell of Whitney's hair and her friends'—and even Will's—the scent I associated with privilege and popularity, beauty, ease, and laughter. Really, it's just the club's Costco brand shampoo.

8

IT'S THURSDAY, SO I'M GOING SURFING WITH DANNY after his tennis practice. He's the only guy I know who does varsity football in the fall and tennis in the spring. Even though the courts are way up by the kindergarten, I always park down by the academy so he can stop by his locker. On this campus, you start at the top, then descend to high school at the bottom.

I watch people going into Montague with their instruments—cellos, violins, and guitars—and then I see Danny walking and I honk. A group of seniors sitting in front of the Mamiya building look my way, and I'm sort of glad to have them witness Danny getting into my car, lending me some cool. His brown hair has a gold tint from the sun. He seems above everyone, so tall that he doesn't notice all the girls looking up at him.

"What's up, Little Donkey?" he says, getting in. He pats me on the head.

"What's up?" I say back. Ironically, if we weren't good friends, we'd probably hug or kiss—everyone seems to do a lot of that here, this effortless affection between people who aren't going out. They hug when they come and go, girls and girls, girls and boys. They walk with their arms over one another. They sit on each other's laps. It's an intimacy I envy and that I look away from, in case the envy is apparent.

I hit him on the leg.

That's as intimate as it gets.

I head out of school, past the science center and theater, then slow at the Wo International Center until security waves me on.

"Tonggs or Diamond Head?" I ask when we've made it to the road.

"Why don't we just go to your new house?" he says. "Paddle out from there."

I never considered doing that. Could I have people over on just my sixth day living there? I drive up the hill toward UH, then wait in the long line to merge onto the highway.

"I don't know if I can."

"Of course you can," Danny says. "It's where you live, right? You have your own access now. It's killer. This is going to be so much easier."

"But I don't know if I'm allowed to have people over." I reach across him to the glove compartment for my gum and hit his knees. His body seems to take up the entire car. "I can't walk up by the house. Yeah. I don't think I can do that."

"It's not like we'll be rummaging through their fridge." I hand him the gum; he takes a piece and puts the pack away. "We'll just walk, walk, walk—" He uses his fingers on the console between us to imitate us walking. "We won't make noise. We won't litter or poop on the lawn—"

"Poop on the lawn?"

"We won't do anything. We will be upstanding citizens. The

West home will not become a Genshiro Kawamoto property on our clock."

I laugh at the reference to the Japanese billionaire who bought more than two dozen properties along Kahala Avenue and invited native Hawaiian families to move in free of charge. Walls have been tagged with spray paint, pools filled with garbage, beer cans, even needles. Tennis courts are cracked and crumbling. He put marble statues around the properties and landscaped with rows of loud and busy plants and flowers. The homes look apocalyptic, like the remains of a once-grand society.

"It's almost like performance art," I say.

"No, I've told you already," Danny says. "It's a social experiment. Watch these Hawaiians ruin their riches. Embarrassing."

"I think he's just nuts." I pull my skirt down because it's creeping up. Danny looks down, then quickly the other way, out the window, chewing his gum.

"You should totally invite him over. You're his neighbor now! These are your peeps." He wiggles his eyebrows.

We cruise down H-1 quickly. The traffic's going the other way. I don't think I've ever driven here without tons of traffic going in one direction or the other, usually both. It's like Hawaii is stuffed to the gills, bringing in but not putting out, like a hoarder. I take the Waialae exit, still not quite used to my new route home.

"It's not my neighborhood. And I'm not inviting anyone over. I still don't think we should surf there." I try to stay immune to his charm.

"Don't overthink, overthinker. Seriously." He does a drumroll on my leg, and I bounce his hands off.

"It's better than underthinking," I say. "And stop distracting me. I'm driving. Your life is in my hands." I mimic his wiggly eyebrow, purposefully doing it in a way that looks hideous. I don't tell him about Will, since I don't know if my experience was good or bad. Was he just doing what his mom told him to do? Did he enjoy it? It was weird, and yet I prefer that it happened versus nothing happening at all.

"We're going to your house," Danny says. "That's it."

"My house," I say. "My house on Kahala Avenue."

"Yup. Your house on Kahala Avenue. Get used to the way that sounds. Own it, baby. You just need to trade this shit car in for a Mercedes, and you'll fit right in."

"I'll need to do a lot more than that," I say, though I couldn't say what that would be. "And it's not a shit car. I love my li'l Hyundai."

"Hurry," Danny says. "Cut in front of the bus. Go, li'l Hyundai donkey."

"I don't want to cut in front of the bus."

"Cut in front of da bus!" He scoots toward the dash and bounces in his seat.

I zoom ahead, cutting in front of the bus and the cars turning into the mall in time to turn right.

"Nice pidgin," I say. "'Da bus.' What's next, saying 'goden' instead of 'golden'?"

"And 'jewry' instead of 'jewelry,'" he says. "I can swing bot' ways, la dat." He finds a mellow song and sits back, relaxed.

He can get so amped up and then just slump into chillness. It's funny.

"So do you like Whitney?" he asks. "You girls going to be friends?"

"Doubt it," I say. "She's probably all set." And yet, who knows? She did seem friendly; she asked me to come over and lay out. "She's okay," I say. "She doesn't phrase everything as a question?"

"Does she post daily bikini shots on Insta?" Danny says.

"I hope not. That is so icky."

"Insta icky," he says with a funny, girly voice. "I'm not discouraging it, though." I look over at him grinning. His legs take up so much room. He drums his hands against his stomach in time to the beat. How does one look so much like a little boy and a grown man at the same time? I glance briefly at myself, my breasts, my legs, and wonder if he feels the same way about me.

"Do you always have to be drumming something?" I ask.

"I don't know. Let me drum up some answers and get back to you."

I imitate an idiot laughing. "Dork," I say.

The homes are getting bigger as we approach the ocean.

"What do you think of Will?" I ask.

"You already crushing?" He smiles, yet his eyes look wary.

"No, I'm not crushing. I'm just wondering what to think."

"I don't know him that well," Danny says. "Different crowd."

"He showed me around yesterday," I say. Now that I think about it, it was kind of nice of him to give me his club number, even though I didn't use it. "It was cool. He took me to the Outrigger."

"Rad," Danny says, looking out the window.

"He showed me Doris Duke's. Have you jumped from there? Will said it was kind of sketchy."

"The jump? Not at all."

"No, like it's kind of local."

Danny rolls his eyes. "Please, are you serious? That is the most tool thing to say."

That seems aggressive for Danny. I rarely hear him speak badly about anyone, and I wonder if he's jealous that I could have another guy friend who's nothing like him.

I drive down Kahala Avenue and recognize that lady from paddling in the basement. She's jogging in a bikini. I wonder if she ever wears clothes. I slow down when we near the house, and then we arrive.

"This is it," I say.

I use my opener, and the gates part slowly.

Danny takes off his seat belt. "I can't imagine being like, "'Dad, I'm home. Can you make me a Hot Pocket?'"

"I can't imagine your dad having Hot Pockets in his house," I say.

"He has laulaus," Danny says. "The original Hot Pocket."

I drive in, scoping things out. The Wests' house always seems deserted to me, and you can't see their garage, so I never know who's here.

"Welcome to my lovely home," I say. "Can I offer you a Hot Pocket?"

"This *is* frickin' lovely," Danny says.

I park in front of our garage. Danny gets out and looks up at our cottage. "You're so stoked."

"I know," I say. For the first time, I feel a sense of ownership, and because of that, I almost want to downplay the coolness of being here. I start to get the boards out of the car while Danny looks around. It's not that we haven't seen versions of this before. That's the thing with private schools—which we've both gone to since kindergarten—we're all bumped up next to each other. In Hawaii it seems to be even more so.

In film and literature class, I'm in a group of five for presentations, and last week we all went to Kayla's house after school to watch one of the movies. Kayla is in that group of girls who hang out with Whitney. She's tall, Chinese, a little ditzy. I went over, prepared for a fancy house, but hers was a bland concrete box in Kaimuki, and her parents were gambling with old people in their carport.

I strip down to my suit—green top, purple bottoms; girls here don't wear matching sets—and Danny takes off his shirt, showing his lean, muscled torso.

"This way," I say, then walk like I know where I'm going.

Danny walks alongside me, waddling a bit.

"What's wrong with you?" I ask.

"I'm, uh, kind of chafed."

"Oh," I say. I look over at the V muscle running down into his shorts, then look away. "Use Vaseline."

"Any other girl would have been, like, *eew.*"

"I'm saying that on the inside." We walk side by side across the lawn. When a breeze hits the palms and the hedge alongside us, it sounds like it's raining.

"How do you know to use Vaseline?" he asks. "I didn't realize you had experience with this matter."

"It just makes sense," I say.

"Balls and Vaseline—"

"They go hand in hand." I bite my lower lip.

Danny laughs, something that always makes me proud—cracking a boy up. I don't know why it matters to me, or pleases me, maybe because I rarely see girls do it. They're always the laughers, and sometimes it's so frequent, it's not even laughter anymore—just space filler.

We're closer to the main house. When we pass the yardmen, they turn off their weed whackers and look down, waiting for us to go by. I try to look at the home without looking, not wanting to get caught caring. I can see right through it—there's a wide entry with glass doors between us and the ocean. I can see the pool on the other side, extending toward the whitecapped sea, making it seem like the ocean has an inlet to the house.

We walk around the side, my heart beating as if we're stealing something. It's like passing a police car and feeling guilty when you've done nothing wrong.

"This place is really nice," Danny says. We're on a little stone path between a rock wall and the side of the house. He stops walking, admiring I don't know what. The garbage cans? Maybe it's because we're on the side of the house, the place that most homes use as a storage area for things that shouldn't really be stored. It's where the junk is kept, where things turn black from dampness and mold, where beach gear and toys and odds and ends are rarely seen and never organized.

I've noticed this before in the homes of super-wealthy friends—everything is so *clean,* and some worker is always there cleaning it. Not that my mom and I are messy, but cleanliness is hard work. I feel like I sweep, do dishes, scrub, sponge, mop—only to see more ants creeping in or more dirt accumulating. This house is probably always immaculate, even in the nooks.

We walk onto the yard in front of the house, and I look down, hoping not to see anyone. The ocean beyond is cast with a peaceful orange and silvery afternoon light.

The waves are washed out, but it still looks good, especially since it's all ours. I look back at the house behind us. Again, my first reaction isn't in response to the beauty and grandeur of the place—it's to the maintenance of all the windows. I feel the wet salt on my face.

"Shall we?" Danny says, looking out to the surf.

I see steps to the far right of the property that lead to a gate.

"Four, two, three, two," a voice behind us says.

We turn to see Whitney.

"The combo to the lock." She's on a daybed on the patio, fanning herself with a magazine. She's in jean shorts and an orange bikini top.

"Thanks," I say, seeing the lock on the gate, though it's short enough to hop over if I wanted. "I hope it's okay that we're out here. We could always use the beach access if—"

"Why wouldn't it be okay?" she says. She's chewing on something—a stick of some sort. Sugarcane?

"I don't know," I say. "I don't really know the rules."

"There aren't any rules," she says.

"Awesome," Danny says behind me.

"Hi, Danny," Whitney says. She smiles while biting on the sugarcane. She looks so comfortable, not adjusting or fidgeting, just lounging in her own body.

"What's up, Whit?" Danny says. I look back at him and notice his Adam's apple bob up toward a flirtatious, perhaps nervous, grin.

I look down at my suit and legs, wishing I had shaved. Whitney's eyes are still on Danny, then move back to me.

"I just didn't know if your parents want privacy on this side or—"

The place is so big, with so many different places to enter, I wonder if they even see each other.

"It's not like you're confined to your quarters," Whitney says. "No line in the sand. Or the grass or whatever." She waves the stick as she talks. "Seriously," she says. "Of course, it's fine. It's encouraged."

"See?" Danny says. He winks at me. "It's encouraged."

I shrug my board higher up into the nook of my underarm. I follow Whitney's lazy gaze out to the ocean, then realize she's looking at Danny again.

"That's another thing," I say. "It's great I'm allowed to use this area and whatnot, but is it okay if I have friends—if I have Danny—around?"

"Jeez, enough with your worrying," she says. "It's fine, it's good. And whatnot." She purses her lips and smiles. She looks like she's on vacation or has just gotten a massage.

"All right, all right," I say, making light of it all.

"Come surf?" Danny says to her.

Of course she'll say no. Her hair looks perfect, the water looks cold, plus she's reading about fashion and sucking on a stick.

"Sure," she says.

She stands, then takes off her shorts, under which are light blue bottoms. She's thin, but fills out the suit in all the right places. Her inner thighs don't touch, and her legs are like a dancer's. I'm aware of Danny behind me, watching the same thing.

9

WHITNEY AND I STRADDLE OUR BOARDS, WAITING for the next set. Danny has already caught one in. Beneath me are the dark shapes of reef and bright strokes of sand. The water moves, glossy and glassy, making the reefscape look like an oil painting. At Ocean Beach or Pacifica, I never looked down, not wanting to know what was beneath me.

I look at the homes along the beach and detect no signs of life. I'm homesick, but I'm not sure what home I'm sick for. Do I miss the smallness of the San Francisco apartment, the noise of Panhandle Park, the rudeness of the cashier at the Cole Street bodega, who always treated me like I was going to steal something? Do I miss the Enchanted Lakes condo, the neighbors barbecuing in their carports, Dr. Rocker and his sexually frustrated wheelchair-bound clients, or the cars driving by, vibrating with bass and top forty? I seem to love places intensely, but only after I've left them.

Whitney lies down on her board. Surf is flat. I lie down too. The sun feels good on my back.

"I could do this every day," she says. "My mom thinks I need more activities. She wants me to join a school club. Says it will be good for college applications. You in one?"

"No," I say. "But I paddled."

"Have you heard of these clubs? I mean, shitballs, they've thought of everything. Anime club, environmental surf club, military history, civil engineering, global grinds."

"Happy club," I add.

"Really?" she says.

"Yes, it already makes me sad."

She laughs.

"Nihonjin, mud, and lemon clubs. What are those all about?" I say.

"I don't know," she says. "Maybe I'll join the Bible study club," she jokes.

"You totally should," I say.

The easy conversation makes me feel like I'm not at the bottom of a huge ladder.

"Go!" Danny calls. He's paddling toward us. We look back, remembering why we're here. We start to paddle.

"We can put surfing on our applications," I say.

I paddle hard, feel the swell lift me, move back a bit so I don't nosedive, then stand up. On the wave I look over, then back. Whitney didn't make it on.

I can only see Whitney and Danny when the swells dip them down or raise me up. They've drifted out of the lineup and aren't making any attempts to get back. She's lying on her stomach, her arms propping up her chest, which makes her lower back arch. She's on full display, her low skimming bottoms showing butt cleavage. Not that my suit is any different. In Hawaii everyone pays a lot for very little fabric, yet somehow my suit comes off as athletic and hers comes off as sultry, Brazilian. I slide my finger along the seam of my suit, making it go in a bit, seeing what that feels like. I look back at myself, and I guess I like the result.

I prop myself up on my forearms, trying to catch Danny's eye, but it's impossible from this distance. I wonder what she's saying that's got him so interested. What are they talking about? School, clubs, the cost of bathing suits? How rich she is, how pretty she is, how weird it is that I live on her property? I can't imagine what it is. If I'm so curious, why I don't just paddle out there and join in?

I can see an island in the distance, a thick slab on the horizon, and I imagine a girl, floating off its shore, looking this way, imagining me. I lick my salty lips and straddle my board again. The sun is beginning to set, the yolky blob of it running down the sky. They don't even notice that they're drifting away.

"Shark," I say out loud, warning no one. It's crazy that there might be one under us and we'd never know it unless it mistook us for a turtle and bit. The ocean is darker now. Who knows what's under my legs, dangling in the water. I must look like a jellyfish.

A wave rolls under me, and I look back to see the set that's coming.

"I'm going in!" I yell, and the wind must have carried my voice, because Danny lifts his arm in acknowledgment. I let the next wave roll under me, then paddle to catch the next one, which I think I'll get before it breaks. I'm with it, and I stand up and ride. You can't help but smile when you're moving fast over the reef, afloat, the spray of water hitting your face, your body able, strong, free. I try to ride the wave to shore, leaving the shark bait behind.

Whitney shows us the outdoor rock shower on the back side of the pool house, and the three of us get in, elbowing for position under the hot stream of water. I am so cold, and the water is so hot. When I get under, I never want to get out. Hot water makes me lazy.

"My turn," Danny says, pushing me aside.

"Mine," Whitney says, pushing him.

We stand in front of her, trying to get splashes of heat. She tilts her head back, letting the water run down her hair and back. She looks slippery. Her bathing suit is the smallest suit I have ever seen. There's nowhere to hide in it.

"'Kay, done," she says. "Meet by the pool. I'll get towels." She walks out, twisting the water out of her hair.

I shoulder him out of the stream, and he pushes back.

"What were you guys talking about?" I ask.

"Life," he says.

"What about it?"

"She's not doing well in school, she's tired of her friends, she wants something exciting to happen, blah, blah, blah."

"'Blah, blah, blah'? But you seemed riveted."

"She's a good-looking female. Of course I'm riveted." He shivers a little. I move out of the water to let him in.

"School, friends, ennui—seems like you covered a lot. Did you get any airtime or was it all about her?"

"I got air," he says. "Come." He pulls me in next to him, halving the water. I close my eyes and let the water run over my face. He tilts his head back and crosses his arms over his chest.

"I voiced my concerns about the lack of diversity in the Kahala neighborhood," he says, "then moved on to the subject of literacy in Hawaii, our crystal meth problem, GMOs, supporting local farmers."

"Cool. What did she add to all that?" I look down, detecting an ugly tension in my jaw, and a restlessness all over. "Did she even know what you were talking about?"

"Yeah, she said there was a lack of diversity in the Waimanalo neighborhood too. Had me there."

I thought he was kidding with those discussion topics, but maybe they really did have this conversation. I look him over while he has his eyes closed. Though Danny is just a friend and I've never wanted him to be anything else, at that moment, I get the urge to press myself against him, kiss him under the hot water, the ocean lapping nearby, the home like our estate, our paradise. It would be a lot different than the time we were twelve.

I don't know what I'm drawn to more—the whole scene itself and kissing Danny, or the thought of him opening his eyes to me, the ability to surprise someone. The ability to act. Like Whitney, I can be riveting. The urge passes when he turns around and pulls out the top of his shorts to let the water in.

"How's the chafe?" I ask.

Whitney is lounging by the pool on a big, circular chair that looks like a throne. When she sees us, she picks up a towel with her foot.

"Thanks," I say, then realize it's not a towel, but a white, fluffy bathrobe.

"Thanks," Danny says, taking one off the chair, but he doesn't put on the robe, just uses it to dry off. She watches him, amused, and I don't know what I'm feeling right now, but it's something unattractive. A jealous kind of possession.

I put on the robe, then wish I hadn't, since no one else has. She's still in just her suit, her legs curled under her, looking relaxed and so much older than me.

"I gotta jet," Danny says. "Picking up my brother at T-ball."

"What the hell is T-ball?" Whitney asks.

"It's a sport with a ball," Danny says.

"What sport *doesn't* have a ball?" she asks.

"Gymnastics," he says. "Running. Kayaking. The list kind of goes on."

"I hate running," she says, sitting up, like she's about to get into a good debate.

I feel stupid standing here, not contributing to anything right after I asked if she added anything to their talk out in the surf. Clearly, they have a rapport. I almost want to take a step back. Then another and another, until I reach my room.

"T-ball is like an intro to baseball," Danny says. "For young kids."

"How young is he?" she asks.

"Four."

"Shit, that's young."

"Second wife," Danny says and shrugs, as if it's not a big deal, but I know he misses his mom. "Her turn."

I feign interest in the setting sun.

"Four," Whitney says, shading her eyes. "That's a fun age. That's what mothers in Kahala say. What do moms in Waimanalo say?"

"Um," Danny says. "They say kids is 'one hassle,' or 'one blessing.' Depends on their mood, I guess. And the kid."

My head goes back and forth. Finally, I sit by her feet. The round chair is large enough, and it's the only way I feel I can insert myself. Danny wipes his face, then hands the robe back to Whitney. She hugs it to her chest.

"You're welcome to surf here anytime," Whitney says. "You know the code."

"Cool, thanks. I'm catching the bus."

"Da bus," I say, but he doesn't react.

"Mind if I leave my board with you?" He looks at me, sniffles, then runs his hand through his hair, making it spike up.

I'm about to answer when Whitney says, "Yeah, leave your board on the side of the house."

He looks at her and then me as if deciding something. It shouldn't matter who he leaves his board with. "Thanks," he says to Whitney. But it does. Why does it feel like she's winning something? And in a game where I can't fairly compete.

"You're catching the bus?" she asks.

"Yup. My dad's using the truck."

"That sucks," she says, and she truly looks pained and incredulous.

"Not really. I do homework or just check out. I like it sometimes."

"I want to try," she says. I'm surprised he doesn't make fun of her for wanting to try the bus, as if it's an activity like kite surfing or something.

"I gotta go," he says.

"Then go already," I say. He looks down at me as if he just remembered I'm here.

Whitney is less enthused and conversational when he leaves. I get up from her chair, feeling awkward.

"I guess I should get back," I say.

"Get back to what?" she asks. Before I can answer, she hands me a mug from the table next to her.

"Thanks," I say.

"Hot cocoa," she says. "Or warm cocoa."

I sit down on the recliner next to her. It's like being at a spa. Afternoon surf, hot shower, and now lounging in a robe. I don't know whether it inspires me, refreshes me, or makes me feel like doing absolutely nothing ever again. I take a sip, trying to shake off the annoyance I had, the feeling that she was poaching my friend. Poaching with access codes and board storage. I need to let it go.

"It has a little Kahlúa in it," she says.

"Great," I say, so quickly that she laughs.

The Kahlúa is creamy and sweet, like a dessert. I take another sip and already can, or think I can, feel the alcohol. A nice heat forms in my chest, and I feel both heavy and light.

I only drink when I go out with Danny to parties, which is rare. I usually turn him down, feeling bad that he's obligated to hang with me since I don't really know anyone.

"Makes dinner more enjoyable," she says.

"Yeah," I say, and feel false. I've never had a drink with dinner.

"You're coming over tomorrow, right?" she asks. "My mom said she asked you guys over for dinner, so we had to be home."

"You don't have to be," I say, so embarrassed that she's being forced to eat dinner with me, on a Friday night no less.

"No, it's cool." She pauses, as if considering its coolness, which makes me think she's okay with it, maybe looking forward to it. "Just hope my dad doesn't get wasted and embarrass me."

I'm not sure if she wants me to respond or not. "Like, what would he do?" I ask.

"Oh, he just drinks and gets angry, or irritable—not like violent or anything. He's kind of losing his memory, so he drinks to cope with that. He gets frustrated. But he's cool. Didn't mean to scare you."

"I ain't skurred," I say, and thankfully, she laughs. I prop my leg up, so it slips out of the robe. The sky darkens, and behind us I hear faint music. I can also hear the palms—now when they move it sounds as if something's sizzling. "It's so nice here," I say.

"I know," she says, and for some reason her saying this is refreshing. Dismissing or not realizing the beauty would be an insult.

"Also just to warn you, my mom may ask you for help," she says.

I turn to face her. She's closing her eyes, as if sunbathing.

"Like chores or something?" I ask.

She laughs, then turns to face me as well. "No. She thinks you might be able to help *me*. Like with homework and stuff. I'm stupid."

"Don't say that."

"But I am," she says.

I don't know what to say. I was behind when I first got here, and I'm sure most of us feel overwhelmed, pressured, and, yes, stupid.

"I feel stupid too," I say. "This school is crazy. Why would she think I could help you?" I want to say that just because I don't have many friends doesn't mean I'm smart.

"I don't know," she says. "Probably because odds are that you're smarter than me, and I guess my dad said you were astound nuts in your interview and testing."

So everyone but me knew that her dad got me in. Rad. I don't mind, I guess—it's just weird to be told your whole life that hard work pays off, but really you need connections.

"I guess I should thank your dad," I say. "I think he got me in more than some test scores."

"Yeah," she says. "He really likes you. Or your mom or whatever."

"Yeah," I say, at a loss, yet somewhat comforted that we both may feel this way. I think the Kahlúa is making me care less about it, though. The sky is dark now, and the pool lights and landscape lighting come on.

"Maybe I should prove her wrong," I say. "Your mom." It takes her a moment to understand.

"You should!" she says. "Prove her wrong and corrupt me further. That would be a riot."

I want to know why she used the word *corrupt.* What does she do that's bad? I want to do it too, and for a moment I see her as a portal into another world, or at least a different plane.

She sits up and gets another mug off the table. "This was for Danny," she says, pouring me some and taking the rest. She's a good hostess. It seems like she's almost obligated to show off all the things she has and the things she's allowed to do.

I hold the mug in my lap. "What are you having trouble with, anyway?"

"French, I guess. And math, English. I like to read, though. I love it, actually. I just don't want to have to talk about what I've read, and I don't want to write about it. It kills the whole experience for me, you know?"

"I know," I say. "I feel the same way sometimes." A trickle of languor moves throughout my body. "It's weird that in French dogs say '*ouah, ouah*' instead of 'woof, woof.'"

I'm looking up at the palm trees when I say this, then look back at her and see that she's laughing.

"*Ouah, ouah!*" she says.

I laugh too, and we go through all the sounds of French animals, a rooster crowing (*cocorico*), a cow lowing (*meuh*), a duck quacking (*coin, coin*) and the one that becomes our favorite: a pig rooting (*groin, groin*). I tell her in Chinese a duck would say *ga ga*. We laugh and laugh, and she reaches down and brings out a bottle, refilling our cocoa without any cocoa this time.

"You're tutoring me already!" she says.

"And I take Mandarin," I say. I lean back and glance at my legs out in front of me. I tilt my head to the dark sky.

"*Oui, oui,*" Whitney says and then a silence comes over us, a nice, comfortable silence.

10

DANNY IS ACROSS THE COURTYARD UNDER THE TREES by the library steps. I walk toward him, self-conscious as usual, even with the understanding that no one is looking at me. I tug my skirt down. It looked good when I was alone, but has suddenly become heinous.

I get closer. He's talking to Barrett Dillingham. They're both holding the straps of their backpacks and nodding. Boys always seem to communicate without using words. I could walk by and see if he stops me, but then I reconsider. One of the things I absolutely need to do is what I want, especially when it's something this trivial.

"Hey," I say.

"What's up, Little Donkey?" Danny says. Barrett looks me over, but keeps talking to Danny.

"Do you know Lea?" Danny says.

"'Sup," Barrett says.

"Hello," I say, because if I said "'sup," I think I'd hate myself forever.

"This is Barrett," Danny says.

Yeah. I know. He's in my history class. He plays water polo. He drives a black Ford F-150.

"I hear the pattern is A, D, C, E," Barrett says. "And if you stick to that, you won't, like, ace it, but you'll do okay."

"Yeah, or you could just, uh, study," Danny says. "It wasn't that bad."

Barrett adjusts his backpack and grins. "My lifestyle is seriously becoming compromised."

"There you go. That's a big word," Danny says.

I laugh to participate somehow, and Barrett looks at me like I have Tourette's or food on my face. I keep my hands down by my sides. I will not check for food on my face.

"What about you?" Barrett asks. "Are you taking the prep course?"

"No," I say. "And if I did, it wouldn't compromise my lifestyle in any way."

No one responds. Please, ground, consume me.

"So glad that's done with," Danny says. "Just wait, little juniors. Senior year cruise."

Danny raises his arms over his head. He's so damn comfortable. I'd raise my arms and not know how to bring them back down. What will I do here without him? With him going to Berkeley, it feels like we're switching places. Why can't we just line up?

Barrett looks over my head. "Hey, girlie," he says.

I turn to see Whitney. She walks up behind Danny, dipping her knees into the back of his legs. He collapses way more than he should. "Hey, now," he says, laughing. Barrett greets her with a hand slap, then pulls her into a hug.

"What about you?" Barrett asks. "Saturday prep?"

"Are you kidding me?" she says. She's wearing an off-the-shoulder T-shirt with a long skirt. "Too early," she says. "I'm hungover now—how would I deal on a Saturday?"

"Such a party girl," Barrett says.

"Party, party," Danny says, and I see a flicker of something—curiosity or disapproval? Something.

"Yeah, you totally missed our après-surf cocktails," Whitney says and acknowledges me.

Again I see that look on Danny's face, like he's trying to seem indifferent, but isn't. I think I'm expected to talk now, and so I say, "Yeah. It was good. We—"

"Got wasted!" Whitney says.

"For reals?" Barrett says, looking pleased, suddenly reevaluating me. I go with it and don't say anything. I didn't think Whitney was drunk at all last night. I wasn't, but maybe she poured more Kahlúa into her own drink or imbibed without me, alone. But why would she want to include me this way?

"Danny, join us next time?" She grins with an open mouth as if posing for a picture.

"Sure," he says. "Next time."

"What about now?" she says.

"Now?" He laughs. "You're crazy." He looks toward the library. "I'm on brother duty tonight."

"Your stepmom should get a nanny or something," she says, and I cringe, but Danny just smiles.

"Yeah, she totes should," he says in a girly voice. "Nanny, driver, gardener, guest cottage . . ."

Barrett laughs, even though he probably has or could have had all these things and more. The theater here at Punahou has his last name on it.

"Mari!" Whitney yells. "Yo! Wait up."

Mari Ito turns. "Yo!" she yells from across the quad.

"See you tonight?" Whitney says, looking back at me. Barrett leaves too, tilting his head in farewell.

"Right," I say. Dinner. I almost ask her what I should wear.

Danny watches her go. "You got drunk with Whitney?" He almost sounds jealous.

"Not really," I say.

"Not really?" He looks past me.

"We had a few drinks, that's all."

"Well, well, well." He smirks and shakes his head.

I recognize his look: fake relaxed. He wants to know more, see more, do more, but doesn't want to appear like he wants anything at all.

"She's a trip," he says.

"Yeah," I say and look down, and then I ask, "How so?"

"I don't know," he says. "Crazy or . . . interesting."

"Interesting," I say. *How so?* I want to ask again, but I can see it. She's beautiful, composed. She's interesting because she's fully herself.

He looks deep in thought, and now I'm back to where I was with my fake-relaxed face, wanting to know more while not looking like I do.

Am I interesting? I want to be interesting. I want to be crazy. I want to be fully myself.

"Like I've always known her as a group," Danny says. "All her little party friends. But alone, I don't know, she's cooler than I thought." He smiles to himself.

I'd be cool too if I had a house like that, a pool like that, a life like that. These thoughts make me feel small, but it's true. She's pretty, but it's as though money gives you bonus points; it makes you prettier. Because if she weren't Whitney West—if she were, say, Gina Crumb from Kaneohe—then she wouldn't be as compelling, as cool, even if her looks remained the same. Money seems to work like yeast, raising people to the top.

"She's . . . irreverent," Danny says, his thumbs tucked into his backpack straps.

He looks like he's still thinking about how to describe her. Is it that complicated? I wait for him to elaborate, but he doesn't. Is she that much more irreverent than us? Than me?

"There's your other roommate," he says.

I look across the quad, and Will's walking slowly with Lissa Sand, a senior who looks like she's twenty-five. She's tall and, in a way, sandy—the same coloring as ground-up coral, cowrie, and the exoskeletons of sea creatures. Ms. Yamada would be so proud of me, the way I've applied school lessons to the real world. She also has sandy-colored hair, highlighted, wavy, and long. She's beautiful and rich-looking, though she seems pissed off about it. In paddling she stroked, the first seat in the canoe, due to the length of her limbs. She's aloof and intimidating, and seems to be always looking at her nails or the ends of her hair. I'm jealous of her and Will, the way they're walking so intimately, like it's no big deal. I'm horrified that he's forced to leave that tonight in order to have dinner with this.

"Now *he's* interesting," I say. "Can't wait to have dinner with him later."

"His girlfriend coming too?" he asks, using a sarcastic and

slightly bitter voice, which is unusual for Danny and has the odd effect of making me want to hear it again.

"Not invited," I say, making it up, suddenly feeling like we're competing against each other. *If you're going to pay attention to Whitney, then I'll pay attention to Will.* Except it's not just a game to me. I genuinely can't wait to see Will tonight.

11

WHEN I WALK INTO THE HOUSE, MY MOM IMMEDIATELY says, "We're going over to the big house for dinner, okay?"

"I know," I say. I close the door, drop my bag, and run my hand through my hair. "I'm very aware of that." I pretend to be burdened by this plan and the constant reminder of this dinner, when really I'm thrilled to have something to do. Something to dress for.

"How was school?" she asks, and begins to make tea. Her hair is in a topknot, and she's wearing all Lululemon exercise clothes.

"Fine," I say, too tired to give her my rambling answer. "How was work?"

"Awesome," she says. "I spent hours in makeup just so they could make me look bad." She tears open a tea package and drops it into the hot water. "I could have worn no makeup and not washed my hair." She takes her mug to the couch, then waves me over. "But they need to make me pretty ugly," she says. "Cute ugly. That's the key."

I sit down and put my legs up, pushing my feet against her thighs.

"Then Les, that guy I was telling you about, he can never

get things right. Not just his lines, but the delivery, and his ego washes out anything the director says."

My mom uses big hand gestures. I love hearing her complain—it's always done comically. "Like, today I had to say—" She starts to laugh and pats my feet. "Today, I had to fend off Jenkins, who of course I'll probably fall in love with by the end of the season—but I had to say, 'You need to find a new cereal.' And then he goes, 'What's that, Dr. Lovejoy?' Then I look at him like this—"

My mom gives me a look that's both attractive and cruel, then says, "You need to find a new cereal that has more fiber, because you are so full of crap."

"Oh my God," I say. "That's really bad."

"Really bad," she says. "*Hawaii Five-0*'s still going, though, so who knows."

"And we always have the Wests," I say.

She doesn't answer, and I wonder what she's thinking about. There seems to be this cloud of mystery around her friendship with them.

"Why didn't we ever do things with them when I was a kid?"

"You are a kid," she says, but looks at me like she can't believe it.

"You know what I mean. You did things, but I never really met them."

"I don't know," she says. She seems to be truly thinking about my question. "It's a different kind of friendship," she finally says.

"You and Melanie don't seem to have a lot in common," I say, and she laughs quickly as though I've made quite the understatement.

"She's part of the package," my mom says in a soft voice.

"What does that mean?"

"Eddie and I are good friends. Or were. We are, but . . . you'll see in life that it's not so easy to maintain relationships with guy friends. You sort of inherit their wives and continue your relationship through them."

I think of the exclusion I felt with Danny when he was with Whitney.

"Not that I don't adore Melanie. Although she can be a little intense, God bless her."

"You always God bless someone you've said something negative about," I say.

"Ha," she says. "I've just tried to put a little distance between us and my friendship with them, that's all. She always went back and forth with me, so I never knew where I stood. It was better to be at arm's length."

"So what changed? They're kind of within arm's length now."

She takes another sip of tea. "I don't know. Seems like we're friends now. And I guess I'm returning a favor." She sighs, then catches me still looking at her. "Don't worry about it," she says.

"Is Eddie sick or something?"

She hesitates, then says, "Yes," and her eyes water slightly. "He's showing signs of dementia, which at his age usually means Alzheimer's. He's slowing down. No one knows what will happen or how slowly or quickly it could go."

"He's a lot older than you," I say. "But you were friends?"

She scratches her head and smiles to herself. "We dated while I was in college and he was working, going back and forth between Hawaii and LA."

"Oh my God, Mom," I say. "That was your boyfriend before Stranger Dad." I imagine her with this mogul.

"He was kind of in love with me but was . . . how can I put this . . . seduced by someone else."

"Oh my God, this is too much! Melanie?" I sink down into the couch and push my feet against her harder.

"She was manipulative, that one. He got her pregnant, then came the wedding. Really, she was perfect for him and his family. Their wedding was like a meeting of island royalty—the networking event of the century." Her voice is cheery. "Don't look so stunned," she says. "It was a long time ago."

"Were you sad?" I ask. It's weird seeing my mom peeled back and bare, like a girl.

"I was a little sad at the time, but more mad that he professed his love right before sleeping with a family friend he'd probably been seeing the whole time." She laughs. "But believe me. It worked out. I could never have been a wife like she is. He's her job. Socializing is her job. I didn't want that."

"And then came the next fine fellow."

"Yup," she says, looking down and patting my feet.

I always skip over the sex part, the fact that you exist because your mother and father did it.

"And Melanie's great," my mom says, looking at me, as if trying to make sure I understand. "She's the most generous woman I know. And I'm having fun. It's fun to socialize with her group. It's fun to be wanted around. And you and Whitney. Isn't it fun?"

Yes, I guess what little contact I've had with her and Will has, sadly, been the most fun I've had since moving here. Even the discomfort, the awkwardness, it gives a charge to my day.

My mom looks lost in thought, but comes to when she notices me staring at her. "I'm going to shower, then head over," she says.

I look at my phone. It's four o'clock. "Already?"

"Melanie wants me to come over a little early. Chat. I think she likes the company. Gives her an excuse to break open the wine early. I'll see you there, okay? Five thirty."

I move my legs, and she gets up and walks to her room; I'm guessing that she's just as eager as I am.

I take a shower, then stand in front of the clothes in my closet. I have tons of clothes and am always feeling like I have nothing to wear. I want to look good without seeming like I've put thought into it. That's how Whitney always looks—carelessly put together, with stylish results. She'll pair cutoffs with a cropped T-shirt, which would look skimpy on anyone else, but then she'll top it off with a silk scarf tied around her head, and the result is cool, possessed, unintentionally sexy. If I put a scarf around my head, I'd look like an idiot who thought it would be cool to have a scarf around her head. I couldn't pull it off and am ashamed that I tried it a few days ago.

I go to my drawers, get out my jeans. Always jeans. That's all I ever come up with. I put them on, flip through the tops in my closet, choose the black camisole and a button-down plaid shirt. I leave my hair wet, twirling it into a bun at the base of my neck. I look in the mirror. I've gotten so tan, and the freckles on my cheeks are more pronounced. Like stars, they come and go depending on the light. I look different, I think. Can a house change you? Do you alter your look, your posture, depending on which door you come out of? I think you do, and know that it's probably one of those things no one owns up to. I put some lotion on my arms and legs so that I, too, am golden and glistening.

It's silly, but I'm nervous. I don't want to go in alone. It's that awkward time of not wanting to be too early and yet not wanting to sit around here doing nothing. Still, I choose the latter. I stall.

I sit down on my bed. I will meditate! But, no, I can't sit still. How people sit in a room trying to out-ohm each other is beyond me. At paddling practice in San Francisco, Ms. Perry would have us visualize before a race. We'd lie down and close our eyes as she guided us through, narrating our canoe gliding across the bay. The canoe in my head would turn into a rocket ship that would shoot out of my vision so I could go over my homework, my schedule, what I was going to eat, what music I was going to add, what I needed to study, all while shaking my ankle and waiting for our canoe to cross the finish line. I always reentered at the end, so I could feel like I'd accomplished something. I could be Zen still.

I get up and look out the window to see if there's any activity at the West house. The sun is making its daily journey to the other side; the ocean looks as though it were under hypnosis. I imagine cavemen doing the same thing, sipping their animal blood or what have you, gazing upon this daily descent, thinking to themselves, *How beautiful* or *What the heck is that thing?* Should that be my opening line to break the ice tonight?

I look in the mirror one last time, then man up, or woman up, and leave this cottage to walk to the big house.

12

IT'S ALMOST SIX, BUT THE LATE SUN IS STRONG THROUGH the clouds. It's a glorious feeling, walking across this sea of lawn. The palms sway languidly, and even though it's sunny, a faint spray of rain comes down at a diagonal. It's like being misted with an atomizer.

The house is so open, and this is both intimidating and welcoming. I go up to the front door, but feel silly about knocking on a glass sliding door. The living room is just there, wide open, so that I can see my mom and Melanie on the patio beyond, though neither *patio* nor *lanai* seems like a big enough word to describe something that's essentially another living room or, for some people, another house.

"Hello?" I say, so I don't scare anyone, though it's not a kind of house where people can really drop in unexpectedly. No Mormons on bikes making their way to these parts.

I take off my shoes, even though I hate that Hawaiian custom of shoe removal, especially to go over to someone's house for dinner. Like monkeys dining at a table, our bare feet gripping the chair legs. Yuck.

The living room is vast and smells like gardenias and candles. I look around for gardenias. I look around for candles, and see neither. The stone floor feels hotel-like, and the inside of their home is beautiful, but sort of similar to all the beautiful houses in Hawaii I've been in. Pillows with coral or turquoise tropical motifs, perfectly plumped and placed. High ceilings, sometimes thatched, lazy fans, tropical paintings, and books about other grand Hawaiian homes. It's like they all work with the same architect and designers or something, and everything is situated as if staged for an open house. There's no debris, no sign of life, until I walk in a little farther and then I see some evidence—a phone, a bag, keys.

"Lea!" Melanie calls out. "Come on out!"

I walk out to everyone on the lanai, which is furnished similarly to the living room, but more rattan and Bali. I could go on vacation here.

My mom and Melanie are sitting in big plush chairs with high backs. My mom gives me the say-something-nice look.

"I love your home," I say.

"Oh gosh," Melanie says, as if I'm crazy and she lives in a sinkhole. "Look at you." She stands, then walks to me and holds my wrists. "You look so pretty."

I seriously wonder if this is something all adults say.

"You too," I say, with a forced smile. She wears a bright, belted dress and petite and skinny accessories, a tiny pearl necklace and thin gold ones with small trinkets that make faint noises. She's fit, but not crazily so like a lot of these moms who belong to the Outrigger or run triathlons and have bodies like the boys in cross-country. It's weird seeing her now, knowing what I know, that she stole my mom's boyfriend. How? I automatically think. My mom is so much more beautiful, so much more chill than you.

"Eddie?" Melanie says. "Eddie!"

I hadn't noticed him since his chair is facing the ocean. He glances at me, then fixes his wife with a steely yet bewildered gaze.

"Yes, what?"

"This is Lea," Melanie says.

"Hello." He almost stands up, then seems to decide against it.

"Hello, nice to meet you." I walk with my mom toward him. I hate saying "hello" instead of "hi," but my mom has coached me to do it, and to her credit, adults totally respond to it.

He doesn't look like he knows why I'm here, but also seems as though he's used to not knowing the kids who come over.

"This is Ali's daughter," Melanie says. "Lea."

"Oh." He grins and laughs, then looks at me again, and something in his eyes clears, as if he'd removed the lens that makes all of us kids look the same. His grin is slightly crooked, and he squints as though he's having trouble seeing me.

"Lea," he says. "Sorry, I thought you were one of Whitney's friends." He speaks slowly, looking at my mom, then back at me. "Great to see you. All grown up."

"Thank you," I say.

"She's going to Punahou with Whitney and Will, remember?" Melanie says, almost as though she's talking to a child.

"Yes," he says, and he and my mom exchange a brief glance. "I know."

"It's great," I say. "I love the school." I'm smiling like a maniac at this powerful man, who is being forced to talk to me. He must be almost seventy years old, but is fit and handsome. He has small, straight teeth, very white against his nut-brown tan. He wears a silk aloha shirt and long dark blue pants. There are little bags under his eyes—like pouches—that have the effect of making him look kind.

"It's good to have you and your mom here," he says.

"Yeah, you guys go way back!" I say, then look down and clear my throat.

He gives me a quick smile that's almost like a signal for me to relax. I return the smile, identically, and feel immediately bonded and comfortable. I expected him to be some kind of stiff, lush tyrant, but something about him and even Whitney, when I was with her yesterday, gives me the sense that they're similar: thoughtful, expected to be someone they're not, and maybe a little tired of hosting.

"Where's Willie boy?" he asks Melanie, and looks prepared for disappointment. I bite my lower lip. *Willie boy.*

"He should be here soon," Melanie says in a singsong voice. "Can I get you anything to drink?" she asks me. "We have soda, Perrier, milk, kombucha?"

"I'm okay for now, thank you," I say.

She is smiling, but her eyes look frantic, like she's entertaining people more important than us. I see a guy walking out from the kitchen and realize he's a waiter, carrying a tray of appetizers. I thought we were just coming over for dinner. I didn't think it was an event.

"Wow, look at this," my mom says when the waiter walks outside.

He holds the platter of wontons in front of me first. It's weird because he's cute, maybe college age. I want to tell him, *You don't need to serve me.*

I put the wonton into my mouth, a mistake because of its awkward shape. I must look like I'm chewing on a lychee, and I quickly work it down to a mush. He waits there, holding the tray in front of Melanie.

"How do you like it?" Melanie asks.

"Yum," I say, chewing and gasping for air. I finally swallow. My mom has taken one and eats it quickly, talking while she finishes.

"Is it poke in a wonton?" she asks.

"I believe so," the waiter says.

"Really good," she says. "Just a little hard to eat."

"That's what I told them!" Melanie looks like she wants to fry someone. "It gives you blowfish face, right?"

"Right," I say, pretending to be appalled.

"The one thing I detest about pupus is they're so hard to manage! You can't talk and walk and eat these things. I'm not going to order them for the party." She looks over my head, all crazy-eyed. "Oh, there's Gloria. Gloria! Come in! How are you?"

A woman walks in, dressed as if this were a party. Melanie grabs my mom's shoulder. "Gloria, this is Ali! Gloria just moved here from LA."

"Nice to meet you," my mom says, with her habitual warm smile.

"You too," Gloria says, looking my mom over and blinking her eyes as if adding something up.

"Gloria's husband owns a tour bus company in LA, and now

they're buying the Wiki franchise!" Melanie says. She gives my mom a look, which reminds me of the ones my mom gives me—the *speak* look. *Converse.*

"Wonderful," my mom says.

"And this is Ali's daughter, Lea," Melanie says.

"Hello," I say.

She gives me a closed-mouth smile. "Hi, there."

Then Gloria and my mom both exclaim and say all the shit people always say: "So nice to finally meet you, I love that dress, where do you live, isn't it wonderful here? How old are your children?"

"Ali and Lea are staying in the cottage while she's filming," Melanie says.

"It's been wonderful," my mom says.

Melanie nods and presses her hand to her chest. "I'm so glad. Have you evened out all the quirks?"

The kinks, I want to say. And it doesn't need to be air quoted.

"What quirks?" my mom says. "It's a smooth-running ship. It's paradise."

"How nice," Gloria says.

"It's nice for us!" Melanie says. "We get to live with a famous person."

My mom looks down and smiles, and I can tell she's uncomfortable.

"So what's Alex Crane really like?" Gloria asks.

"Oh, he's wonderful," my mom says. I always sympathize with her when people ask this. She needs to be gracious, feed them an anecdote, perform.

"Have I seen you in anything?" Gloria asks.

"I highly doubt it." My mom laughs. "Unless you watch Lifetime or have an uncanny memory and remember me from . . . let's see . . . *Law and Order*, *Parents*, lots of canceled shows—*Grownups*, *616*, *Chasers*. I've been on . . . *24*, *CSI*, a cable series about ancient Rome—"

"I've seen that!" Gloria says. "It was . . . well, it was like a porno version of Rome."

My mom laughs, genuinely laughs, and I do too. I didn't expect Gloria to say something that could possibly be offensive. "Exactly!" my mom says, and looks at Gloria in a different way.

"I don't know how *Chasers* was canceled," Melanie says. "Now, that was a great show."

"It was horrible," my mom says, touching both sides of her face and laughing. "That's why it was canceled."

"The one about the attorneys?" Gloria says.

I nod. Gloria makes a comical kind of grimace. I like her.

"It was genius!" Melanie says, trying to recruit Eddie into agreeing with her, but he shrugs and turns away. He's not part of this girl talk.

"Anyway," my mom says.

"*No Borders* will be a hit, though," Melanie says. "Ali is genius in it."

My mom makes a dismissive sound that's a bit halfhearted, maybe from having to do it so often. I wonder how many people Melanie says the same thing to—how many geniuses there are in her world. Another woman is walking through the living room. Her nose looks flattened by surgery, a bold necklace nestles into her cleavage, and she's being trailed by a guy who's looking at his phone in a way that makes me think he's fake-looking at his phone. Melanie imitates this woman's thrilled expression as she walks outside. I don't know what the shit is going on, but my mom looks just as surprised by the company.

I turn to the ocean, noticing Eddie still sitting there, ignoring everyone, but the woman's husband comes by, shakes his hand, then awkwardly backs off to the bar like Eddie is some kind of head boss. My face is tired. I stop smiling.

"Punahou's a great school," Eddie says as if we're talking about it for the first time. "I'm glad you're there." He looks out to the ocean, shakes his glass and takes a long sip.

"I love it there," I say and laugh, even though nothing he said was funny. "Thank you for . . . everything."

He looks disappointed in my answer. He doesn't want to be thanked. I see this immediately.

"Sit down, relax," he says, gesturing to the chairs and daybed.

I don't dare sit on the daybed. I sink into a lounge chair. The waiter guy comes back with a different platter. He serves the women who are by the sliding doors, then walks over to me and Eddie.

"Thank you," I say. I take a chip and dip it in a gray substance.

"Smoked ahi," the waiter says.

It's really good. I could eat the whole bowl. I wish Whitney and Will would come out or that I hadn't come so dorkily early. I bring my legs under me so I don't look like I'm sunbathing in jeans. Though now I probably resemble the small Alice in Wonderland. I sit alert, like I'm going to be interviewed or tested.

"I hate that daybed," Eddie says. "It's ridiculous."

"Hard to get adjusted, I bet," I say quietly.

I put my hands on my knees.

"It's a good test," he says. "When I have guests over. If a guy sits there, it means he's a pompous ass."

I laugh and can see exactly the kind of man he's talking about. Polos, sockless loafers, big white teeth, kind of like the guy who just walked in.

"I hope this isn't hard on you," he says. "Moving all of a sudden."

"I wouldn't call it *hard,*" I say, gesturing to the things around him. He looks at what I've fluttered my hands toward, then gazes back at the ocean.

"I like having your mom here." He seems saddened by this, but it may just be the way his face naturally falls.

I don't know how to respond, so I remain quiet, something he doesn't seem to have a problem with. It must be hard for him to talk to people, like he can't totally trust his words and expressions anymore. He glances at the guests behind him, then back to the quiet view.

Whitney has finally come out of her room. She walks out to us, and Melanie trails her closely, looking vexed.

"You didn't even start the paragraph?" Melanie says softly. "It's just a paragraph. It should take no time at all. What have you been doing all afternoon?" Melanie shakes her head and looks bewildered.

"If it's *just* a paragraph, then I can do it after dinner," Whitney says. "It should take no time at all, and it's the weekend!"

Whitney looks at me as if we're in on something together.

"Do you procrastinate?" Melanie asks me. Her friends are out of earshot, lingering by the bar.

Whitney snorts.

"Um," I say.

"Answer!" Whitney says, throwing her hands up in the air. "You're procrastinating!"

We laugh, and Melanie tucks her chin and appraises her daughter, then turns her head to me and raises her brow.

Eddie just looks confused. "Isn't it Friday?" he asks.

"Yes, it's Friday, Daddy," Whitney says. She kisses him on the top of his head. "Pace yourself with that," I hear her say.

"How are you, Whitney?" my mom asks, walking over. Eddie looks at my mom expectantly, as if she's about to ask him to dance.

"I'm good, thanks," Whitney says and stops scowling. Melanie, too, eases up, maybe remembering we're supposed to have a nice dinner together.

The other women and the man have gone inside. They're exclaiming over something, and I realize it's Will. He walks out to us holding a box of pizza. I stand up, feeling awkward on the chair.

"Finally!" Melanie says.

I look at my mom, confused. This is hardly the sit-down dinner I was expecting. They're going to have waiter dude serve pupus and then pizza?

Will puts the box down and removes his hat, revealing his light brown hair.

"Will, you know Ali, of course?"

"Of course. Hello, Will," my mom says.

He moves swiftly to my mother. "Great seeing you," he says, kissing her cheek, and I'm slightly jealous of their easy interaction.

"And Lea."

"Hi," I say.

He leans down for a brief kiss on the cheek, but I automatically hug him instead, which he belatedly returns, and because he's tall, I kind of get stuck in the embrace. I make my way back down, chiding myself for failing to master this greeting. *Brief kiss on the cheek. No more. Don't get stuck in hugs.*

"You showed her around?" Melanie asks.

"Yup." His smile is so warm and open. I almost look behind me to see if someone else is there. I pull my hair out of its bun, feeling dowdy and clumsy.

"I saw you guys filming by Olomana golf course today," he says. "How's it going?"

"It's going well, thanks," my mom says.

"Thanks for bringing the pizza, love bug," Melanie says, and he doesn't cringe.

"Right on my way," he says.

Whitney's curled up in her chair and looking at her phone. "What kind did you get?"

"Mushroom," he says.

"I wanted the basil tomato," she says.

"Well, close your eyes and imagine it."

He winks at me, and I blink, lamely. Melanie looks at him in an entirely different way than she does her daughter. I glance at my phone: it's been an hour since I walked over to be on time. My mom doesn't seem to know what the pizza's all about either.

"Okay, kids," Melanie says. "We're off. I'm so glad we could all get together."

"Are we not eating here?" my mom says.

"No, I didn't tell you? Where is my mind? We thought we'd take Gloria and the Rowes out—just going to pop into this fantastic event the girls are chairing. You don't mind, Als, do you?" I've never heard anyone call my mother Als.

"That's fine," she says, widening her eyes at me in a silent apology.

"We'll let the kids have the place to themselves," Melanie says, something my mom can't really argue with, and neither can I. Anyone would be happier without the adults, though for me, sometimes I like having them around. They provide a kind of safety, a time with no expectations.

"Except be sure to get to your homework," Melanie says. "You can all do it together. Study buddies!"

"Weekend," Whitney says.

"I keep forgetting," Melanie says. "Oh, and Ali made an amazing pie. You guys can have it for dessert."

I want to say that my mom made it for the dinner tonight, the dinner we were all supposed to have, and how does she know it's amazing? It could taste like gecko for all she knows.

"Hey, can I grab some of that, guy?" Will says. The waiter stops walking in and turns to Will. Will pops the appetizer in his mouth, then gives the waiter a kind of nod of dismissal. I don't dare take one, not wanting blowfish face.

"You like mushroom pizza?" he asks.

"My favorite," I say. A breeze comes off the ocean, moving my hair off my shoulders.

This isn't so bad.

The adults make their way inside. Eddie seems unsure of his steps and is looking around like he's lost something. I bet he's looking for his phone, the one I happened to see inside.

"It's in the living room," I say to Eddie. "On the table by the couch."

"What is?" he says.

"Your phone."

He laughs and looks up at my mom. "Smart girl you got."

My mom looks at me, proud.

"See you at home," I say, tripping over the word. I want to talk with her about how this welcome dinner has turned into a pizza party, and I can tell she knows this. It's irritating the way both of us are so buttoned up, like we can't communicate freely anymore. But once they leave, I'm thrilled to have weekend plans, even though they were forced upon all of us.

13

WILL COMES OUTSIDE WITH PAPER PLATES AND PLACES them on the table in front of us. He sits next to Whitney.

"Thanks," I say. I take a small slice, even though I'm starving. If Danny were here, we'd fight for the biggest piece.

"Now I remember seeing you before," Will says. He takes the largest slice. "Around campus," he says. "With a paddle."

"I paddled," I add, ridiculously.

"You did?" Whitney asks with her mouth full. She licks her fingers.

"Yeah. I missed most of the season, but they let me practice with them, since I'd been doing it in San Francisco." I wish the season wasn't over. I miss the long paddles out in the open ocean, where we'd sometimes be accompanied by dolphins.

"You steered," Will says, and I'm surprised he knows this. "Like a blind woman."

I want to tell him that we won all of our races, so I couldn't have been that bad, but I can't tell if he's joking or not. He looks carefree and light, his eyes warm, welcoming, like you could fall into them.

"How do you know I steered?" I ask.

"Lissa," he says. "I came to a few of her races."

"She seems nice," I say with a note of insincerity.

"She's very nice," he says with a slight grin. I can't tell if he's making fun of her or me.

Whitney smirks.

"What's the paragraph?" I say to Whitney. "The paragraph your mom was talking about."

"Oh God," Whitney says and puts her feet up on the chair. "For French. 'Write a paragraph about Olivier's weekend and include the animals above.' Like, I'm sure Olivier's weekend included an elephant and a spotted owl."

"Just make it up," Will says, picking a mushroom off the pizza. Why am I noticing everything he's doing, and why do I think it's adorable? "Make up anything. The teacher—you have Schappel, right? She just wants to make sure you know the words. It doesn't have to make sense."

"But I don't know any of the shit I'm supposed to use. Like *passé composé*?"

"What?" he says. "Where are you, dim Whit? How do you miss this stuff? Like, where do you go in your head? Kahala Mall? Claire's?"

"I don't shop at Claire's!" She elbows her brother.

"Ow," he says. He looks poised to say more, but can't seem to come up with anything, so takes a bite of his pizza instead.

"Can you write the paragraph?" Whitney asks. "You're so smart, Will. What happened to me?"

"I have no idea," he says. "I like this song." He leans back and nods his head.

I listen to the music. I love this song too, in fact, though I don't know what it's called and don't want to ask Will and give him the satisfaction of teaching me something. I kind of like the unpredictable terrain between us, like we're both not sure where to step. It's an old song, from the sixties or seventies, and it sounds kind of country.

"What happened to you is that you don't try," he says. "You don't want to work for anything."

He says this in a soft, sincere way, and I want him to continue, to understand what he's getting at.

"Can you write it?" she asks, and I realize she's talking to me. Before I can answer, she gets up and runs inside, probably to get the assignment.

"Don't help her," Will says, but again, he doesn't say it in a mean way. With Whitney gone, I feel like we're the adults talking about our wayward girl.

"I may not be able to anyway," I say. "I only took French in seventh and eighth grade."

He looks across the table, scanning me. "You'll be able to."

"Why do you say that?"

"Because a blind woman would be able to." That slight, highly effective grin.

"What do you have against blind women?" I ask.

"They can't steer," he says.

We don't break eye contact. Again, I'm off balance, not sure of his tone, but liking our rhythm. I don't know if this is naive of me—like a bird enjoying the growling of a cat. I can't tell if he's flirting with me or just treating me like his sister's friend, or maybe both.

Whitney comes back out with her laptop and two mugs that

I assume are filled with Kahlúa. I lean down and look at the assignment. I guess I still remember a few things.

"Can you?" she asks. "Then I have nothing this whole weekend, and my mom will back off."

"I guess," I say.

It really isn't that hard a task, and I wonder if I'm missing something. I type a paragraph about Olivier's animals getting loose. A goose has babies. A cat lives on rib eye made from a cow. An elephant crushes a spotted owl. *Il meurt.*

C'est terrible.

I don't put it in *passé composé,* but figure she can do that, or attempt to. I sense Will's disapproval. I also realize that leaning over to type has made my camisole hang down. I take a quick glance, then decide not to adjust. I look up, and Will looks away.

"Here." I push the laptop toward her. "There are all the animals. See, I used *suivre, vivre, naître,* then you can just rewrite it with *passé composé.*"

I can't help but look at Will again to see where his eyes are. They're on me.

"You could be her tutor," he says.

I lean back onto the couch, pretending to be at home, at ease.

"Maybe you can even get community service credit for it, since, you know, you'd be working with someone with special needs."

"Says the idiot who flunked kindergarten," Whitney says.

He doesn't color externally, but I can tell she's triggered some kind of insecurity mechanism. "Because I switched to Hanahauoli and was too young," he says.

"I just love that story," she says. She rubs her hands together.

"Because you can't find anything else that's wrong with me," he says. "You can have it."

I laugh, and he looks at me and smiles like we're sharing a secret.

"You guys done?" Will asks. There's still half of the pizza left. Whitney takes one more bite of hers, then slings the rest onto the box. Will gets up and takes the box.

"Want me to foil it up?" I ask.

The siblings stare at me as if I'm talking French.

Will looks down at the box and wrinkles his nose a bit, as though it's a week old. "I'll just throw it out."

After dinner, Whitney brings out dessert. I take a sip of my drink while looking out, still wondering what to make of Will—is he just trying to be a good host like his mom would want him to be? I take another sip, not wanting to make anything out of anything. I need to float a little more, let things roll under me like swells. I need to enjoy the movement. The lights from the coconut trees cast a glow on the ocean. I wonder how cold that dark blue water is. I wonder what vacations feel like when you already seem to be on one every day.

"What kind of pie is this?" Will asks.

"It's not exactly a pie," I say. "It's a Pavlova. The only kind my mom makes."

"What's a Pavlova?" Whitney asks. She slurps from her mug.

"Basically a meringue, with fruit and whipped cream on top." I say.

"Is it called that because it makes you salivate?" she asks.

I see she's made a reference to "Pavlovian response" and am almost proud of her, but realize as a peer, I shouldn't really have that right. I don't know if I'm smarter than her, necessarily. As Will said, I think I just work harder.

In class, I hold back answers, depending who's in the room with me. Sometimes knowledge impresses, sometimes it just alienates you further, but something about Will makes me want to show off what I know.

"It's named after the Russian ballerina Anna Pavlova," I say. "She was the greatest ballerina of her time."

Will and I lock gazes for a moment.

"When she danced," I say, "she seemed to soar and float, like she had wings. The Pavlova is named after her because it's light and airy. Graceful."

"That's nice," he says.

"I still keep thinking of the dog," Whitney says.

I feel bad for wishing she weren't here.

"Like it?" Whitney asks, after I've taken another sip from the mug. The drink has created a heat under my breastbone.

"What is it?" Will asks, looking into Whitney's cup.

She hands it to him. He takes a sip, then keeps it. He looks down at the Pavlova. It's truly beautiful—strawberries and blueberries cradled in a cloud.

"Looks too nice to eat." He looks at me over the rim of his cup. I take another sip.

Whitney stabs a fork into its middle and carves out a scoop.

"What are you doing!" he says.

"I forgot plates," she says. "And we're going to eat it anyway. Why does it matter?"

"You could show some respect," he says. "Get a plate."

"It's fine," I say, almost touching his hand to put him at ease.

"Relax," she says. "You're getting uptight in your old age."

I take my fork and scoop out a bite. The cream fills my mouth and I chew the fruit. I love the sweetness and air.

"My mom would have wanted it this way," I say. Will follows my lead.

"Oh, wow," he says.

"Good, right?" I say.

"I can feel my thighs growing," Whitney says, leaning down for more.

Will and I look at each other over her head.

14

MONDAY MORNING, I WALK BACK FROM THURSTON Chapel alone, but migrating with the group. I don't mind chapel—the stained-glass windows, everyone singing, the time it allows you to do nothing. Sometimes I tune in to the chaplain, or watch Ms. Freitas playing the organ, her spastic energy and the way she seems unaware of anyone else in the room. The music thunders through the cool space and makes me feel like I'm taking part in something ancient.

When I signed in this morning, I noticed Will's signature and looked down the row. He was slouched on the hard pew, eyes closed, mouth parted, chin tilted up to the ceiling, a cap on his lap. Just blatantly asleep. I couldn't imagine doing the same. His seems to be a life without consequences. I keep expecting to see him around campus, wondering how he'll greet me after our night on Friday, but I haven't run into him yet.

The air is humid and voggy, stifling. I don't recognize any of the people I'm walking alongside. There are so many faces here. Even if I had started in kindergarten I doubt I'd know them all. I'm almost to the other end of the Olympic-sized swimming pool when I hear Whitney calling my name. I turn back and see her with Danny. He's laughing at something in that Woody

Woodpecker way of his. I slow down a bit and nearly get crushed by the other students headed to their next class.

"Hey, guys," I say.

Whitney is wearing a maxi dress, which she pulls off despite her smaller stature. I've always wanted one, inspired by all the Japanese tourists in Kailua, who look stylish yet super comfortable at the same time. I tried one on at Fighting Eel, loved it, but looked like I was drowning or playing dress-up.

"What's up?" she says, with a nice note of familiarity.

"I like your dress," I say.

She lifts a side of it. "My hausfrau dress. Love these things. You should borrow it."

"Want to come surf with us?" Danny asks. Today's Monday, the day he usually can't surf, and shouldn't the question be rephrased? Shouldn't we be asking Whitney if *she* wants to surf with *us*?

"I can't," I say. "History exam."

"Boo," Whitney says. "Join us after, then, at home?"

"Yeah, maybe," I say.

I expect protests, begging, or just a simple "come on," but there's nothing. I begin to veer off toward class.

"See you guys," I say.

"Late," Danny says.

"Bye-eee," Whitney says. She always drags out the *e*. She's got all these language tics, like word special effects.

"Oh, my mom says you're coming for dinner tonight, so I'll see you for sure," she calls out.

"Okay," I say, knowing nothing about it.

"Meet earlier for cocoa, 'kay-eee?"

"Okay, already," I say. "My arm has been twisted."

She makes a victory gesture, pulling her elbow down and mouthing, "Yes."

I bump into someone during this exchange. "Oh, shit, sorry," I say to a girl with thick glasses and hair that goes past her butt. She apologizes profusely and has a look about her that says this was some kind of fun incident.

"Hard knocks," she says and laughs nervously.

I don't disguise my confused look, and I walk away.

When I get to the library, I wonder if that's the way I acted when I first got to Punahou, or even until recently—needlessly apologetic, fumbling, and, well, lame.

After history and Chinese, I'm done. I walk toward the exit by the pool and see Will, farther up the hill by the bench-encircled tree. I almost turn and walk the other way, but don't see why I should. Still, I slow my pace, but he's moving slow as well, so I have to go even slower. He has a girlfriend and treats me like a kid. I need to get it together.

He turns then, sees me, and hesitates, maybe deciding whether to stay or go. He turns back, facing away from me, then stops walking until I get to his side.

"Hey," he says.

"Hey," I say, not meeting his eyes. I look at his 808 Skate hat, and he lifts his eyes as if to see what I'm looking at. You skate and golf? I want to ask. 'Cause that goes together like wrestling and synchronized swimming. Or maybe he just wears it to look like he skates. We walk slowly, as if through thick sand.

"This vog," he says.

"I know, right." Volcanic ash and fog. It makes my eyes itch and water. I swear it affects your mood and energy too. You can just feel it in the air.

On the walkway, he turns toward the road. "You going this way?"

"Yeah," I say.

"Are you going anywhere for break?" I ask. Spring break starts next week.

"No," he says. "I've got this tournament thing. You?"

"Nowhere," I say.

We walk out of school, stopping in front of the rock wall to wait for the light to change. The wall runs alongside the campus, so you can only see the tops of the buildings from the street. I always feel like I'm in a different world when I leave, like this wall shelters us from the real world, and then our real world is surrounded by the ocean, like a castle's moat, guarding us even further.

"Have you been here at night?" Will asks.

"At school?" I ask. "No."

"Or driven past?"

"I don't know," I say, trying to remember if I've driven this way after paddling.

He looks over at me, then past me. "These flowers." I look at the spurts of white among the cacti that run along the entire rock wall. "They open at night. Night-blooming cereus."

"Serious?" I say.

"Yup," he says, and I hide my smile, since he didn't get my joke. He steps off the curb, and I walk alongside him in the crosswalk, conscious of wanting someone to see us. "Little trivia for you," he says. "It must be hard coming to this place so late in the game."

"It is," I say. "But I'm liking it now." I touch my neck.

"Let me know if you need anything," he says. "I can give you more tours." He looks straight ahead.

"I like your tours," I say. It's requiring a lot of energy to maintain this even walk. My arms are relaxed, but my fingers tap nervously against my thighs.

"Yo, William!" I hear from behind us.

"Thaddeus!" Will says. "Give me a ride up the hill. I'm in bumblefuck."

"Shoots," Thad says. "We can smoke a bowl!"

Will shrugs his backpack off. "Need a ride to your car?" he asks.

We're standing close to each other. He looks at me, waiting. Yes. I want to hang out, want to be with the boys, want to smoke a bowl, but my nerves make me respond, "I'm good."

"Okay, see you at home," he says, and we both smile a little. I wonder if it's because he feels the same way I do: like we've been caught playing house.

15

AFTER STUDYING, I CHANGE INTO SHORTS AND A LOOSE top stamped with anchors. I put my hair into a high bun, then swipe on some lip gloss and head out for après-surf.

I walk across the lawn with less hesitation today. Danny's truck is parked in front. I go around the house to the pool, but no one's there, so I go to the gate to look out onto the ocean. I scan for bodies, but no one is out there either. A strong breeze comes up off the water, and I can't help but see myself from afar; in anyone's eyes this scene would look majestic. I don't know if Will is here or not, but it seems that everything I do, every pause or glance or move I make, is done just in case he's watching.

But now I'm the one watching him. He's by the pool house with his mom and one of her friends. I linger here, admiring his dapperness and the way he talks to his mom's friend as if he's on her level. I realize I'm smiling all alone while looking nakedly at him like an admiring girlfriend.

They notice me then, and Melanie yells, "Lei!" Then they all make their way back up, the women holding glasses of white wine. I walk to the lanai to meet them.

Melanie introduces me to her friend, a beautiful woman with

high cheekbones and Disney-girl eyes. Her boobs couldn't possibly be real—and with her tight yoga gear on, I keep thinking of the words *prison break.*

"Hi, sweetie," Melanie says and kisses me on the cheek, something I don't think she'd do if we were alone. "This is Vicky, Lissa's mom. Will's future mother-in-law."

They both laugh, and Will rolls his eyes and scratches his ear.

"And this is Ali Lane's daughter," Melanie says.

"Ah, hello," Vicky says, and she looks at me differently, like she's trying to understand something.

"So fun to have Hollywood here with us every day!" Melanie looks at Vicky searchingly. Vicky doesn't seem that impressed.

"Mel, you're like a patron of the arts," Vicky says. "So have you met Alex Crane yet?" she asks me.

Here's where I recite, "Yeah. Really nice guy." And it's true. He's always been nice to me, kissing me on the top of the head and asking me about school and actually wanting to hear about it, like it's some fascinating foreign world.

"I'd love to have him over for dinner one night," Vicky says. "We should set that up."

"Yes!" Melanie says. "Absolutely."

Why is it that wealthy people just assume an actor will come to their house, or even want to? Alex would rather be at home, drinking beer and watching basketball.

"Oh, say, hon?" Melanie says to Will. "Do you happen to know whose truck that is out front?"

"That's my friend Danny's," I say. "I hope that's okay. He's out surfing with Whitney."

"Absolutely!" Melanie says. "I've never met Danny, I don't

think. But of course, you can have anyone over!" She moves toward Will and says something to him. Vicky and I smile at each other, then look away. She's like Lissa. Smiles come off as expressions of annoyance.

"You're at Punahou?" Vicky asks. She takes a sip of her wine and looks me over.

"Yes," I say, and I smile again—how I hate smiling for politeness—then look out at the sun going down with a harsh glare.

"These sunsets never get old," she says.

"I wonder if cavemen thought the same thing," I say and am appalled that I let that slip.

"What, sweetie?" Melanie says, walking to us with Will.

"Um," I say and laugh and catch Will's eye. "I was just wondering if cavemen liked to watch the sunset. I mean, I wonder if they appreciated beauty and watched the sunset with cave cocktails or whatever. Animal blood. Ha, like cheetah Bloody Marys." I may as well keep going with this weirdness. "Or if they were just practical. Like—oop, there goes that light, time to mate. But they did art, right? Cave art. So they must have had an eye."

No one speaks for a moment.

"That's right!" Melanie says. "Cave art." She looks at me as if it's something I've invented.

"Though maybe that was more of a form of communication," I say, then sigh. "Anyway."

"Go on," Will says. He looks like he's holding back a laugh, and yet his look is conspiring, like he's entertained and charmed by me. I get stuck for a second, looking back into his green eyes, his long lashes. He bites his lower lip.

"Maybe the art documented their migrations or just told the daily news," I say. "Jojo caught a fish. Fi Fum killed a bear." Holy what the face am I talking about? Melanie keeps looking at me like I'm saying something incredible, and yet these are expressions, not actual reactions, I think. Things she pulls from her social reserve.

"You are so wise," she says. "So soulful." She looks at Vicky. "Well. We should get going."

"Okay, nice to meet you!" I practically scream.

When they've said their pleasantries and left, I look at Will, and he's covering his mouth with his hand. His eyes are bright from grinning. I reach out and move his hand away from his mouth.

"'Fi Fum'?" he says, laughing. "That was hilarious."

"I am such a shitshow," I say. "Sorry."

The gate by the ocean opens, and Danny and Whitney walk in. Danny looks up at us. They cross the lawn toward the shower.

"You make me laugh," Will says, as if a funny girl were something he doesn't know how to operate.

"I'm glad I can do that for you." I'm also glad I'm not exploding right now, because it kinda feels like it's going to happen.

He looks toward the pool where Danny's standing.

"I'll let you go," he says.

"Oh no, I'm—" *Don't let me go.* I hope he'll be at dinner tonight.

He turns to go in, but then says, "Not a big deal at all, but my mom likes when people park over by the big tree on the other side of the pool house. If you could let Danny know?"

"Oh." Melanie could have just told me that, but then I realize

Vicky was there. Just like a kid, she didn't want to seem uncool. "Totally," I say. "I'll tell him."

Whitney's in a different bikini; it's coral and blue, with string straps on the sides of the bottoms. Her top is brown and strapless, and I don't know how she manages to keep it up when she surfs, but maybe she and Danny didn't surf and just lay there like last time. I walk to the pool where she's bending over to flip her hair. She's wearing low-grazing bottoms, the back narrow, revealing a round, lifted ass, flecked with sand.

Danny is standing—strategically, I believe—behind her, and I feel foolish for thinking my prior scene was majestic when the sight of her in front of this pool is by far, in anyone's eyes, the more magnificent.

"You still got sand," Danny says.

"Where?" She straightens up and turns her head to look down at herself.

"Right there," Danny says and slaps it away.

"You can't slap my ass!" She laughs.

"I just dusted it," he says. He seems lit up, and I want to flip a switch, turn him off.

"You dusted my ass?" She laughs again. "I'll dust your ass."

"Be my guest." He juts his ass toward her.

She gives him a spank, and he says, "That was nice. Could you do it again?" And I'm uneasy, feeling like the younger sibling they've had to drag along.

Danny stretches his arms toward the sky, showing his armpit hair. It's weird when you know boys when they didn't have any armpit hair and then, suddenly, they do.

He brings his arms down, one almost hitting my shoulder.

"Don't come near my ass," I say.

"Wasn't planning on it," he says, hitting the side of his head to get water out of his ear.

Why is it sometimes more insulting *not* to be harassed by a guy? And why won't he look at me?

"I'll get some towels," Whitney says and walks to the cabana while securing her hair on top of her head just like mine.

"Did you guys actually surf this time?" I ask.

He stretches out on a lounger, and I take the one beside him.

"Little bit." He rubs circles onto his stomach. "Kind of choppy."

"I heard east side is supposed to be good this weekend."

"Yeah," he says. "I might check out base."

He's talking about the military base, where you need to sneak on or know someone with a pass.

"Maybe I'll go to Flat Island," I say, hoping for an invitation to base or for him to change locations.

"Cool," he says. He finally looks at me. "So how's the old sport up there?"

I realize he's talking about Will. "I like him," I say. "He's nice."

"Nice," Danny says. "Posing with his skate hat. I think a fish could skate better."

"You don't like him much, huh?" I say, turning to face him.

"He's kind of a dick." He shrugs and smiles. "Sorry."

"I don't see that," I say. "You just don't know him, I guess."

"And you do?" he asks.

I turn back away from him. "I'm getting to know him."

Whitney walks over and drops a towel onto Danny.

"Thank you, my dear," he says, and sits up.

I don't really understand what's going on here. His voice, his entire posture, is different toward me, and I can't think of a single thing I've done wrong. Cool—he likes Whitney, but that doesn't mean I have to get canceled like a shitty show.

"Whit, you want to surf with me this weekend?" I ask. "Kailua side?" She doesn't look at Danny to see if he's coming. She doesn't show any hesitation.

"This weekend is crazy, but next weekend for sure," she says.

Danny stands, preparing to leave. I touch his arm. "Oh, Will said you should park your truck on the side of the house next time." I say this like it's a comeback, but I don't know what I'm coming back to.

"'Kay," Danny says.

"Oh, please. Lissa parks in front all the time," Whitney says. "So do my friends."

"I think your mom just wanted—"

"Lissa drives a Range Rover," Danny says. "Looks mo' bettah." He says this in a funny voice, no bitterness at all. He has always managed to be this way.

He slaps his hand against his stomach, and it makes a loud smack as if he's hit a piece of wood. It's funny how he does this, as if he needs a slap like a horse to move. "Gotta go," he says.

"T-ball?" Whitney says, lounging and relaxed, so familiar with Danny and his schedule.

"Yup," he says. "See you guys. Be good."

"Bye-eee," she says, the coyness of her voice making my jaw flex.

• • •

Whitney and I are on our second cup of Kahlúa-spiked cocoa.

"I need to stop drinking these things," she says and pinches some skin on her stomach.

"I know," I say, lifting my shirt, but knowing my stomach is flat and strong. Whitney's too.

The sun hovers over a freight ship. I wonder what it's carrying. Ninety percent of our food, Ms. Leinweber would say. We watch the clouds become a vivid pink spray above the horizon, and then the sky gets cast with a sepia light.

"It's so different from the windward side," I say. "You're more aware of night coming."

"What do you mean?" she asks.

I try to think. In Kailua, after that magic hour of light seeping through the clouds and mountain peaks, night sort of just falls. You don't see the sun's descent.

"Well, in Kailua, the sunset's almost like one of those searchlights, signaling a big event that's far away."

I expect her to make a joke, like I'm being too deep or not making sense. Why do I keep talking about the damn sunset, anyway, like a total wad?

"That's kind of cool too," she says. "The Kailua version." We sit in the cool silence.

"What were you and my brother talking about?" she asks, picking at the towel.

"Oh God," I say. "Who knows. I get so flustered with him, and I just drop nonsense."

"Does he make you nervous or something?"

She keeps her gaze trained ahead. She doesn't look comfortable, like she usually does. Her slouch seems forced.

"I'm a nervous person," I say. "Shy, I guess. New."

"I remember being new," she says. She turns to the side, leaning on her elbow. "Seventh grade. I was really quiet. Total bookworm." She shakes her head and sits up.

"Then my mom threw this party for my birthday—had a rock band, dancing, sushi bar. She invited all the cool kids I didn't even know, and I swear ever since then, I got a rep for being this crazy, extravagant party girl." She pauses, and I don't say anything. "Then I just . . . became that. Maintained. My friends don't know that about me. They don't know much."

I'm not sure how to respond to this, all of it. She sits back again, but this time seems relaxed.

"I felt that way about my friends in San Fran," I say.

"Yeah?" she says and looks over.

I want to go back to talking about Will, but I think this would be a wrong move, a step back.

"It's been kind of nice," she says. "Not going out as much. Not caring where everyone is. Not doing anything spectacular."

"Um, hello." I gesture to myself. "Is this not spectacular?"

She tucks her chin and laughs. "Oh, and postscript, thanks for your help with French. You're welcome to help me anytime."

"Oh, thanks," I say. "So nice of you. And postscript, I'll let you write my paper on Virginia Woolf." I can't believe I need to do more homework tonight. It doesn't seem possible. The freight moves out of the sun's path. Now the clouds look splattered with peach paint.

"I like that shirt," Whitney says.

"I like that suit. I need a new one."

"Acacia," she says, snapping one of the bottom straps. "You can borrow. Unless you're grossed out by your vagina parts touching the same place as my vagina parts."

I start to laugh, and she does too. "Vagina parts," I repeat. "Vag areas."

"Vagarea!" she yells, and we let out some serious honking laughter.

"Oh, shit, there's our 'rents," she says.

I turn and see my mom. She waves, and I wave back.

Whitney stands up. "Let's do this," she says, and we walk to the lanai.

My mom has on a flowing dress, almost like a beach caftan. Her hair is in a braid to the side. She looks gorgeous and chic. "This is so nice," I say, touching the fabric.

She looks down at it, as though unsure. "I got it at Rebecca Beach. At the Royal Hawaiian."

"You have to go," Melanie says. She wears a similar dress, but it's short and her heels are too high. "I took your mom today. Everything there would look so fab on you." She walks inside, then calls, "Whit, can you come in here for a second?"

"Okay." She rolls her eyes. "Homework, mark my words. Hi, Ali."

"Hi, Whitney, how's it going? You guys having fun out there?"

I cringe.

"Fun, fun!" Whitney says and walks inside.

My mom looks at me almost guiltily. "You have a good day?"

"Yeah," I say. "Same old."

"God, it's nice out," she says. "Look at those clouds."

"I know," I say. "Believe me, I've said my piece." I look inside. "I'm starving. What are we having? You didn't even tell me we were eating over here."

My mom takes a sip of her white wine. "I was going to tell you when I got home, but you were gone. I didn't find out until this afternoon. Dinner's ready if you're hungry," she says. "Simple. I made ham—"

"You made dinner?" I ask. Eddie is walking into the kitchen, holding a cocktail glass. He's dressed in silky pants and has on black sunglasses.

"Yeah, this morning after Rebecca Beach we stopped at Whole Foods. She was going to pick something up for you guys, so I just offered to make something. I had time."

You did? I want to ask. It seems Melanie, the one with no job and a housekeeper, would be the one with the time.

"It's not a big deal. You know I like it."

"What do you mean, for us guys?" I ask, now seeing Melanie come from the kitchen with a huge, floral-printed handbag. I register my mom's outfit and realize she isn't dressed to stay put.

"They want to take me out again, so I thought why not?" She runs her tongue over her teeth and twists her braid.

"Why don't they go out with their whole family?" I ask.

"I'm sure they do," she says.

Will appears in the living room, and I wonder where his room is in this house. What does it look like? What are on his walls and shelves?

"'Kay, bye, have fun," I say.

She follows my gaze to Will. Her eyes narrow briefly. "Be good," she says.

"My mom killed my buzz," Whitney says when she comes out with plates, napkins, and forks and starts to set the outdoor table.

"That's what moms do," I say. I walk over to help her, but since there are just three settings, she doesn't need much help.

"How could *your* mom possibly be a buzzkill?" Whitney adjusts the centerpiece, a white wide vase with short-stemmed tulips. I smile to myself, thinking that she looks like her mom in this moment.

"Your mom is so cool," she says. "She's an actress! She at least does something with her life. She doesn't breathe down your neck about everything—homework, college, tennis, my bill at the club, my table manners, fuuuuck," she roars and throws up her hands. "Rum and Coke. That's what we need. Diet Coke. We'll rebuzz."

"'Kay," I say, eager to have fun.

"'Kay," she says and heads back in.

Will comes out with two platters of food, so I refold the brightly patterned cloth napkins to have something to do. My heart beats fast.

"Hello again," he says.

"Hello," I say, and my throat is dry.

He places the platters on either side of the centerpiece, and it feels like prom, like we're mimicking the customs of our elders or getting a head start on becoming the people we're bound to be.

"Where's this food from?" he asks.

"My mom."

"Your mom cooked again?"

"Yup," I say, embarrassed.

"Nice," he says. "I was wondering why Maya isn't here." He puts tongs on my mom's spinach salad, scattered with raspberries and caramelized chipotle pecans.

"And what's this?" he asks, putting a serving spoon next to the main dish.

He's just showered, but still has stubble on his face, which, again, makes him seem so much older than me. His skin is lightly tanned, his damp hair a soft brown like his dad's. He catches me looking at him, and I quickly say, "Ham. It's ham."

He smiles, and I'm taken aback, the way it changes his entire face and seems to occupy most of it. His eyes brighten, and his cheeks color. He has a dimple on the left side.

"You sure don't try to dress it up, do you?" he says. "First you can't stop talking. Now all I get is 'ham.'"

I laugh, relieved to let it out. "Well, that's what it is. Ham."

"I guess there's nothing you can say about a dish when all roads lead to that."

I speak in a posh voice. "This is dressed in a lovely pomegranate reduction and served on a bed of roasted leeks. And what is the meat?"

"Ham," Will deadpans, then laughs, his shoulders moving up and down twice. "I guess you could always say *jambon*." He clears his throat. "Vog's still getting to me."

"We should swim it off," I say, and hold my breath.

"We should," he says, a response I never like. *Should* could mean now, or in the near or distant future, or never. "Or we can take out the boat sometime. I could take you for a sunset cruise. Can't wait to hear what you'd have to say about it."

"Oh my God, you need to drop it."

"Cave art," he says.

"What are you guys talking about?" Whitney says, coming out with drinks. She looks different, smaller, like there's been a reversal and she's the outsider. She hands me a glass. I shake it to hear the ice cubes rattle and have a sip that I nearly spit out, the rum is so strong.

"We're talking about *jambon,*" Will says.

"What the hell is jam bone?" she says.

Will and I exchange brief glances, and I think to myself that out of the three of us here, she's the only one taking French.

"It's 'party' in French," I say, then look down. That was mean.

"Well, let's get this jam bone started!" Whitney says and sits at the head of the table.

It is all very civilized. Platters get passed, napkins are put onto laps. I wonder if they're used to this, if it's ritual, the two of them eating alone after Maya has cooked for them.

"Seriously," Will says, taking a serving, "what is this? Does it have . . . you know . . . a title?"

"Ham Impossible," I say, and I see a smile almost blooming, but it doesn't quite get there. He twists his mouth to the side.

"It's one of those dishes everyone ate in the seventies," I say. "Ham and cheese, Bisquick. My mom makes it with cottage cheese, sour cream, Parmesan, and she uses smoked Gouda. And cornbread mix instead of Bisquick."

"Gouda." Whitney laughs. "That sounds funny." She takes another drink, tilting the glass all the way back.

"Jesus, Whit," Will says.

By the sound of the cubes, I can tell her drink is gone. She acts the same buzzed and sober, so I never know what state she's in. I take another sip.

"What?" she says. "Why are you always Jesusing me?"

He doesn't answer, just chews his food, and I take another sip, trying to be discreet, but the ice falls onto my face and Whitney laughs. She takes our glasses and goes back in.

"This is good," he says, still looking down. "Impossibly good. Tell your mom. I mean, I'll be sure to thank her, but—"

"I will," I say. "She likes it. This one's easy. Comfort food." *You need to describe a dish in a way that won't scare Republicans,* she has said, the tip of her tongue touching her bottom lip, something she does when she hopes to have sounded funny. The thought makes me smile. I think of her tonight with Will's supposed in-laws. She'd be the better in-law. I look quickly at Will, then take a bite, savoring the cheeses and dough. Whitney comes back out and places the glass in front of me.

"Mmm," I say. "There's nothing better than—" I stop myself, thank God. I was just going to say *than warm cottage cheese on your tongue,* which sounds absolutely vile.

"Than what?" Will asks.

"Than a rum and Coke. Want?" I move the glass toward him.

"No, thanks," he says, and I feel like a disappointment. I wonder if his disapproval is because of his dad. If he doesn't drink because his dad supposedly drinks too much. And Whitney drinks because her dad drinks too much.

"Will's wearing his golf goggles," Whitney says. "He sees nothing but the hole."

She gives me a quick glance, and Will furrows his eyebrows as though she's said something ridiculous.

"Big game?" I ask.

"Yes," he says. "I'll have one with you after." I think he winks at me, and I close my mouth and swallow.

"He's actually pretty good at it," Whitney says, which seems to annoy him more than an insult would. He takes a sip of water and looks down, something my mother does when faced with praise.

"I want to watch sometime," I say, suddenly interested in something I'd never consider watching before.

"Only after he advances," Whitney says.

When I think of golf, I think of green jackets and alcoholics, white men, bad pants, and money, but imagining Will play makes me think of expansive greens, blue skies, elegance, and a beautiful precision.

All of our plates look practically licked clean, but Will and I both go for more of the salad. I'm glad, because I don't want things to be wrapped up yet. My house seems so far away and lonely.

"You girls don't have homework tonight?" he asks.

"I do," I say. I want to tell him I'm only having a drink since I'm over here. It's not something I would have done on my own.

"Do you?" I ask.

"Not much," he says. "But I have some things to do."

"I can't wait until next year," Whitney says. "Senior slacking."

"I think you're getting a head start," Will says.

"You going over to Lissa's tonight?" Whitney says, glancing at me.

"I'm helping her with her thesis," he mumbles.

"Oh yes, helping with her body of work," Whitney says.

My heart beats as if caught.

"God, even I look smart next to her, but I guess she has other strengths." Whitney looks at me, and I sort of laugh, wanting to show I don't care, that I wasn't misled, that I'm in it somehow, digging on her. I'm the cool, funny friend. But here he is, sitting with me, the soft whisper of palms, the salt in the warm air, the boom of waves, and I don't want to be his friend. I imagine being in the ocean with him, close together in a ray of moonlight. I shake it off.

Whitney gets up. "Want another?" she asks.

"No, thanks," I say. "I need to study." She goes in and soon after a song comes over the speakers, an upbeat top-forty song about partying all night. I immediately miss the other music, the trance it put me in.

"Sorry about the Lissa thing," he says.

"What?" I pretend I didn't notice a thing.

"Seems like twice today—"

"I don't care," I say. "Girl trouble?"

He laughs. "Always." Then he looks at me and smiles. "You don't look like trouble." I resist answering, fearing it may sound like some cheesy line pulled from *No Borders*.

"Your mothers seem to think it's serious," I say lightly, the voice of the girl bro. "Is it?"

"No," he says. "I'm a senior, you know? Time to . . . learn

new things, explore—so I can bring back new knowledge." He smiles, recognizing his cheesy line.

"Good to be adventurous," I say, and I think I manage a flirtatious look. We lock eyes and smile at everything we're not saying, and whatever else we're imagining. Whitney's still in the house, and I want her to stay there for a little longer so I can be alone with him. It feels like this is our home. He'll inherit all this one day, I realize. I hope Lissa won't inherit it alongside him. They'd be like Eddie and Melanie the Second.

"Honestly, it's a bit much," he says, looking down at his plate. "She's going to California for school too, and I just want some solo time, you know?" He glances back up, serious.

"I'm sure," I say.

"Maybe we can take the boat out or do something soon," he says.

"Okay," I say, feeling his leg next to mine. I'm too shy to ask when.

"Maybe without Whitney, though," he says. "Can't hang out with my little sister all the time."

"Right," I say. I can't believe this is happening. He wants to be alone with me.

Whitney comes back out. "You guys are so quiet," she says.

I take the last bites of my dinner. When I'm done, I put my fork down, and Will gets up and clears my plate. He was waiting for me to finish.

"I gotta go," he says. "Have a good night, kids."

"All right," I say, and add a horribly lame clicking noise. "You too!"

After he has gone, it seems so sad and boring. Whitney looks at her phone, texting someone. "Helping with her thesis, what a joke," she says.

"So are they going out or what?" I ask.

"I'm sure she thinks so," Whitney says. "But he likes new things."

I'm about to ask her to explain, but she clearly doesn't want to talk about him, and I think I already know what she means.

16

I WATCH THE SENIORS FROM THE WINDOW OF MY creative writing class. They're kicking a beach ball. Everyone around here is hyper on spring break, coming up in three more days.

Nalani Ogawa kicks the ball, following through with her long-ass legs. She makes facial expressions indicating that she's having more fun than you ever will in your lifetime. From here she's beautiful, even though up close she has the features of a Siamese cat, but if you put a bulldog's head on her body she'd still look good from a reasonable distance. She's one of the Angels—the group of girls who, at the Halloween dance, came dressed as the Victoria's Secret angels. Underwear, wings, and stripper heels. It might not have been such a big deal if they hadn't looked so good, like actual supermodels. They got kicked out of the dance, yet as Danny said, "left everyone's spank bank full."

Lissa was another one. She's sitting a bit behind me, so I can't look at her, even though I've been trying to. She's magnetic. You're drawn to her face, her body, everything she's wearing, even if, like today, it's just jeans and a white button-down shirt. It would be weird to be the kind of person who's always looked at.

"Lea," Mr. Spitzer says, "stop looking out the window. You're on the clock."

The class laughs, which kind of gives me a thrill, and I look back and lock eyes with Lissa, but can't tell if her look is congratulatory or annoyed. I wonder if she knows I live in Will's cottage. I feel like I have so much on her. *Will the Explorer. He doesn't want to be with you.*

"As I was saying, folks," Spitzer says, "we are a country that makes things like pastrami burgers. A huge burger patty with pastrami layered on top of it. Do you understand the implications of this? Do you get it?"

I must have spent too much time looking out the window, because I don't get it at all. Spitzer's one of the younger teachers here, and he tries to emphasize his youth—talking casually, being provocative, chatting with the boys after class. The teachers I like best here all seem to moonlight as coaches after school.

"I grinded one of those last weekend," Raj says. "With cheese too." Everyone in class seems to look at him shyly, then back at the teacher.

"Me too," Jon T. says. "It ruled." Jon T. is one of those guys who's a bit overweight, but also super athletic and confident.

"But the breakfast burger blows it away," Raj says. "It's got eggs, sausage, cheese, and then burger."

"I'd have to be stoned to eat something like that," Jon V. says. "Weed is insurance. Movies, TV, food—weed guarantees it will all be good, worth the money spent. I learned that from my dad—the importance of insurance. He sells it. Not weed, but life insurance."

The class laughs, though some of the quiet boys seem annoyed.

"Okay, clearly, you're not understanding my point," Spitzer says.

I want to tell Spitzer that this is his doing. By trying to be cool, he has allowed students to talk about things that shouldn't be talked about. This school isn't like Storey, where teachers lectured and we sat. We say anything we want here and rarely sit still. There are more investigations, questions, collaborations, and inventions. I haven't been to a lecture yet, only Skype sessions with experts and kids in other countries.

"What is your *point*?" Mikey Sharp asks, giving Spitzer a look I don't think most kids would dare express. He has freckled skin and big green eyes, and his voice is scratchy, like he's been up all night shouting.

Spitzer looks like he always does whenever Mikey says anything. He has a closed-mouth, weasel-like grin that's both condescending and contrite. He doesn't like Mikey. It's pretty clear. He doesn't seem to tolerate kids who attend this school and give no glimmer, present or latent, of intelligence or curiosity.

"My point is I've heard enough about your stress, how you can't come up with anything," Spitzer says, looking like he's shrunk a few inches.

And how is this connected to the pastrami burger? I wonder.

"Just sit down and write." He leans against the desk. "You're in America. You have an endless backyard of inspiration and ideas and absurdities to draw from. You are interesting. Your lives are interesting. Write what you know, write your complications, what you're passionate about."

"Like pastrami burgers?" someone says, just as I'm thinking the same thing.

"If it's so easy, then why haven't you published anything yet?" Mikey asks. He holds eye contact with Spitzer—it's both appalling and amazing.

The whole class oohs and ho snaps, except for Jon T., who is smiling and looking around because he knows someone made a joke, but he didn't hear what it was.

"I have published something, thank you, Mikey. And my next book will come out shortly. Very soon. I take time. I'm not an assembly line. I don't just churn them out like Danielle Steele."

"I've met her daughters," Ian says. "In San Francisco. Buns of Steele for real."

Everyone laughs. We all know Ian also has a home in San Francisco, a kind of second life. I can't tell if Whitney's friend Mari dates him or hooks up with him or if they just hug all the time as so many of these kids do.

"Your authoring project should be fun for you," Spitzer says. "And from what you've handed in so far, I don't sense that you're having fun."

"How will it be graded?" Kat Muller asks.

Spitzer seems to deflate. He leans against the desk and takes a drink from his aluminum water bottle. "Don't worry about that."

This is an impossible thing to ask of us. Many of these kids have been coming here since kindergarten and are primed to excel, and excellence is measured by grades. Grades get you into college. Ninety-nine percent of Punahou students go to college.

Our fates are published in the alumni magazine, displaying what we're capable of—Princeton, Smith, Vassar, Colgate, Williams, Harvard, MIT, Berkeley. The alums here include Steve Case, founder of AOL; Pierre Omidyar, founder of eBay; our president, Barack Obama. You can't remind us of the success of the present and past student body, then tell us not to worry about grades.

I've maintained a 3.5 average, and know I could use some more distinguishing marks. I look around and can tell others have been prompted to think about their record. Even the wise-asses care.

"Writing isn't easy," Spitzer says. "But I promise if you just keep at it, you will start building up enough to work with. You need clay to mold, and once you get enough clay, then you can actually sculpt it into something functional and beautiful, and that part is fun. I promise."

I look down at my journal, then over at the others. What's in them? I wonder. What in the world are they writing about?

When I think about the books that have been assigned to us—*A Separate Peace*, *The Catcher in the Rye*, *Of Mice and Men*, *Lord of the Flies*—they're all about complications and longing, I guess. They're also all about boys.

Maybe Spitzer's right. Our lives can be interesting, as long as we show the specifics, the little details.

"Write what you know," Spitzer says again. "What you're inspired by, passionate about. Write about what frustrates you, confounds you, and all the things that make you feel out of place."

I look out the window again at the seniors whose exaggerated expressions of joy make them seem as if they're acting in a play. I look down on them, yet want to be them. I want to have so much fun just kicking a ball, and look cool and sexy doing it. I want to not want that too. Is that my complication?

"So, tonight, write a monologue," he says. "Pick a topic and write."

"How will that be graded?" Jenny Hee asks.

Spitzer sighs, probably thinking that the last thing Jenny Hee needs to worry about is grades. I like this assignment because people like Jenny will struggle with it, a task with no right answer, something she can't research. She has her laptop open, fingers ready to type whatever Spitzer says.

"Your effort, okay? I want to see effort."

She types, her forehead wrinkled with stress. "Could you give us possible topics?" she asks.

Overambition, I want to say. *Predictability. Lack of a life.*

I feel like I don't suffer from this anymore.

"No, I don't have topics," Spitzer says. "It's your life. You have your topics spread out in front of you." He opens his arms, displaying our array of topics. Jenny looks angry—like she's going to call someone to fix this.

"Look," he says. "You have jobs. Write about your jobs."

Before anyone can correct him, to let him know that they don't have jobs, he continues: "Maybe your job is to be a son. Maybe your job is to be a football player or the most popular girl in school, or"—he looks briefly at Jenny—"the smartest. Maybe you literally have a job as a babysitter or a cashier. Think of it in those terms. Write about your jobs. Write about what it takes to do your job."

I like this clarification. Jenny does too, it seems. Her eyes are intense, and she's typing rapidly.

My job is to see if Will wants to jump in the water or take the boat out—today. To not overthink it, to say what's on my mind instead of holding it under my tongue like a lump of gum.

We get up and gather our things. I glance back, and Lissa has a smug look on her face, like she expected me to look back because everyone does. It's a strange sensation to feel sorry for someone like that, and it feels kind of great.

And so I'll do it. I will go to the main house after I change my clothes. When I open the door to the cottage, my mom is there at the kitchen counter, leaning over a script.

"What are you smiling at?" she asks.

"Nothing," I say.

"That's a boy smile," she says, but then lets it go.

We've never been the kind of mother and daughter who talk about boys. She would be if I let her. Even when I was ten, she'd ask me about the boys at school, teasing out responses, which always brought on a kind of fun mortification. She separates the script into two piles.

"Good scene?" I ask.

"So good," she says. "I mean, Pulitzer material. Deep characterization, moving dialogue."

She runs her finger down the page, and I know she's looking for something to read.

"Okay, here," she says. "'Samantha: You're an animal, Jenkins. Jenkins is looking through binoculars at a young woman on her knees in a revealing bikini, rubbing wax on her surfboard.

Jenkins: Well, yes, by definition. I am an animal. He looks at Sam with a charming smile and winks. And so are you.'"

"Awesome," I say.

She picks up a script, but leaves one behind. "And it's a rewrite!" she says. "In the old one, bikini girl has her back to him, but now because of her other assets—which are out of control, by the way—she will face forward."

I pick up the script. "Can I read?" I ask, picking up the other copy.

"Go for it," she says. "But homework first."

"Can I go over to Whitney's real quick?" I ask. I smile and blink, move my shoulders to my ears.

I can tell she's charmed by the way I pleaded, by my sweet face, and by the fact that I have a friend.

"Real quick," she says.

I hurry across the lawn, then slow when I get closer to the house. Whitney's not here. She usually parks her Mini Cooper by her room, which has its own entrance, a room I have yet to see.

I've brought my backpack, and my strategy is to go and read by the pool, so Will doesn't think I came over just to talk to him. Maybe I've taken his invitation too seriously. It could have been just friendly conversation, hypothetical. Chitchat, air filler. Or he's still being the good host.

I go around back to the pool. It's windy out, something I didn't feel just moments ago, shielded by the house. The wind thrusts right off the ocean, which is choppy and scattered with tufts of whitecaps. At the edge of the property, a coconut falls from a tree. The pool water moves in wrinkles. I wish Danny were here to break open that coconut, something he always does when I go to his house. We drink the water, eat the meat. When we were young, we'd pretend we were castaways, foraging in his yard, surviving on coconut and lychee and mint for our breath.

It would be awkward to sit by the pool, like someone sunbathing in a hurricane, so I go to the lanai. I like being over here more now. In a way, it feels silly not to be, like holing up in the locker room at a water park. Since I was planning on sitting on a recliner by the pool, I choose the daybed. This seems like something you'd do when you want to read and be alone, which I ostensibly do.

I look into the living room—empty—then hoist myself onto the daybed and get situated, sitting upright, my legs together at the knees. I didn't want to look like a total nerd, reading for school, so I brought the old draft of the script. I always loved to do this in coffee shops or at a park or even at my old school, how it would make me feel so adult and make people curious about me. They always were. Read a book, no one looks. Read a script in public, and people always do.

Besides, reading this script is actually more appealing to me than *To the Lighthouse*, which is boring me to death. I open it and am already smiling a bit. I like its badness. Then again, if there's something that draws you in, something you can't help reading or watching, then how can it be bad? It's almost like a villain winning while showing his cards. Not his fault he won.

"What are you smiling about?" I look up, and there's Will, standing on the step down to the lanai, his hands holding the doorway over his head. I can't imagine being able to do that. I run my eyes down the length of him, then back up to his face. He rubs his chin and looks like he's recalling a good joke.

"It's been a smiling day," I say. "I've been caught twice."

"Just twice?" he says. "That's not enough."

"It's still early," I say, surprised by my ability to talk smoothly.

"You reading for a role?" he asks and brings his arms down.

I feel misplaced on this bed now. I don't know what to do with my legs. I sit up straighter, cross-legged, and regret my choice. "It's my mom's. She likes me to read them over."

"And read with her?" he asks. "So she can practice her lines?"

We never do this. "Yeah," I say.

"Cool," he says. "Maybe you'll be an actress one day."

"Yeah, right."

"Why not? You've got the look." He grins, and I don't know whether he's being sincere or polite, or if it's just what you say next to keep things going. He steps out and ducks a bit to see the ocean. The light catches his eye. I want to tell him that *he's* got the look. He could be an actor. There's really no difference between him and the guys on screen everyone thinks of as heart-throbs.

"Kind of windy for the boat," he says.

"Yeah," I say. "Surf was nice last week. I only got a day in, but—"

"Longboard?"

"Short."

"Sweet." He looks at me as if I've said something that has changed his perception of me, and for a second, I wonder if my ability to surf has lessened me as a girl in some way, or at least a girl he would like. I can't imagine Lissa doing it. Or him, for that matter.

"Must have been nice to grow up with a surf spot right out your door," I say.

"Yeah, it was great. I'm not really a water guy, though." His confidence in saying this makes me think of surfing as immature. Unsophisticated. I wonder what Danny would think.

"Golf's your thing," I say.

"Yup. Love it. Today was great."

He tells me a story about today, and I shake my head, I open my mouth, I say "really?" and "oh my God," all those things you do when someone is telling you a story. Boys do this all the time with sports—they'll talk about a canoe race in detail, or a wave they caught, and after the first sentence, you want to say, "Okay, you paddled a canoe. Can we leave it at that?" They occupy your ears for way too long with sports tales.

I don't have the same sensation with Will because I love that he's talking to me, and I like watching him. It's just that I feel like I'm performing, and I'm running out of lines and gestures and don't know how long I should hold his gaze, which is making my throat dry. I look down, I look up. I cover my mouth in wonderment, I nod in understanding. It seems I'm almost in the end zone. I think he's about to wrap things up. He shakes his head, and I do the same. I put my legs out in front of me and glance down at the script.

"Sorry," he says. "You're working."

"No, not at all. This is . . . nonsense. I'm just . . . nothing better to do." Loser.

"What's nonsense about it?" he asks.

"Oh my God," I say. "Read it." I hand it up to him, but he doesn't take it. Instead he sits down and leans toward me. I scoot up and, in the same movement, slightly away. I can smell him—sunscreen and that cologne of his—oranges, sandalwood, laundry detergent.

He reads to himself, but out loud at some points. He laughs sometimes, not unkindly, but in a sort of wonderment. "This is great!" he says.

Our heads are so close. I feel like it would be so much easier to jump on him than sit here. It's like someone pretending to tickle you—they're not touching you, but you feel it anyway, and it's unbearable.

"Okay," he says. "Let's do this."

I didn't notice the sun was behind a cloud until it comes out and lights up the lanai, heating my hair.

"Do what?" I ask.

"Let's read it." He flicks the script. "Out loud."

"Oh. Okay," I say in a funny voice, my default-setting voice to hide behind. I'm rolling my eyes at my own damn self. I flip through the pages, looking for a scene, but then I indicate that I'll randomly open to something, not wanting to be responsible. I turn to act 3, scene 2.

"So," I say, "I'll be Samantha."

17

WILL ADJUSTS HIMSELF, SITTING UP, AS IF HE'S REALLY about to audition for something. He clears his throat, then reads as Jenkins:

"'Wow. Look at that . . . asset.'"

I've turned to the same scene my mom and I had read in the kitchen, but we have the version where we see the back of the girl bending over and waxing her board.

"Go on," Will says. "Your line. Say it like you mean it."

"'You're an animal, Jenkins,'" I say, sounding like my mom when she read the line to me.

"'Well, yes, by definition. I am an animal.'" Will looks at me and winks. "'And so are you.'"

I smile back, even though I'm not supposed to. I'm supposed to be disgusted. I look back at the script. A local surfer is coming out of the water, his ripped body glistening. My character takes the binoculars from Jenkins and looks at the surfer.

"'Yes, I guess I am,'" I say.

Seen through the binoculars, the girl is standing now. She stretches before going out into the surf. She twists and reaches and bends and is very flexible.

"'I guess it's your turn,'" I say as Samantha, and pantomime handing him the binoculars. Samantha looks down at the book on her lap and feels his gaze. He isn't looking at the hot girl in her bikini. He's looking at her.

"'What?'" I say, and feel what Samantha is feeling—a kind of flushed yet empowered kick.

Will says, "'Nothing, I . . .'"

"'What?'" I say. "'Spit it out.'"

"'It's just been nice hanging with you, that's all. I know at work we've been all over each other, our egos colliding and—'"

"'No, no, no,'" I say, liking our timing and rhythm. "'Your ego colliding with your own ego and sending shrapnel into everyone's hearts.'"

In the script, Samantha looks shy after saying this. The word *heart* was too much.

I take a breath, get my emotions under control. It doesn't say she does this, but it feels right. "'Our heads, I mean.'" I tap my head, improvising. Will, or Jenkins, sits up a bit, pulls away.

"'Now, that's no way to speak to your elder.'"

He's kidding, but his voice has softened.

Will is good at this, or we're good at this together. It's almost easier this way, and I wish I always had a script at hand. I feel like myself even though I'm not myself. I've warmed to the script as well, as if saying the words out loud not only brings Samantha to life, but makes Jenkins more likable. More than that. As Samantha, I want his attention.

"'I know what you mean,'" I say. "'About hanging out. It's nice to get out of the so-called office.'"

"'I don't mean to be a jerk in there,'" he says. "'Is that what people think?'"

I put my hand on Will's leg, then take it off as if it burned me. It's what Samantha does in the script, and yet it's what I would have done if I were her too, and I even probably feel the way she's supposed to feel—embarrassed but good, and needing a response, needing him to say something to erase the awkwardness and fill the silence. Then I realize it's my turn. It's my line.

"'I take it back,'" I say.

Will laughs. "'You can't take it back.'"

"'No, but I do.'" I glance at the next line, then look at Will as I say it.

"'You should act exactly how you do in there. That's what makes you a great surgeon.'" I look back down and read, "So whatever you're doing, or however you're behaving, it works, in the long run.'"

Samantha turns to him, and Jenkins looks back at her.

"'It works?'" he says. "And there's a long run?'"

"'It works,'" I say. "'And there's always a long run.'" And then he kisses me. Will kisses me, and I kiss back. Our lips are parted, our tongues touch, and I wonder if it will turn—

"'Sorry,'" he says. "'I shouldn't have.'"

"It's okay," I say. "That was . . ." I look at his lips and let my sentence trail off because I can't think of anywhere it could go. My body is working overtime—my head grasping for coherent thoughts, my heart walloping me from the inside. I feel a connection like a string running from my stomach to down between my legs. The string is taut and keeps being pulled.

“I guess we should call it a scene,” Will says, looking down at me.

“Sounds like a good plan,” I say, relieved by the steadiness of my voice. It will be okay. It’s better than okay. This is a good kind of crazy.

“That was fun,” he says, his voice light. I realize what a good actor he is, how his Jenkins voice and demeanor were so different from his own. He inhabited the character so well that I wonder if, when I actually see it on television, I’ll be able to believe in that version. Ours was so real. It’s then that I realize the possibility of something, which gives me the feeling of being on an airplane that's dropping from turbulence.

Will gets up. “It got beautiful out,” he says, and goes to the edge of the lanai, looking out at the ocean. “Look at that light.”

I don’t look at the light. I look down at the script, at Jenkins kissing Samantha, then pulling back and saying, “Sorry. I shouldn’t have . . .”

I had said, “It’s okay,” but Samantha says, “You’re damn right you shouldn’t have,” then gets up and walks away.

Will turns back toward me, and I flip the script over.

“Do you know when Whitney’s going to be home?” I ask. Anything to squash my mortification.

“No,” he says. He walks toward me, and I hold my breath. I wish I could get off this damn bed, or at least adjust my position.

“I have to go,” I say. “Write a paper.”

This is so awful. So good. It’s gawful.

“All right, then,” he says.

I stand up to leave.

"Let me know if you ever need to rehearse again," he says, turning his head.

I grin, then look up to a face that tells me it's all good. It's wonderful.

"Practice makes perfect," I say.

18

THE SAME THING THAT HAPPENED LAST NIGHT HAPPENS again; my mom makes dinner for us and goes out with the Wests. But this time I don't flinch. I can't stop thinking of Will, his hypnotic green eyes, his expert, dizzying kiss, the way it seemed to reel me in. It was way too short.

When I go over to the house, music is playing loudly, thumping through the living room. Who knew a Tuesday night could be so fun? I find Whitney in the kitchen.

"Hey!" she yells over the music, and I yell back. She's wearing a scarf tied around her head, a bathing suit top, and a pareo around her waist. She gets out the plates—just two, I notice.

"No Will?" I ask.

"What?" She takes her phone off the counter and turns the music down. Now that the music is low, I'm self-conscious of my question. "Just the two of us for dinner?" I ask.

"Yeah, Will's at Lissa's."

I look down at my jean skirt, not wanting to admit even to myself that I put it on because I guess I have nice legs, if I had to pick a strength, and I was hoping Will would think that too.

"What's wrong?" Whitney asks.

"Nothing," I say. And it's true. It needs to be true. I like hanging out with Whitney, and the charge I get from knowing we can talk about what we did the night before in front of her friends. When she's with her friends and I walk by, she'll wave or stop to talk and her friends will give her a look like someone pulled a lever and replaced her. By their expressions, I can tell she must have been different before I came along.

Whitney should be enough.

"Catch up," Whitney says, handing me a bottle out of the fridge. It's some kind of canned fizzy daiquiri.

"Perfs," I say, twisting the lid. She sort of smiles to herself, and I wonder if it's because I used one of her words. Oh God, don't let me be that girl who copies the popular girl. I can see the movie sequence: me rising, then burning like frickin' Icarus and, in the end, rising back in my own way, on my own terms. Gag. I take a sip. "Invigorating," I say, and she laughs.

"Should we eat right here?" she asks.

"Yeah. It's just us."

We load up our plates and sit at the bar stools. She turns on the kitchen TV. It's funny the way we switch around—pizza on paper plates, then a set table with cloth napkins, and now, eating in front of the television. I guess it's just like the way my mom and I do it.

The spread tonight: steamed miso butterfish and an edamame, corn, and red onion salad with chopped celery and red cabbage, which I know has been tossed in my mom's homemade dressing—a creamy tarragon concoction that I could pour on absolutely everything.

"Oh my God, these chicks are so busted," she says. "Let's hatewatch."

On-screen are the Real Housewives of wherever. Must be Beverly Hills or the OC.

"They're like—" I don't continue my sentence, knowing I'm bound to insult someone she knows.

"They're like my mom's friends," she says. "Look at that one! She even looks like Vicky. Lissa's mom."

She does look like her, like a human version of a thoroughbred.

"Eeew, and they all talk the same."

I listen to the women at a cocktail party—complaining about someone who said something to someone else. Their voices are appalled, yet simultaneously delighted: a little drag-queenish.

Whitney is rapt either in the drama or perhaps the familiarity of it all. Melanie comes to mind when I watch these women, which brings along an uncomfortable image: my mom in the mix, leaning in with the other ladies, whispering something unkind, getting caught up in things that never would have interested her before.

"They're going to do one here," Whitney says. She points to the TV with her fork.

I take a drink, and realize I'm almost done with it. "*The Real Housewives of Kahala*," I say, imitating their oh-mah-haw voices.

"I'm serious," Whitney says. "They're recruiting the elite of Honolulu. The richest and most fabulous and social, blah, blah, blah, and my mom said she knows tons of people who are trying out but won't admit to it."

"So funny," I say.

"My mom and Vicky totally want to be on it. So embarrassing. They've filmed themselves doing yoga with their trainer and want to film a video of themselves at your mom's premiere. Can you imagine if my mom is on a show like this? I will go into hiding."

"Shit," I say. "I hope that doesn't happen. What about your dad?"

"My dad doesn't even get it. But there's no way he'd let them shoot at the house. Who knows when they'll film, though. Could be years away, and . . ."

"I'm sorry," I say.

"I know," she says. We watch the show again, but aren't laughing this time. It just seems so awful. I wonder if that's why Melanie has attached herself to my mom. Whitney goes to the fridge and gets us more drinks, but pauses when headlights shine through the kitchen windows.

"It's just Will," she says, and I try not to adjust my clothes or hair, but end up doing both. She puts our drinks on the counter and sits back down.

"What's up, ladies?" Will walks into the kitchen, his hair ruffled. He wears black jeans and a long-sleeved dress shirt.

"Hey," I say. I grip my cold drink. I sense him behind me and imagine him leaning down to kiss my cheek.

"What are you having?" he asks.

"A seriously awesome dinner," Whitney says. "Made again by not-our-mom."

He looks at the TV. "Hey, it's Mom's friends," he says.

Whitney laughs and looks at me. "See?"

Will picks up my drink and reads the label. His hands are big, nails short and clean.

"Try it," I say, and he does, licking his lips after. I move my plate over, making room in case he wants to sit down.

"Not bad," he says.

"Do you want one?" I ask.

"Uh, sure," he says after looking at his phone. He goes to the fridge.

Whitney's zoned out on the TV. He comes back beside me and puts his drink on the counter, his hand next to mine. I feel like I'm about to shatter. There are all these things we can't say, and I just wish he could give me some sort of sign that this afternoon happened and mattered.

Someone on the television yells across the pool at another woman, who says, "I'm out of here," while all her friends plead with her not to go.

"There's your future, Whit," Will says, and I smile when he looks at me.

Whitney doesn't respond. She looks over at us, and I get a hollow feeling.

"Do you want some?" I ask Will, gesturing to the food.

"Thanks, but I'm on my way back out again. Just came to pick something up."

"Where you going?" Whitney asks.

"Morimoto's."

"Ooh," she says. "Can we come?"

I picture a dog at the beach, shaking off water. That's what my insides do. I have a drink to calm myself and communicate somehow that I don't care about what his answer will be.

"Will, what the hell?" Lissa comes to the doorway. She's wearing a short green dress and high heels. If I got off the bar stool, I'd fit under her arm. "I'm waiting out there." She looks down at me, then back at him.

"Hi, Lissa!" Whitney says, in a way that draws attention to Lissa's rude inability to say hello.

"Oh, hi!" she says. "Sorry, but I would have come in if I had known you were going to be taking so long."

"I just wanted to hang with my little sister and her friend," Will says jokingly, and Whitney throws a wadded-up napkin at him and smiles.

"Okay, but can we go now?" It's like she just walked out of the television show we're watching.

"Yes, dear," he says, which makes a nasty vibration go through me, a manic drumming.

"Have fun, girls," she says, which makes her sound like a mom leaving the little ones behind.

"No love," Whitney says, after she leaves.

"It's this senior dinner thing the girls have planned forever," Will says. "Otherwise, it would have been fun to have you there." He puts his hand on my shoulder so it feels like he's just addressing me. Whitney raises her eyebrows as if she's not sure whether he's being sarcastic or not. She looks back at the TV.

"Bye," he says. He seems to be communicating so much more than farewell. His eyes, his bearing, tells me he'd rather stay.

"Bye," I say, hoping to communicate both my disappointment and understanding.

"Lissa's a bitch!" Whitney calls after him.

"Noted!" he yells back. When I hear the door shut, I ask her why she said that.

"She got all close to me so she could hang out with Will,

and did you see that? She doesn't even say hello. I mean, catchphrase, right?" She is smiling, and I manage a small laugh.

On TV I watch the women fight, the husbands in the background in bright shirts and slim pants, sunglasses and sports coats. They're drinking cocktails, and one is laughing like a hyena while holding his hand up for a high five.

"This is not my future," she says. "More like Will's." I'm about to ask her to say more, but then she says: "Ooh! I want to show you this thing on YouTube, reminded me of our French animals. So funny." She looks down at her phone.

Will's headlights shine in, then turn to the edge of the yard. I feel so left behind.

"What's wrong?" Whitney asks, and I realize she's looking at me.

"Nothing," I say, and for a moment, she looks incredibly annoyed.

19

ON THE WALK BACK HOME FROM WHITNEY'S TONIGHT, I trip on a sprinkler, fall, and laugh hard under the moon. I immediately want to tell Whitney, then think how nice it is to have someone to tell things to. We ended up having a really fun night, and I have the sensation of finally clicking into something. While it's been a little unplanned—like I'm a doctor on call—it's still satisfying. How was I ever hesitant? What about Kailua was I homesick for? It doesn't miss me.

I continue across the grass, the cool night blowing through my clothes, a smile on my face from imagining Will driving through the gates, seeing me in the moonlight like an innocent heroine in the fields or the moors. *Lea in the Lawns* by Leahi Landscaping. He has come back for me. He couldn't wait to leave the dinner. I play the loop of our encounter, both the real one on the daybed and the imagined one, until I get to my front door.

At home, I watch a cooking show on TV and eat a huge piece of the cake Melanie got for us. I may have drunk too much. Drunk? Drank? I stand up to test my skills, balancing on one foot, then the other. I laugh, keep balancing, then lean forward, arms out like Superman, one leg extended behind me, and of course, that's when my mom walks in.

"What are you doing?" she says. "It's eleven thirty and a school night."

"Then I should probably stop doing my yoga routine," I say, articulating each word, which is kind of hard.

I sit back down on the couch, little stars blinking around my head.

She puts her keys on the counter. "Did you have a good time?"

I watch the television. I can tell she's looking me over.

"I wouldn't call it a good time," I say, because I want her to think that I've sacrificed something.

"What would you call it, then?"

"Call what?" I should have escaped and gone to bed earlier.

My mom stands across the room by the kitchen, then slowly walks toward me. She looks so composed and beautiful, it scares me.

"I asked if you had a good time," she says. "You said you wouldn't call it that, and so I—"

"Just a time," I say. "I had a time. We ate, that's all. Devoured your meal like savages. And the cake." I shove my hand toward the cake. I am the savage. I had a little delicate piece with Whitney, then a much larger one alone. "Whitney said to bring it back here. Her mom got it at Diamond Head Market—"

"Yes, I know," she says. "As a way to say thank you for the dinner I made, and for all I've done." There's a strong note of tiredness in the way she says this, as if she's repeating something that's been said to her over and over again.

She gets a fork from the kitchen and walks over to the table. She looks at me curiously, then sits down and takes a bite from the cake without cutting a slice.

"Did you have fun?" I ask. "Doing whatever you were doing?"

"I was at the club," she says. "Dining."

"Dining at the club," I say in a posh voice that doesn't quite deliver. "Didn't you go there last night too?"

"No," she says. "We were going to, but then we went to some food and wine festival. Tonight was just a casual dinner with some of their friends."

"Sounds lovely," I say and put my feet up on the coffee table, which makes one of the magazines fall. "Ouch," I say, and don't know why.

"It was lovely," she says. "It's so pretty down there. And good to meet people outside of work."

She's like a new girl at school, finally making friends, and I don't know why I can't be happier for her. She's feeling the same way I am, experiencing that same satisfying click.

"Gloria's great, and this one girl, Pi'i?" She laughs to herself. "She's hilarious. You should meet her. She's just so witty and out there. She says these outrageous things—"

"Like what?"

My mom puts the fork down, still smiling over the memory, still sailing on the buzz created by connecting to someone. "I can't think of anything on the spot. Just everything. I guess—"

"I had to be there."

I've brought her down from her flight. "Yeah," she says. "I talked all about you. Mostly everyone there has kids who go to Punahou. You probably know a lot of their daughters. Whitney's friends . . ." She looks up at me, and I can see something awful: pity. "A woman named Vicky said she met you. She has a place on the Big Island she said we could use."

"Vicky Sand?" I say, much too loudly.

"Yes, on the Kohala coast. I guess it's this super-private—"

"God, she's horrible! She's like Boobzilla. She wants to be on that Real Housewives show. They're filming it here, you know. That's why they're nice to you in the first place. They want you to help them get on the show or have you introduce them to Bradley Cooper or some crap."

My mom gets up and takes the cake into the kitchen. I look ahead, but can hear her doing dishes, putting things away. It all seems to take forever. I should have stormed out, but I feel glued to the sofa. I can see out of the corner of my eye that she's walking my way, and then she sits down next to me, making the sofa dip.

"Breathe," she says.

"I am."

She puts her face right up to mine. "Breathe in my face. Blow out air."

I inhale and blow, moving my lips so the breath goes to the side.

"You've been drinking," she says.

"So have you." I try to scoot away from her without her knowing.

"I'm allowed to drink," she says. "Put your feet down."

"Why?" I say.

"Because it's bad manners, that's why."

"No one's here."

"Lea!" she says—the hard emphasis on the *e* like she always does when she's angry, which isn't often.

"What?" I say. I put my feet down.

"Where were you drinking?" She looks both angry and worried.

"At your friend's house," I say, emphasizing right back. "Where you put me."

"That is totally unacceptable."

"Yes, I know," I say. We are locked in angry stares, and I can tell she's out of her element. She doesn't know what to do with me, having never been in this situation before. Tears are beginning to glaze her eyes, and her weakness makes me bolder, meaner.

"I only drank because Whitney offered it to me," I say. "Just trying to have good manners."

"Cut the sass," she says. I scoff, and she looks tempted to smack me. Her hands are in fists, and I imagine her heart is racing. Mine is.

"You cannot drink here," she says. "Or anywhere. If Whitney does it, or offers it, it doesn't mean you have to take it. If she jumps off a bridge, you don't have to jump off a bridge too." Even she looks disappointed with this statement.

"But I would," I say. "If it was into deep, clean water. That's my favorite! And you do whatever Melanie does."

She closes her eyes and takes a long breath, and I take one too, in imitation, but then I get tired. Tired of my own behavior, tired of this fight. I know I will cry when I get to my room.

"Help Whitney out, okay?"

My anger comes racing back. "What do you mean, help her out? What is that? One of your job requirements? Cooking, socializing, and outsourcing me?"

She looks toward the television. "I don't want . . . tension. These people are being very nice to us, and—"

"What does that have to do with anything? So I owe them something too? Is this part of the deal?"

"There is no deal," she says. "Stop saying that. There's no obligation. We don't have any obligations. I want you to have friends. I'm happy you're getting along so well, but now I'm in an awkward position. I'm going to have to tell Melanie."

Now I wonder what's made her angrier: that I was drinking or that she'll have to tell Melanie, putting an end to both my playdates and hers. I shake my head and smirk when she looks at me.

"So tell Melanie," I say. "Maybe she'll replace you with someone better."

"You don't know what you're talking about," my mom says in calm way, which makes me feel just that, like I don't know anything.

"And I *will* tell Melanie," she says, challenging me right back. "I don't want to, but I will. We talk, and . . . I know Whitney is a bit distracted in school. She's going through things. Her dad—"

"Whitney's probably going through things because her parents just leave her home alone all the time and her dad's losing it. You're the one who's put me in this environment."

"Don't speak that way about Eddie," she says. "It's horrible what he's going through."

"Sorry," I say, ashamed. How hard it must be. "I know."

"I realize I've been out a lot. I . . ." She stops, and I look at her. "I don't think Melanie accepts the severity of it all."

Before I can ask her to explain, she continues, "And the kids are having a hard time with it too. It's a big weight. I think Melanie was looking forward to having someone sensible around. Someone with her head on her shoulders."

"I'm not the nanny," I say. "And who says I have my head on my shoulders?" I want to go wild. Drink and drink, never come home, have guys touch my body of work. I'm tempted to start now—strut right out of here, find Will, and tell him to get all Jenkins on my ass. Though I wouldn't know where to go. And I'd be afraid an alarm would go off at the gate. And he's with Lissa, who I thought he was tired of! He's supposed to go forth and bring back frickin' knowledge!

"I think you should get to bed," my mom says. She looks so tired. "We'll talk tomorrow. We both need to get up early."

I think of Spitzer and his assignment.

My job is to help my mom look good. It's to be her junior, her daughter, to be the daughter of someone who will always be bigger than me. My job is to be a good houseguest, a good recipient.

But right now I want nothing more than to be an owner, a giver, a person who has her own fabulous life, wearing heels on a Tuesday night. I want nothing more than to quit my job.

"Maybe I'm having a hard time too," I say. "Maybe not having a dad is a big weight for me. Ever think of that? That I have my own issues?"

"I think of that all the time," my mom says. "You've always said you don't, but I've wanted you to admit that you do. You care. You feel things."

I'm stunned that she threw this back on me, almost like a trap.

"I love you," she says. "I'm proud of you."

Don't say that. That's what makes the tears come, and I'm glad I'm facing the other direction.

20

FRIDAY AND SPRING BREAK IS HERE. HOPEFULLY, I WON'T still be grounded for it, though compared to everyone else, I may as well be. Everyone on campus seems ecstatic, and I'm only pretending to be. It's like New Year's or Halloween, something you're supposed to be excited about, but if you have no plans, the holidays seem to be making fun of you.

All day there's been chitchat across the campus. I overhear the same people talking about their plans and using the exact same lines.

Malia Lautenbach: "My mom's making me go with her to Tahiti. She dives for shells for her jewelry line? So . . ."

Chris Watanabe: "Tavarua, baby." Followed by a high five. "Let's do this."

There's a bunch of guys going on this surf trip, apparently, and it's something they've done before. They surf all day, then return to their own island and drink kava, whatever that is. "Do you all jack each other off, too?" I hear Coco Kettley ask.

Celeste Baldwin will go to her cabin on Molokai; Isabelle Kehau's going to her family's house in Vail; Emma Emerson is off to Park City. Everyone has GoPros to put on their boards, just in case we want to see pictures of them shredding.

Skiing in Vail/Steamboat/Park City. Going to the Molokai/ Maui/Big Island house/cabin/condo. Surf trip: Tavarua/Indo/ Kauai. The variations on the lines.

What are you doing, Lea? The question I've been dreading every day this week before realizing no one really cares. Just chilling here, I say when someone happens to ask. Or I say that I'm planning on surfing a lot. The most common reaction to my plans is that the person I'm talking to sometimes just loves staying home. "It's just so easy." Then they'll look at me as if I'm doing something they envy, but I know they don't.

The school day feels illegitimate, a charade that even the teachers are playing at. I walk out of math at the same time Danny gets out of his class. We bump into each other, a silent hello and agreement that we'll walk somewhere together.

I take off my sweatshirt that I keep for classes and remove once I hit the humid air. Danny sniffles. "Fuckin' vog," he says, and hocks a loog.

"Only a guy could do that," I say. "Can you imagine if I just spat?"

I try to make the sound he just made and sound like a hissing cat.

"It would be cool if you spat."

"No, it wouldn't," I say.

"What are you doing for break?" Danny asks. We stop by the steps to the library.

"Nothing," I say. *I just want to hang with you,* I don't say, mainly because the thought surprises me. I miss this. Being with someone who knows me, someone who knows both my strengths and weaknesses.

"I'm not doing anything either," he says. He puts his hands in the pockets of his jeans and clears his throat again, then spits. "Sorry," he says.

That's another thing about guys—they can get away with this behavior and look good doing it. I don't wish I were a guy, but I love being around them—their humor, their wildness, and how these traits seem to lend themselves to me in their company. I don't feel this way with Will, though, not yet. I'm more reserved with him, still nervous, and yet the true parts of me seem lit up, or at least like they have the potential to shine with him.

Laura Sherman walks by, a cute girl with freckles as big as papaya seeds. She's in practically all of my classes. Months ago, I'd have considered her a friend.

"Hey, hey," she says.

"Hey, hey," I say, matching her tone.

"See you in Chinois." She walks past us.

"Can't wait," I say, in that singsong voice that I realize I only use with other girls and always when I don't know them that well. It's like a shield from awkwardness. It's small-talk voice. I use this voice a lot.

"We should surf over break," Danny says in a flat voice.

"Oh, *now* we should," I say, remembering his dis last week. "Now that Whitney's going to."

"What?" he says. "No." He looks away. I feel like we're arguing. There's an awkward silence.

I don't want to ask if he likes her, knowing how I'll sound. Why should I care?

"I want to jump off Waimea rock," I say. I've never done that before."

"I should take you," he says. "You're too haole to go by yourself." He steps closer, peering down at me and puffing out his chest.

"Oh, please," I say. "You're perpetuating stereotypes. I can handle, Randle. I go huge."

"Oh my God, Donkey, was that your pidgin? That made King Kamehameha roll in his grave."

"He wouldn't have spoken pidgin, idiot."

"Still, he's rolling." Danny sniffs, something he always does after being cute.

"You're rolling," I say, and can't help but look around. It's fun to laugh with someone in public. That may be superficial, but it's true, and it feels good to have our rhythm intact.

I take a few steps back so he's not towering over me.

"Don't," he says. "I like how much taller I am than you. I like looking down on you."

"Impossible," I say, rising up on my toes. "That needs to be earned, and not by inches."

I see a few of his football buddies walking over and know our easy banter is going to be usurped by grunts and high fives that are less high and more like swinging a tennis racquet. I'm not crazy about the football players. They're so serious and stoic, which I think is really a cover for a lack of speaking skills. They're not funny like Danny, or friendly, and they always seem to look at me as if I'm some kind of weirdo.

Here are Ryan, Luke, Kalani, and Win Wong (everyone calls him by his first and last name—both just roll off the tongue). True to form, they go through the whole hand-slapping, "waddup" routine and then they mumble to each other quietly and far above me physically, and I just stand there and nod while they form this kind of arc and gaze out at nothing.

Seriously, no one is talking. It's like they're bouncers, looking all tough and flexing. Girls cross in front of us, and if they like them, they'll tilt their heads in hello. If the girls aren't up to par, they do nothing at all. If they're super hot, they'll pass and the guys will turn their heads ever so slightly and mutter things like "chee" and "shaddup."

These are expressions everyone around here uses when something pleases them. "Chee" is said enthusiastically; "shaddup," dryly and in response to something that looks good, like a pizza or a girl. "Shoots" means "okay, let's do it."

Michelle and Liana pass and receive a "damn" and a kind of sucking noise.

I sort of get Michelle—she's all sporty and cute—but Liana Carriage is normal looking. I may even be prettier. It's that yeast additive thing again, her clothes, her voice—that popular-girl, clipped-alto drawl—the fact that her dad owns all the Carriage car dealerships, this retrofits her look, making her hot.

Mike Matson and Maile Beaucage walk by, holding hands and looking like they're strolling the grounds of their kingdom. I consider saying something—commenting on something or asking about these guys' plans for break, but know I'd embarrass Danny or myself. I imagine them not even answering.

"'Kay, I'm out," I say to Danny. He holds out his hand for me to slap. Really? Must I? I hate high-fiving or low-fiving, and he wouldn't do it if these guys weren't here, but maybe he's helping me out, showing he's down with me and not just letting me shuffle off, muttering spastically. I slap.

"Hit me up over break."

"Yeah, okay." I will hit you up. Maybe this is male singsong. I walk away toward Griffiths Hall, and Danny calls, "You're going to the hotel, though, right?"

"What?" I turn back. "What hotel?"

"The Wests' hotel. One of 'em in Waikiki."

I shrug. I have no idea what he's talking about. "Yeah, um, no," I say. I want to keep walking, so he doesn't see my irritation, and I need to keep walking to get to class. The quad is emptying, and there's something horrifying about getting yelled at in Chinese.

"I'll talk to you after class," I call.

The campus looks empty—like everyone's gone, say, skiing or shell diving. I hurry off, seeing Laura heading into the room and am annoyed by the late reveal. We could have been talking about the hotel the entire time instead of grunting like gorillas. What is happening there? I want to know, and I don't want to know. Or, I want to be told, but I don't want to have anyone see my reaction, pretending not to care that I didn't hear it first or, worse, faking indifference to not being invited. Sometimes when you think everyone is doing something better than you are, you're right.

In the classroom it hits me: an idea about why I wasn't invited. Actually, a few theories, one of them being that Whitney is mad at me because maybe I got her in trouble. My mom hasn't told me whether she told Melanie, so I don't know for sure. I haven't spoken to Whitney since Tuesday night. I've been grounded this week, which has pretty much made no difference in my life. I've basically continued on my not-awesome trajectory. School, home, studying, cheehoo. We're not texting friends—I don't even have her number—so I have no idea what's happening on her end.

Maybe I'm not invited because unbeknownst to Danny, the whole hotel thing is canceled due to her grounding. Maybe I'll be the one who has to say to Danny, "Oh, you didn't know?"

"Lea, will you read the next paragraph aloud, please," Ms. Chun says.

I look down at my book, searching for *fuyu*, the last word Derek Kwan read. I glance up at everyone in the circle we've formed with our desks, feeling their gazes. I bring shame to the class—everyone teases Laura and me with this saying, since we're the only ones who aren't Chinese. This seems to give us a little leeway to be idiots.

"Um," I say.

"Um," Ms. Chun imitates me. "I don't see 'um.'" Her derisive jokes are never funny, even though by her puffed-up follow-up expressions, she must think they are. She doesn't hold humor right. She's all thumbs.

I place my finger near the bottom of the page. "*Wǒ míngtiān kàn zhè běn shū,*" I say with confidence, then keep reading. I've always enjoyed reading aloud and am glad to have gotten through the paragraph. Ms. Chun looks contrite, or like she's hiding a small bird in her mouth. Why do some teachers seem to want you to fail?

This thought stays with me during the rest of class as I'm thinking of break and plans and friends and why we all can't want what's best for one another.

21

WHEN I GET HOME, I WANT MY MOTHER TO BE THERE SO I can ask her what happened with Melanie, if she told her or not. Other than grounding me, she hasn't said a word about that night; she's using the power of scary silence.

She seems to be waiting for me when I walk in. She's standing in front of the counter, sorting through the mail. She smiles, then looks down, probably remembering that I'm grounded and shouldn't be encouraged to smile. It must be a nuisance to have a grounded kid after a while—it's like being happy to see a friend, then remembering you aren't speaking to each other.

"I'm sorry about the other night," I say, which feels funny to articulate because it seems so long ago. "I've had all week to think about it . . . so . . ."

She sighs and leans on the counter, then pats her palm down hard, which has the effect of a judge using a gavel.

"I'm sorry too," she says. "I haven't been home. I haven't been here for you. I've been traipsing around town—"

She's about to cry. I put my backpack down and walk closer to her. She smooths my hair, and I sit down on a bar stool next to her.

"It's okay—It's not like I need you to be here all the time or anything. I wasn't rebelling or—"

"No, I know," she says, and she's regained the strength in her voice. "And I'm not excusing your behavior, and me being gone doesn't give you license to raise hell."

"I really raised hell," I say flatly.

"You know what I—"

"I know. I know. I'm sorry, I got—"

"Caught up," she says, and I let it go with that. I don't feel that's what it was. I didn't feel pressure to do the things I did—I wanted to drink. I want to go out, I want to do things with Whitney to pave the way for more adventure. I want to go to the hotel and party. I like it. I like kissing Will.

Still, I'll pretend to be caught up in someone else's desires, someone else's poor judgment, even though I'd think she'd understand me, respect me for my curiosity and yearning. She was young too. She must know. But then again, I'm glad she's not too lenient.

I remember in San Francisco going to Tanya Rowley's house. Her parents let us drink, and she had a guest cottage, which basically served as a romper room. She had a party one night, and tons of people came. The music was loud; there was a keg, and her parents were there, standing in the kitchen, hitting the joint that was being passed around. I nursed a beer, feeling prudish, the thought *who will take care of us?* ringing in my head. Her parents were laughing with the other kids in the room, and Tanya's mother was sort of the center of attention with a story she was telling. I thought she looked pathetic, that the kids' laughter was tinged with a kind of pity and politeness. I guess I prefer the mom who says no.

"So now what?" I ask. "Am I still grounded?" I look up at her and grin, showing my teeth.

Her hair falls in front of her face, and she leans over and swoops it up into a ponytail high on top of her head, looking like a cheerleader. I think people assume she's a mom not quite like Tanya's, but someone who'd abide more. Because she's an actress. She's cool and pretty, and maybe when you're a pretty mom, people assume you're lenient.

"I'm not a very good grounder, am I?" she says. "Grounding you during the school week."

"You're great," I say. "I like the way you ground."

"Well, then, you're free," she says, then at the sight of my smile adds, "Free to make good choices."

"Did you tell Melanie?" I ask.

"No."

I'm relieved, and yet it puts a twist on things. Whitney has no reason for having excluded me from the hotel. Maybe it's just because she hasn't had the opportunity to tell me.

I stand up, bouncing a bit. "Can I go over to Whitney's?" I almost said *Will's*.

"Okay, but I want you to think," she says. "To respect and take care of yourself."

"Deal," I say.

And it is a deal. I'll take care of myself. I am good, I'll be good, but I also want to get a new job.

22

NOW, THIS IS SPRING BREAK. SUNNY, NO ONE HOME. Will's car outside. I will make my own plans and maybe make him clarify his own.

Will? For break you're hanging out with Will West? That guy is, like, dreamboat, like, dream yacht; he's, like, Kelly Slater kind, and his body is ohmahhaw-mazing. As soon as I think this, though, I rethink. Will isn't the tan surfer type. Danny's the one who looks like the pro surfer. Will is classy, sophisticated. I imagine him taking off a suit jacket and putting it over my shoulders.

Will West? Golf pro. That guy is such a boss.

I know! And he is so sweet and sexy.

I'm on the daybed again, reading the script. It may be a setup, but I'm going with it.

I hear music coming from inside, and I cross, then uncross my legs. I will lounge. I will be cucumber coolness.

And then I sense him there in the doorway, and when I look over, I act as though I was in deep concentration.

"Oh, hey," I say. "Thought you'd be off spring breaking."

"I'm here spring breaking."

We smile at each other, and it's as if we've both agreed to bypass the shyness and admit something.

“I’m glad,” I say.

He holds his hands out in front of him, framing me. “I think we need to do a retake. The light is perfect.” He looks down, then back up, his face coy and confident.

“Take two?” I say.

He sits next down on the edge, and I sit up and move my legs so they hang next to his. “I haven’t seen you this week,” he says. “This is a nice surprise.”

“I’ve been busy,” I say.

“Hey,” he says, his face close to mine.

“Hi, there.” I almost reach out to touch the stubble on his face, his hard square jaw. I want to bury my face in his shirt that smells good and worn. His body looks strong beneath it. I move back, not wanting to be looked at so closely.

“You look nice,” he says, in a way where it seems as if he’s still deciding on it.

“Are you in character right now?”

“Maybe,” he says.

Something has changed. It’s as though we’ve skipped ahead or something happened off-screen. This feels so easy.

He looks at the script and reads a few lines in a jokey voice.

“We could change it up a bit,” he says. “Improvise.”

I swing my legs back and forth. “Okay, Dr. Jenkins,” I say.

He reaches for my hand. “Okay, Samantha,” he says. It’s sweet, the way he’s holding my hand, like we’ve done this before.

“We could start where we left off,” he says, and before I can think about anything, his mouth is on mine.

It’s more urgent this time—not a test, inquisitive kiss. This kiss lands and stays to explore. We do this for what seems forever and could be forever. I could do this all day and night.

"What about Lissa?" I ask.

"What about her?" he says.

"Are you with her or not?"

"No," he says. "I told her I had other things on my mind." He lies back and takes me with him, pulling me between his legs. I can feel him. His hand moves up my shirt, one on my back and one on my breast. He groans a bit into my mouth. He moves us so we're facing each other on the bed and presses his body between my legs, and I imagine us having sex this way. There's so little fabric between us, I feel like we already are.

We haven't stopped kissing, and a breeze moves my hair over our faces. He pushes my hair away, then presses me on my back. He begins to bring his hand under the buckle of my shorts and part of me is mortified, anticipating what he'll find, the evidence of my total desire. He finds it and sighs, "Lea," and though I'm a virgin and want to be one until the time is right, the way he's moving his fingers and the naked desire on his face make me want to throw caution to the wind. I move into his hand, closing my eyes, but seeing us here with the ocean, the wind, the ripples on the pool. The time seems beautiful.

I open my eyes, and we lock gazes, then kiss again. I reach for his buckle to feel him too, and his hands find mine, helping me. I feel I need to give him fair warning that I'm a virgin and while my body wants to swallow him, my brain, my being, would like a first date.

"I think . . . ," I say, but don't get anything else out, hoping my hesitation conveys everything for me.

He holds my hand again, then brings it to the outside of his boxers. He kisses my neck. "We can go in," he says.

A car door slams, and we jump. Will faces the ocean, getting himself together. I sit up, then get off the bed.

"I'm going to go," I say.

"Yeah, okay." He turns, and there's something distant in his eyes, like nothing happened just now. "That was a good take," he says with a laugh.

It takes me a moment to understand what he's talking about. "Take two," I joke again.

He walks over to me and ruffles my hair, making me feel like a Labrador or, worse, a shih tzu. "See you soon."

"Right," I say. Is this my cue, then? Will there be a take three?

"You okay?" he asks. "We cool?" He wipes his hands on his pants.

We cool? I think so. I'm cool, I'm hot—flushed, fiery. I'm cold. A little sour, but, ah, what happened—this moment—I'm a little sweet too. I'm all over the map.

"I should go," I say, and am left feeling both exhilaration and shame. I walk to the side of the house, where the garbage cans are, so that whoever's coming in won't see me.

23

THE WIND CAME BACK AND, ALONG WITH IT, RAIN, which is rare in Kahala. I miss the rain in Kailua, the way it cleans the slate and makes it okay to stay inside. In Hawaii you always feel you have to be outside doing something.

The sound of the rain is faint. In the cottage, we are too sealed in to really hear or notice it. There are no glass jalousies that let the outside in. I can see the rain, though, through the kitchen window, and a rectangle of night sky softly illuminated by light from the coconut trees.

I tried to read in my room, which is to say, I had a book open and was looking at the words and reading sentences over and over because I couldn't focus. I looked out at the main house, wondering what Will thought, if he even thought anything at all. I was straight-up mortified right after everything happened, but now that time has passed, I find myself smiling at the memory, smiling at my mortification, smiling at the event of it all, the way he touched me. The script was an alibi. Whatever happened I chalk up to Samantha, so it was all a wonderful fiction. I think of his hand. I would like more fiction. I close my book because it's not nearly as good as my own story.

I go to the living room and switch on the TV, which is giving me something to look at, but I'm not really hearing what anyone's saying, and when my mom comes out from her room and asks what I'm watching, I tell her, "I don't even know."

She stands by the couch, watching.

"You're not grounded anymore, you know," she says.

"I know," I say. I guess I'm grounding myself. Friday night of spring break. Girl gone wild.

"Want to watch this Netflix?" she asks, and I see the envelope in her hand. Her face is so open and eager. She'd be so disappointed if I said no.

"What is it?" I ask, moving my legs, inviting her to sit.

"A documentary about African lions." She walks up to the TV as if she's been waiting to do this all night.

"Really? Why do you get every animal documentary ever made?"

"I love them!" she says, and the thing is, once they get started, I usually do too. Still, now I'm adding documentary to the list following *Friday* and *first night of spring break.* I am so punk rock. Just when I thought I liked my own story, the reality settles in. I am home with my mom. And yet, the residue of today still lingers, and I realize no matter what I'm doing I have the memory and the sensation in my reserves. My face warms, and that string pulls, and I feel like I can't move. I'm like a wildebeest near a lion; my mom will find me. She'll detect something new and awful about me, like alcohol on my breath, something she'd be able to smell. *Breathe in my face.* She'll sense dirtiness, inappropriateness, or maybe just something adult. I want to be an adult, but not with her. The things in my reserves that are making my body pulse are mine.

"Popcorn?" she asks, after setting up the movie.

"Yes!" I say, feeling kind of spoiled that she's making it for me, even though I know she wants to.

After she pops the corn, she sits down with the bowl, puts the blanket over our legs, and we move into a broad shot of the Sahara.

We reach into the bowl at the same time, grabbing our handfuls. I feel that this will always be what I think of when I think of home. This is something we do together and have always done. I can remember the movies we had when I was little, all on rotation—*The Sound of Music*, *The Parent Trap*, *Whale Rider*. There were *The Perks of Being a Wallflower*, *Emma* and *Clueless*, *Annie* and *Fantastic Mr. Fox*. And of course, animal documentaries. I know everything there is to know about penguins.

The cubs are playing, pawing one another. The mother licks a cub, lifting it off the ground with her tongue. We both laugh. "Love it," I say, feeling so myself and absorbed. When the film nears its heartbreaking conclusion (one of the cubs taken, devoured), both of us cry, but that's what happens out there in the wild. Why can crying feel so good? I'm happy to feel something, sad and tunneled out, convinced it makes room for something else.

24

I WAKE REFRESHED AND READY TO MAKE SPRING BREAK official.

The thought of Will has given me a buzz, a spring in my step, a confidence. Whitney hasn't said anything about our plan to surf, but I've decided that I am going to Kailua, and she can come if she wants to.

Just days ago, I'd have felt cautious; I'd have looked out the window, not sure if I should remind her or worry that she wasn't serious about coming with me. Now I walk across the lawn to knock on her bedroom door with an assuredness that makes me feel like a new person. I like my outfit—short jean shorts and a white T-shirt that falls off my shoulders. I've borrowed my mom's black Ray-Bans, and I like the way they look so much I'm hoping she forgets to ask for them back.

I see Will and slow my pace. He sees me, but from this distance, I can't read his expression. He's putting clubs into the trunk of his SUV.

"Morning," I say.

"What's up?" he says. The familiarity, the easiness, everything is gone. He looks preoccupied, his face pinched in irritation or anger. Aren't we supposed to be climbing the ladder to something? Or are we going back down again? I want to shake him, throw myself at him, kiss him, and say, "Remember this?"

He's wearing a baseball cap, light gray shorts, and a green golf shirt. "Nice outfit," I say.

"Yeah, you too," he says.

"What's going on here?" I ask. He seems to scoff, but then his face settles down into something normal.

"Sorry," he says. "I suck at this. And I'm stressed. Big tournament today, and my dad had me up all night helping him out with work stuff."

"Oh," I say, comforted by the fact that he was just sitting home with his parent too. It also makes him seem so in charge, the fact that his dad needs him in that way. I love this light he's in—both a caring son and a responsible heir. "Is he okay?"

"Yeah," Will says and takes his hat off, wipes his brow with his forearm, then puts it back on. I'm so tempted to touch him as a girlfriend would.

"He's just worried about everything, a little paranoid," Will says. "He had me go through all his finances—again—things he wants kept from—" He stops suddenly.

"That's a lot to deal with," I say.

"Yeah. Anyway." He touches me lightly on the waist, his hand bringing comfort and relief. "You okay?"

I laugh. "I'm good."

"I'll see you soon?"

"Yeah, okay," I say. "Good luck today." We make eye contact while walking backwards in different directions. He holds his hand out toward me as if he were palming a basketball, then turns to his car.

• • •

Whitney opens one of the doors to her room. She looks like she just woke up. She's wearing a large Billabong T-shirt, and I imagine it being handed down from Will. It looks like something he'd wear when he's out of his golf costume.

Will has deflated me a bit, but I want to patch up that hole and keep my good-mood momentum. I've missed Whitney this week.

"Let's surf!" I say.

She covers one of her ears, indicating a headache, a hangover. Something—a ring or a bracelet—catches on her T-shirt, which gets momentarily lifted, revealing that she isn't wearing anything beneath it, not even underwear. I try not to react to the sight of her body, but it's jarring to see it—she's completely shaved, and my first thought is that it looks so cold.

She groans. "Too loud. Too happy."

"Sorry," I say. "I'm going to Flat Island, if you still want to come with."

"What time is it?" She hits her forehead repeatedly with the palm of her hand.

"Almost ten, I think."

"Oh God," she says. She looks behind her, then moves out a little more toward me, holding the door against her. I almost ask, jokingly, *Hiding someone?* then realize that maybe she is. The thought, coupled with her bareness down there, makes me feel incredibly childlike.

"I guess I'll go," she says. "Give me a sec. You want to load up the boards while I get ready? Mine's on the side of the house."

"Sure," I say, and she closes her bedroom door.

• • •

My board is already on the roof, and I put hers on top of it. It's a Saffron James board and has a batik-like white-and-blue print. It's like a beautiful cake you can't bear to cut into. Still, I'd love to have one. It's achingly cool.

I knock on her door again. She opens it, all the way this time, and looks like she went back to bed.

"Are you kidding me?" I say. Her hair is in a sloppy bun, and she's wearing the same thing, her legs bare.

"What?" she says. "I'm ready."

"Oh," I say, and see the straps beneath the T-shirt. I get glimpses of her room while she gets her bag and sunglasses. There are glass doors on the other side facing the ocean, the wooden blinds up. The room is very adult, but not necessarily in a good way. It looks designed and decorated by someone from a place like Martha's Vineyard who wanted a Hawaiian theme for the guest cottage.

I want to wander around—I love people's rooms, but this doesn't look like it would reveal anything true about her. I glance at the unmade bed. I look for clues, but the only thing that strikes me is that the bed is fully turned down. Whenever I wake up, half of my bed is still partially made—I just tuck myself into one side—but I know this doesn't mean anything. She could just move around a lot. She could kick off all the covers. I stay pretty still when I sleep, and maybe I've just gotten in the habit of not disturbing the other side so I don't have as much work to do the next day. She probably isn't forced to make her bed.

She closes the door, and we get into my car. Would Danny sneak over here? Would he sleep in her bed? I could just ask her—was there someone in there?—but worry it would come off sounding pathetic.

On the road, my mood is back to soaring again, triggered by the sight of Nu'uanu and driving up the Pali toward the tunnel. The air is cooler, the sky sunny but muted, trees and wildness on both sides of the highway, all varying riffs on green. Some of the mountain's sharp wrinkles are lined with waterfalls, though the wind is making them spray in the other direction. Waterclimbs and waterfalls.

Whitney has her bare feet on my dash, and she's texting someone, which reminds me of the hotel. I want to ask about it, but don't want my voice to betray me, revealing me and my longing. I'm sure she'll tell me about it sometime today.

The stereo goes out when we go into the tunnels. When we get to the other side, my heart swells from the feeling of returning home, as if I'd been away for years. Whitney puts her phone down.

"Epic day," she says.

I carve down the Pali, looking out at the blues of the ocean, the whiteness of the sandbars. I take the big curve by the lookout and see Mount Olomana, which is different from every angle. Of course there's a helicopter over its peak, rescuing someone who's overestimated themselves. On the way to Waimanalo, Olomana doesn't even seem like the same mountain, and I'm always surprised by how something can seem so looming and regal from one side and then, from another, like a mere bump.

"I haven't been here in so long," I say. We pass the Kaneohe Ranch building, and the traffic slows.

"That's right," she says. "This is your 'hood. Lucky. This place is so much cooler."

Lucky, I think. She's right. I was lucky to have lived here. Something I've noticed since moving to Hawaii is that everyone kind of feels this way about themselves no matter where they live.

"I'm definitely going to come here a lot over break," I say. This is true, but I'm also fishing.

"Totes," she says. "Oh my God, shaddup, love this song." She turns on the stereo and dances in her seat, nodding her head and slapping the air overhead, something I do too when I'm with Danny, but now I feel I can't with her, like she's claimed it. Shaddup, hand flicking—it's hers. I'm left with lame gestures. I imagine saying "coolio" and raising the roof.

"What about you?" I say. "What are you going to do the rest of break?"

"I don't know," she says. "Eat. Just kidding. I've been eating like a frickin' . . ." She can't seem to think of a simile.

"Whale shark," I say because I hate unfinished sentences.

We get to the entrance of Kailua town, and again I'm warmed by its familiarity, the way I feel an ownership over it, despite not having lived here that long. But my grandparents did, so that counts. Even though I didn't grow up here, I feel I've grown from them, like I'm something indigenous and not a Norfolk pine.

"Oooh, can we hit up Mu'umu'u Heaven on the way back?" Whitney asks as we pass the store.

"Shoots," I say. We turn at the banyan tree, and Whitney sees more shops she wants to stop at on our way back, which sounds fun. We'll make a day of it, hanging in my sweet hometown.

• • •

The surf is, indeed, epic. Glassy and fun. Whitney follows me wherever I paddle, and when I catch a wave and paddle back out, she always looks a bit lost. She's out of her element, shy; I can still feel that way surfing—intimidated, embarrassed to be seen falling—but maybe since she looks nervous, it takes that all away. She's holding it for me. I know exactly how she feels—like a tourist and like a girl.

But I'm not a hostess. I can tell she wants to go in, but I paddle past her to get farther out and closer to the island. I sit in the lineup with the boys, nodding at a few I recognize and even those I don't. Some people ride standup boards, some are on one-man canoes. From Lanikai, a four-man yellow canoe points toward us, a few kids hanging off the ama.

It's one of those crowded days when you don't mind the number of people—it's like everyone here came alone but is now in on something together, bonded by these hours, by one of the choices they made today that happened to be the same choice as everyone here.

When my arms can't take another paddle back out and my ribs hurt from the board, I go for one more, then paddle to Whitney.

"Grab lunch?" I ask.

"Yes!" she says, looking burnt and weak.

I catch a wave in for as long as I can, then paddle the rest of the way to the boat ramp. When I look back, Whitney is far behind.

We're giddy eating hamburgers at Kalapawai. Sun-soaked sore bodies, salty skin, and huge plates of food. "This is some bomb-ass shit," I say with a full mouth, and she laughs—*honk!*—which makes us both laugh. She honks again, then takes a sip of her soda.

"Bomb-ass shit," she says and we both nod. "Nom nom."

We finish the rest in silence, and when we walk to the car, she burps and we rub our stomachs.

Before we hit the shops, she asks to stop at Lanikai to take a picture of the Mokuluas. It takes forever to find parking—there are rental cars everywhere.

"So many tourists," I say, as we walk down the beach path. "So annoying."

"I know, and what's up with the kayaks?"

"Rides of shame."

She's puts on her oversized cap with bright flowers on the face. I'm wearing my favorite—a Mike Field design that I haven't seen on anyone else yet. The beach is so packed that it resembles Waikiki. When Target is built, this will all get worse.

We're both still in our bikinis, but have pareos tied around our waists.

"Let's just take the pic, then ditch." She stands in the ocean so she's situated between the two distant islands. Everyone takes their picture between them, and at least for me, it never gets old. It creates a perfect symmetry and is always exotic and captivating. The subject is between two everlasting things.

She poses, and I snap the picture with her phone. She laughs while she smiles, that uncomfortable laugh everyone uses when waiting for a picture to be taken.

"'Kay, come," she says.

I walk to her, and she takes the phone and holds it out in front of us. "Selfish," she says through her teeth. I like selfies. You can really pose because you're not being looked at.

"Cheese," she says.

"Cheesy," I say.

"*Fromage!*" she says.

"Aw," I say. "You're learning!"

First we go to San Lorenzo to look at bathing suits. We both try on countless tops and the teeniest bottoms I have ever worn.

"Come out," she says from the room next door.

"I am not coming out," I say, looking at my ass in the bright light.

She slides my curtain open. She's wearing bottoms with a thick, low white band and about an inch of purple fabric covering the essentials. I guess that's why she waxes it all off: mere safety precautions.

"Oh my God, that looks so dope on you," she says.

I grabbed it from the back of the shop. The sides of the bottoms are strings that connect the block-print fabric. The bandeau top is pulled together in the middle by a set of strings.

"Your body is, like, banging," she says. "Is that Acacia?"

"What?" I turn and look at my ass in the mirror, the fabric riding up then out.

"Acacia," she says. "The brand."

I look at the tag to see the brand and notice the price. One hundred and twenty, which I've come to realize is kind of standard for a suit, but then in the mirror, I see a tag coming out of the top too. I try to lift it a bit and read: $110.

"Holy shizz," I say. "Not happening."

"I know. They're super *cher*. You could buy just the bottoms."

"I'm not spending that much on just bottoms. And, dude, good job with your French."

"Do you like mine?" she asks.

She turns around and does what I just did—looks at her ass. Bikinis and jeans—the way the ass looks determines everything.

"I like the pattern," I say. "But honestly that band bottom thing I see everywhere. It's not the most flattering."

"I know," she says. "Kinda played. 'Kay, I'm going to go with the bunched one. You know the ones that bunch in the butt?"

We both laugh. "That sounds so wrong," I say.

She goes to her room, and we change back into our own suits. When we come out, she asks if I'm going to get anything.

I tried on four sets of suits. "Nothing really worked," I say. "Except the one."

She looks forlorn or pantomimes the look of it. "Let me get it for you," she says. "It was so cute. And you drove today."

"No!" I say. "It wouldn't cost me two thirty to fill a quarter of a tank."

"Come on," she says. "We had the best day ever."

I shake my head.

"Yes," she says, using a businesslike decisive tone. "I'll get one too. We can be twins."

I notice in her pack of suits she has also tried on an Acacia, though the pattern is different, and the style is slightly different too. I guess I can now officially recognize the brand.

I'm touched and follow her to the counter, part of me dragging, part of me feeling like I do when my mom brings home swag—getting to have something I'd never buy for myself. We did have the best day ever, and it's still going strong, yet it's the recognition of this that makes me say, "No. I'm not letting you get it for me."

"Aww," she says, "boo." But I wonder if she's partly relieved.

She goes to the counter and hands over her suits to the young, dark-haired woman who has a friendly plumeria tucked behind her ear but a not-so-friendly face.

I wander around the clothes section of the store, looking at airy dresses and their accompanying price tags. I said no because I don't want to be—or worse, feel—indebted, but also because I don't want to set a standard. Like how the snot bubble came out of her nose the first day we talked—it set a tone for us, and this would set a tone too, but the wrong one. I like that we're different but can still be ourselves. I didn't hold her hand surfing, and she's not going to hold my hand now. I think about her seventh grade birthday party, how she became known for providing a good time. I'm sure she's set herself up for this with her other friends, that they expect her to cover things for them.

I walk back over to the register and see she's buying just one suit. She has put the Acacia to the side and I wonder—no, I know—that she's not buying it out of respect for me.

Transaction complete. We walk out of the store to a cheerful *ding* and the bright sunshine and music coming from Island Snow next door.

She holds the little plastic bag with her finger and makes it spin.

"Butt buncher," I say. "Let's get shave ice."

• • •

Lilikoi, li hing mui, guava for me. Vanilla, coconut, li hing mui for her. Before we head back, we go to Fighting Eel, HIC, Twin Islands, then finally Mu'umu'u Heaven on our way out of town. I try things on along with her and buy a Samudra clutch at Fighting Eel. I don't want her to feel guilty about buying things in front of me. I tell her when things look good and when they look bad, and she does the same for me. She buys something at every store except Mu'umu'u Heaven, a store I loved and that had tons of Japanese tourists saying "Kawaii!" after every dress they touched.

On the way to the car, she tells me she thought the dresses were way too expensive and they looked like cut-up muumuus.

"That's what they are, genius!" I laugh.

"Oh!" she says.

"They're like, old-school, vintage muumuus cut up, then re-designed."

We get into my car and drive out of town, and she looks deep in thought.

"What's wrong?" I ask.

"It's just kind of sad," she says.

"What's sad?"

"To cut up old Hawaiian dresses. My grandma had the prettiest muumuus."

"So did mine," I say, and we're quiet for a while, both thinking about our grandmas, perhaps, or thinking about each other, having never really considered each other's roots or lives as little girls.

"But they're using the past and making it . . . I don't . . . something we'd wear. Young, you know? New school."

"Yeah," she says. "That's true."

We drive back over the Pali, listening to music and looking out, alone with our thoughts together.

25

IT FEELS A BIT AWKWARD WHEN WE GET BACK, LIKE we don't know how to part. I drive up to the main house, realizing that I've completely forgotten about the possibility of Danny being in her room, and I've forgotten about Will. What happened with Will had just recently consumed me, entertained me, but today all thoughts of him vanished. The whole event seems like it happened long ago, or even to a different person. And what now? I just wait until he comes around again? And when he does? I hate that I can't talk about this with Whitney.

I park near her room, but keep the car running as she gathers her stuff.

"Fun," she says. "Thanks for today. For driving." She opens the door and gets out. "Oh, my board," she says. "How do I—" She looks up at the racks.

"I'll get it," I say.

I turn the engine off and get out, then stand up on my car to undo the straps. She gets up on her side, and I edge the board to her.

"Can you carry all that?" I ask.

"Yeah, yeah," she says.

"I'm going to go rest," I say.

"I know," she says. "I'm beat."

We both stand there. I'm going to ask her about the hotel. "I'm just going to watch a movie or something tonight if you want to—and—"

"That sounds so good," she says. "But I told Mari and the girls—"

"Cool. See you later, then!" I say. I *enthuse.* I can feel myself enthusing all over the place. Mari, the very person she was complaining about over hamburgers. All her friends, in fact, who she can't be herself with—she's always playing a role. Quote, unquote. Is that why she didn't invite me? 'Cause I fit with her, but I don't fit with them? I'm not sure what's more insulting. The fact that her friends won't accept me or that Whitney's not making any efforts to include me. Is it like my mom and Melanie? I'm only allowed to hang with the others when I've done something right?

Whitney shrugs the board up onto her hip, then makes a sound of enthusiasm, a half *woot,* to sum things up. She closes her door with her foot, and I drive back to my house, seeing her in the mirror struggling with her board and the bags.

I was having so much fun, but now the whole day feels crossed out. I wasn't a friend, I was a tour guide, a frickin' sherpa or something. These West kids are making me go up and down, up and down, and it hurts.

That night I pace and I snack, all while enduring the blaze of headlights that indicate people leaving, going somewhere, doing something with friends, having destinations on this Saturday night. One flash must be Whitney, one flash must be Will, one belongs to the parents who have taken my parent with them. The cast of my mom's show is attending an event for the Hawaii International Film Festival, and of course the Wests are also going to the very same event, so Melanie exclaimed, "Why don't we just go in the same car?" I imagine Melanie there now, edging close to my mom whenever the photographers come around.

After such a long day, I'm still wired, as if waiting for guests to arrive at my long-planned party. I'm even dressed cute, in a long, low-riding cotton skirt that hugs my thighs and a tight top that tucks into the skirt, fitting like a one-piece bathing suit. All dressed up and nowhere to go. All dressed up and hoping (though not admitting to hoping) that someone will come over. I wait for Will while telling myself I'm not waiting for him.

And then I think of Danny, how I haven't really hung out with him in so long. I want to tell him that we can all be friends even if he's hooking up with or likes Whitney. There's room.

I call him, and he actually answers. "Yo," he says.

"Yo," I say.

"Where you at?"

"I'm at home," I say. "Like a rock star." I look in the fridge at the same things I saw when I looked in the fridge just moments ago. That's what tonight feels like. Like I'm expecting something to change, for some kind of treat to suddenly appear.

"Did you have a good day?" I ask. "We haven't hung out forever."

"Stellar day," he says. "You?"

"Same," I say, picturing him standing there, running his hand through the tips of his hair.

"Let's cruise soon," he says, and I hear some guys in the background and know he's drinking and having fun like every other kid in the whole wide world. I liked picturing him alone. *Aha!* I think, and pour some wine into a cup from my mom's open bottle in the fridge. I take a big sip.

"Yes, I want to," I say. "When?" I ask after I take a huge sip and then another. "When should we cruise?" I'd like to think that the drink is loosening me up, making me assertive.

"Whenever!" he says. I hear the music in the background, and I walk to the stereo to put something on. Ideas all over the place. I'm virtually partying.

"Or I'll see you at the hotel," he says, then sings, "Hotel, motel, Holiday Inn, say what?"

Before I can say, *Um. Yeah. Not invited 'cause I'm a rock star,* Danny says, "Whit said you're coming. I just talked to her."

"I haven't heard a thing about it," I say.

"I'm sure you'll get the four-one-one." Why am I even hearing this from Danny? Why does she tell him things? I was just with her.

"When did you talk to her?" I walk like a toy soldier across the room.

He shouts to someone, "One for me too, 'kay shoots!" then says, "Like just now. Downstairs. We're at Mari's house."

I take a sip of the wine, then another. Why wasn't I invited to Mari's house?

"'Kay, it's too loud," he says. "I'll talk to you tomorrow."

"Were you at Whitney's last night?" I ask, moving my hips side to side.

"Say what?" he says, but since I can't see him, I can't read him.

"Are you guys going out, or what?" I ask.

"No, we're not going out. Aren't you with ill Will, anyway?"

The question is phrased weirdly. *Anyway,* meaning if I weren't, then . . . *Anyway,* meaning why should I care about Danny?

"Where'd you hear that?" I ask, glad he can't see me smiling.

"I don't know," he says, sounding annoyed. "Around. The coconut wireless. Watch out, though, Little Donkey. Lissa's bigger than you."

"Whatever," I say. "They're not together."

"Yeah, when you're with him, they're not together. That's true."

My heart beats something fast and ugly. I want to talk, milk all the details. Do people know about me and Will? And am I totally embarrassed or totally proud? Proud. Happy. I love the idea of him talking about me.

"What else?" I ask. I do a pirouette.

"What else about what?"

"Like exactly who—" The music goes up on his end, and I hear guys yell in unison as if someone scored a goal. I want Danny to be here so we can talk about the things we're experiencing without each other, and so we don't have to talk in riddles. We've never spoken to each other this way before.

"Are you there?" I ask.

"Yeah, I'm here," he says and I'm surprised how near he is, like he's been just listening to the phone and nothing else, thinking and waiting just as I had been. I hear someone call his name. I'll let him go.

“Hey, what’s the song you were just singing?” I ask. “The hotel motel one.”

“‘Rapper’s Delight,’” he says. I smile and imagine him doing the same.

“Okay, I’ll talk to you later, then,” I say. *Let’s just be like we’ve always been.*

“Bye, Lei Lei,” he says, and a warmth rises in me. He hasn’t called me that since we were little.

I search for the song on Sonos. There it is. “Rapper’s Delight.” Sugarhill Gang. The name itself already makes things better, and when I play it, the beat and funny lyrics automatically cure what ails me. Forget Mari’s house and the hotel and the fact that I’m alone. Forget waiting for Will. Though I do wish Danny were here, because he’d be doing what I’m doing—rapping and dancing like an idiot. I wouldn’t have to hold anything back.

26

I WAKE UP TO THE SOUND OF MY MOM MAKING breakfast. I had fallen asleep on the couch. I sit up. My mom's back is to me. On the low coffee table in front of me is my empty cup with the telltale redness of wine lining the bottom. Well, I guess the more telltale sign would be the empty bottle itself, which is on the counter, to the left of my mom.

Holy majorly busted.

Has any teenager in history been so stupid besides the ones whose parents allow them to be? What do I do? Tiptoe out like a cartoon character? Make a joke? Weep at her ankles?

She turns her head. I raise my hand, say, "Hi."

"What the hell is going on?" she asks and slams the spatula down on the counter.

I look around, as if for someone to blame . . . *The Sonos made me do it.*

"Should I be worried?" She faces me with her arms crossed.

"No," I say. My head is pounding like surf. I put my fingers to my temples, then think better of it. She knows, though. She knows everything; every move I make she is adding to the roster. I decide to be honest.

"I was bored," I say. "Everyone was at a party I wasn't invited to. I was just trying to . . . make my own fun."

She scoffs, but right before she does, I see a glimmer of recognition. I, too, can tally up the moves.

"There are other ways to have fun," she says. "Go . . ." She falters. Score for me. "Go play!"

Oh my God, triple points.

"Go play?" I say.

She turns back to the stove to save herself. "I mean, if this is what you do when you're not invited to parties, then we have a problem. A big one."

"Yeah," I say. "Because that would be a lot of bottles." Oh my God, I'm killing it.

"That's not what I meant," she says. "I don't drink every time I don't get invited somewhere."

"You have wine every night," I say. Her shoulders lift then lower as she lets out an exasperated sigh.

"Because I like wine, not because I'm trying to escape!" This still doesn't sound very good. She clenches the spatula, her hand shaking a bit. "And stop. Just stop. You cannot drink. You are grounded. Again, or still."

"Okay," I say, indifferent, since I have nothing better to do. Besides, she's never home at night. To ground me is to ground herself. "Are you going out tonight?"

"Yes!" she says, and now I think she might cry. "I have to. Something for autism. The show is donating us"—and she breaks—"you know, 'cause that will really help autism! A dinner with us! Or a golf package at Koele!" She weeps, and I get scared.

I don't know what to do. Her shoulders tremble, and she lets out little high-pitched bleats.

I get up and turn off the stove, where the scrambled eggs have become a solid patty.

"I'm sorry," I say. I touch her shoulder. "Mom, are you okay? Honestly, you don't have to worry. I got carried away. I was dancing—" I look around the room. "And playing ukulele, evidently. There are worse things."

She sniffles and laughs. "It's not funny, and, yes, I'm fine. I'm just tired. Tired of smiling." She smiles.

We stand side by side, leaning against the counter.

"I'm sorry you were lonely last night," she says. "This seems to be a pattern."

"No," I say. "Last time I was with Whitney."

"I meant the pattern of you drinking, me yelling, then me feeling guilty that this is somehow all my fault."

"I can go with that," I say.

She elbows me, and we stand in silence for a little while, which clues me in to the sounds of mynah birds squawking outside. I wonder what she was like when she was my age. I think she was much wilder.

In her stash of photos, I've seen her posing with friends in low-riding bikinis, the boys in tight short shorts. In some she holds a cigarette. In one she is joyfully yelling on the Hanalei pier and raising a can of Budweiser. In another she's asleep, her head on a guy's lap (again with the short shorts) while he plays guitar.

"I tried to tell Melanie," she says, "about the first time." Her eyes are zoned out, not focusing on anything. "I told her you girls were drinking, and she just interrupted me. She said that she buys those drinks for Whitney—they're kombucha spirits," my mom says, imitating Melanie's pushy voice, "which are very healthy, but have a little alcohol in them. Healthy alcohols."

"Are you serious?" I ask, disbelieving, amused, and envious all at once. What would it be like to have such a dumb mother?

"I don't know if she's oblivious or if her kids just run all over her," my mom says.

"I'm a good girl," I say. "Despite it all."

Her eyes come back into focus, and she looks me up and down. "I can't believe you were in me."

She always does this, reminisces about me as a baby and being in her womb. She'll tell me the same stories sometimes—my first laugh, my belly button falling off, having to use Pez to bribe me to leave the park—and I'll laugh every time, as if hearing it for the first time, fascinated by myself, by this life I don't remember.

She hands me a fork, and we eat out of the pan.

"Look," she says. "You can do something during the days, but at night I want you here."

I don't answer.

"I don't want to do this on your spring break, but I can't just let it go."

"Okay." I leave it there, not adding anything, afraid I'll say the wrong thing or she'll figure out how lenient she's being. I can't help but feel like I'm getting away with something. It's weird to be trusted. I've always been trusted, but I've also always obeyed until now.

27

AFTER MY BIG BUST, I GO OVER TO WHITNEY'S TO SEE IF she wants to jump off Waimea rock.

I knock on her door, but she doesn't answer, so I go around back. Will is there with his dad, reading the paper and eating breakfast. He looks up at me, then back down, shifting in his chair. Eddie doesn't seem to recognize me.

"Hi, Lea," Will says.

"Lea," Eddie says, looking at me as if with fresh eyes.

"Hi, Mr. West."

"Your mom with you?" He takes a sip of what looks like a Bloody Mary.

"No, just me here."

"We used to date, you know," he says.

I laugh, uncomfortable, and Will immediately says, "Dad. Can I have Sports?" I think as a way to change topics.

"It's really nice having her around," Eddie says.

"Dad," Will says. "Sports."

"Sports," he says. I wonder how many Bloody Marys he's had.

"Is Whitney around?" I ask.

"Kitchen," Will says, looking down at the paper.

"Thinking of going to the North Shore," I say. "If you want to go."

"Golf," Will says.

I stand there, insulted by something intangible.

"Another big day," Eddie says. "My boy."

Will looks like whatever he's reading about is paining him. I want to run away before Eddie says anything else. I don't want to think about his sickness and weirdness with my mom. I want to flee and get in the ocean.

Will looks up and finally flashes me a small, private grin. I want to sit on his lap, tell him he's hot, mysterious, cool, and charming—and hot, did I mention that? I want to be seen with him and not seen with him as we hook up on the daybed, or in the ocean at sunset. That would be nice. I glance at the daybed, then back at Will.

"Lei!" Whitney says. She walks out in another long T-shirt. "What's up?"

"Want to go to the North Shore?" I ask. "We can jump off the rock?"

"Totally," she says. "Let me get my act together."

Will jostles his newspaper, holding it in front of his face, concluding something that never quite began. I feel so bad for him, taking care of a father who sometimes seems like a child. That same tension is on his face that he had the other day after being up all night, caring for him. And yet, his compassion keeps him going.

"You girls need some cash?" Eddie says.

"Sure, Daddy," Whitney says.

She take a few bites from his plate, and I get a surge of sadness, thinking of how their family will cope. I'm watching Whitney, but can feel Eddie looking at me as he hands her a stack of cash. I quickly look at him and smile, and have the sensation that he's gazing proudly at something that belongs to him.

28

I FEEL LIKE WE'RE ON A DIFFERENT ISLAND, ON VACATION somewhere far from home. I drive down the country road, flanked by rows of sugarcane, getting closer and closer to the dark blue sheet of ocean. It's like we're marching down the aisle to a vast, liquid altar. We listen to Johnny Cash for a while, then switch to A Tribe Called Quest, which makes me feel older, wiser, above the teenagers we know.

The sky before us is cloudless; to the left along the mountain range, the clouds hover, seeming still as wallflowers.

We've driven in silence for most of the ride, but now I tell her about last night, how I drank, got caught, and am grounded.

"That sucks," she says, and then, "What were you thinking?"

I laugh. "I don't know. I wasn't, clearly. How was Mari's?" I try to measure my voice, but it gives something away.

"Oh God," she says. "She wasn't even supposed to have a party. People just invaded. You should have come."

How does one say *I would have if I'd known about it* without sounding defensive? One doesn't. I go with sarcasm. "I was busy," I say, "dancing with myself."

"So gangster," she says.

And since I went there, admitted my loserness yet infused it with a bit of nonchalant badassed-ness, I continue on and ask the questions I want answered.

"Danny says he's going to your hotel sometime this week? You guys having a honeymoon?"

"I wish," she says, and tries to evaluate my reaction. I smirk, look ahead. "I don't know how you've been friends so long," she says. "You've never hooked up?"

"No," I say, keeping the times we kissed each other to myself—that was more like playing house than hooking up.

We are driving through Haleiwa now, and I go slow to participate somehow in the scene around us. Shirtless surfers with low-riding trunks, lowriders and trucks pumping music, tourists eating their shave ice on the bench in front of Matsumoto's. Everyone looking at everyone else.

"So you don't like him, right?" she asks.

"Me?" I say. "No, he's like a brother. He's . . . Danny." And yet my voice is funny, like I'm trying to convince her or myself.

"Have *you* guys hooked up?" I ask. My jaw tightens, and I hold the steering wheel with one hand, assuming a relaxed pose, which also betrays me to myself. I don't know why I feel threatened.

"No," she says teasingly, as if not telling the whole truth. "I wouldn't mind, though. Last night . . ." She smiles to herself.

"Yes?" I say.

"Last night was cool," she says, again with the secret smile. "I like him, but . . . it's cool you guys are such good friends. Jealous."

This feels both nice to hear and yet, lately, untrue.

"It's not just the two of us at the hotel," Whitney says. "I've been meaning to see if you're free. Friday—just one night."

"I'm super busy," I say.

"Yeah, that's what I thought. Anyway, it's fun. We have the suite. Everyone just crashes wherever. Mike makes brownies. Hopefully you won't be grounded by then."

The knots in me finally untie. I don't know what upset me more—not being invited or the thought of her and Danny doing something without me.

We drive across the bridge, its structure like a double rainbow that signifies something different to everyone. To me, it's a kind of crossing into the wild, into anonymity.

"Does Will go to the hotel?" I ask.

"He might," Whitney says. "He doesn't stay at night, though. You like him, don't you." She's stating this, versus asking, and something in her voice sounds annoyed.

"I mean I like him, but . . ."

"It's a little weird," she says in an assertive way. Her face is calm yet strong, set. "Since you're my friend."

"Right," I say.

"And he's dating Lissa."

I look out at the road, but feel her watching me.

"But he's not," I say and glance over.

She holds my gaze for a moment. "Doesn't matter anyway," she says, then turns toward the mountains, clearly not wanting to talk about her brother. It's all I want to talk about, and I want to confess, but I don't want to leave her with the feeling I have when I think about her and Danny, the knowledge that something will be changed. And I don't want to be like Lissa—close to her to get to him.

Even though we've gone through the main strip and are back on the country road, the air still smells of barbecue and wood chips. We're a world away from everything. I turn the music up and try to get our rhythm back again.

Soon, Waimea Bay glistens below us, the stretch of white sand like a tiny desert, the ocean moving slowly up and down as if it were taking deep breaths. We watch guys jumping off the rock, arching their backs, then tucking before landing. One does a goofy, yet ultimately graceful backflip. My heart beats with the thought of us not just jumping, but being watched, being surrounded by the guys down there who look so at home. Why do guys get to be so free and stupid? Why do we giggle, as if we'd unexpectedly landed onstage? We pretend we're afraid when we're not. We pretend we're unafraid when we are.

"Let's just do this," I say, and she seems to know what I mean.

The sand is hot on my feet and burns between my toes. It's deeper here, thick, harder to walk through, which makes my hamstring muscles flex. It feels like we're crossing the desert. We put our towels down near the rock, but up far enough to be safe if the tide gets higher or the waves bigger. We strip down to our suits and load up on sunscreen.

"What about our phones?" she asks. I was thinking the same thing, not about them getting stolen, but about how we'd take pictures. The event doesn't exist without the pictures.

"Forget the phones," she says. "If I see another post of my friends posing in their bikinis, I'll die." She imitates them posing, shots I see all the time on Instagram—the bikini shot, hair falling over their eyes so you can see just their mouths, smiling as if shy. Whitney does this perfectly.

"Oh, and then this one," she says, and turns, arching her back a bit so her butt sticks out, her head slightly turned, gazing at the beautiful world.

"Oh my God, so artsy," I say.

"So artsy," she says.

We leave our phones and walk toward the water, and then we hear the shrieking noises I recognize as the sound of a girl seeing a girl she knows.

"Whit!"

Down the beach, walking languidly, are her friends Mari, Sobey, and Brooke. Whitney, I notice, doesn't seem as thrilled to see them as they are to see her.

"What are you doing here?" Sobey asks, giving Whitney a hug. She looks at me, wide-eyed, with a huge grin, and yet her eyes dart from my head to my toes, then back up again. I hate that question: *What are you doing here?* as if you're in a place you're not supposed to be and it's a replacement for a simple *hello.*

"Sweet, are you showing Lea around?" Mari says. I feel like saying it was my idea to come here and that, like them, we are friends going to the beach. I'm not a visiting cousin or something.

"We're just chilling," Whitney says.

They say hello to me with small, closed-mouth grins. They all are wearing the thick-banded bikini bottoms, the ones I told Whitney were unflattering. When we happen to look at each other, I believe we're communicating our understanding of this—both the memory of me saying it and my rightness. Not that these girls don't look good. Sobey, especially, with her long, strong flank of tan torso, her heavy-looking boobs and high, perfectly rounded butt—pick your fruit, then double it. The other two keep adjusting their suits, and though they're not at all fat, their tummies sort of spill over the band, and when they face the water to look at the jumpers, their asses look like they're somewhere they shouldn't be—like dough in a cardboard tube, oozing out after the first twist.

"Oh my God," Mari says. "Was that not insane last night?"

Brooke laughs. "I have, like, a bruise on my leg—I have no idea why."

"Probably from jumping into the pool," Mari says. "Like a loon."

"I swan dove!" Brooke says. "Or dived." They laugh at whatever was not insane. I twist my foot into the sand and look down as if something there is fascinating.

I am not a part of this conversation, and so I won't pretend to be, and oddly for a moment, I'm comforted by the thought of Danny, of having him by my side, looking at them in the exact same way.

"You want to swan dive off the rock?" Whitney asks.

No! I want to say. This is my plan, my excursion, and Whitney knows this—because as soon as she asks, she looks at me, quickly, with guilt and apology.

"That's what we're doing," Mari says. "But no swan diving."

My plan now seems clichéd, and again I feel Danny, but this time the smirk is back, the belief that I'm just like everyone else. I shake him off—why is he here anyway, like some kind of angel/devil on my shoulder, either grinning approvingly or making wisecracks? I summon the feeling I had in the car—this isn't cliché, and who cares if it is? It's just about wanting to jump off a goddamn rock, take the plunge, feel alive and scared and thrilled for a moment.

"Have you guys done this before?" I ask.

"I have," Brooke says. She runs her finger under her suit, adjusting so the fabric goes in. "Before you land. Make sure to close your legs."

It's an easy climb up, but for some reason, Mari is having trouble. In one section she scales the rock like a crab and is unsure of every step. I like climbing rocks, getting into the rhythm and making quick choices. When we get to the top, there are about ten other people, and no one is jumping. It reminds me of going to the terrain park in Tahoe—everyone waiting before a jump or rail slide, seemingly planning their trick, but most likely waiting for everyone else to go so no one will be watching if they screw up.

I look out at the beautiful bay, the white sand and reef visible under the slow swells. The expanse of ocean, the varying blues that seem to inhale and exhale. Spray from the surf mists my face, and on my shoulders is a thin layer of powdery salt.

I look back, and Brooke is taking pictures of Mari and Sobey, who are laughing hysterically, but every so often freezing their laughter for the pictures.

"Wait, take one of me on the edge," Sobey says. She goes to the edge of the rock and does the arched-back, butt-up pose while contemplating the jump, her arms up in diving position. Then she comes back to look at the picture. "Nice," she says.

"Are you going to jump?" Whitney asks.

"No way," she says. "I just got my hair blown out."

Whitney looks at me and rolls her eyes. It's weird to think that I saw her as part of this group, even the head of it, with no difference between her and the pack. Now I don't see her fitting in at all. She must fit only when she hides the things I get to see—the weirdness and vulnerability.

Mari runs her hands up and down her arms, which are shaking a little. It's funny the way another person's fear sucks yours away, so all that's left is a little residue, a little dust. Brooke, the expert, looks like less of a rock scholar now, adjusting her bikini, making the chin-tucked frown face required when checking one's boobs.

"I'm going to go down to the beach to get pics," Sobey says.

"It's so far," Whitney says. The blue water churns below.

"I know," I say, but we both smile.

A few guys quietly trickle off the rock, and we watch them land and splash below. It's not so intimidating here after all—it's less local and more Texas, or wherever these guys are from. Mainland guys are just plain dorky, no matter who they are back where they're from. It's like HNL has a customs that confiscates anything cool or desirable. We have Hawaii boys to compare them to—Asian, Caucasian, Hawaiian, it doesn't matter. They are mysteriously more capable, attractive, effortless.

"You girls going to jump?" a sunburnt auburn-headed guy says with a drawl. The thing is—he'd be attractive on, say, Clement Street or the Marina. Anywhere but here.

"Yes, we're going to jump," Whitney says, as if he's a first-grader. "That's kind of why we're here."

His friends laugh, then one suddenly runs to the edge and throws himself into a sideways tuck. That's why people wait too, I guess—they wait for girls to watch, or for the perfect audience.

"Your turn, ladies," the drawler says.

"You guys go ahead," Brooke says. She has a hand on her waist, daring them.

The one sitting down on the uneven rocks, who looks like he's chewing tobacco or something, eyes Brooke and squirms a bit, and I wonder if he's getting a boner.

"What's you girls' names?" the bonified guy asks.

"Grammar," I say. "Grammarcy." My friends, or Whitney's friends, all laugh.

The two boys speak to themselves, then the auburn-headed one stands at the precipice and jumps, yelling the mainland equivalent of *chee-hoo,* which is *yahoo.*

A new batch of guys come up, slick like eels, tan, and wearing low-riding shorts revealing the smooth bumps of their asses. The mainland guys aren't so loud anymore. They're mumbling to themselves, shy and deferential. It's funny that moments ago our group was practically a Hawaiian sovereign nation next to these haole boys, and now, in the newcomers' presence, I don't even feel like I live here. My Hawaiian blood cowers in some corner of my body, tucks itself into my spleen. The girls they're with are wearing baggy soccer shorts and T-shirts, and look at us like we've insulted them without having said a word. One carries a cooler, which I've come to think of as a local's accessory, like a watch, or no—something necessary—a wallet. In

Hawaii we all give ourselves so much credit for being a melting pot, but I don't think we melt—we just pick from one another's cultures, then carry out the things we like best.

"Let's jump already," Whitney says, and we all look at one another.

"I'll go," Brooke says. She walks to the edge, looks down, then back at us. She pushes off, and I realize I'm holding my breath.

"Oh my God," Mari says. I feel embarrassed for her.

"Go," Whitney says to her.

"You!" Mari says, laughing to hide her self-consciousness. She darts her eyes around.

"Want to all jump together?" I say.

"Too crowded," Whitney says.

We stand at the edge. "Oh my God, it's so far," Mari says.

"It's deep," Whitney says. "Don't psych yourself out. You can always go from the lower ledge."

"'Kay, jump with me," Mari says.

"I'm going with Lea," Whitney says, and Mari blinks at me, then looks away.

"Should we go first, or do you want to?" I ask. Mari checks out the strangers on the rock, as if deciding between two dark fates. If we go, she'll be alone. "I'll just wait," she says.

"Let's go," Whitney says.

"I'm going to dive," I say.

"Not!" Whitney says. Mari's fear and Whitney's alignment are fueling me.

We creep up to the edge.

"Ready?" I ask.

"Ready," she says. "One . . . two . . . three!"

I dive from the rock. We don't have a picture, don't have proof, just the feeling to go on and trace back to. I feel the air swallow me, the chill on my skin, a pure and solid fright, and then the shock of hard water. It's breathtaking, disorienting, like I've been hit. Then things clear. I know where I am, and I'm safe. Underwater it's so quiet. I open my eyes, see Whitney's legs above me fluttering. I kick up, then break the surface with a grin and somehow feel the beauty around me, actually in me, tingling. And then I feel something else. "Oh my God."

"I know, right?" Whitney says. "That was killer. Let's go again."

We tread water, circling our legs like propellers.

"I can't," I say. We move toward shore. I go underwater to look around, then come back up. "My bottoms came off," I say, and feel close to tears.

At first she looks incredulous, then stunned, and then on the precipice of hysterics. I automatically mirror this progression.

I go back down, swim around, and see her too. Our hair floats above us, and we share an underwater break, looking around, then back at each other. We are wordless, weightless, and hopeless. We both emit a huge bubble of air, then rise to meet above.

"Holy shit," she says.

"What do I do? How am I supposed to get out?"

"I could go buy you a suit," she says.

We tread water, my heart races.

"And I just stay in the water?"

"Or no—easy," she says. "We'll swim to shore. I'll get your shorts."

"Oh yeah," I say. "That works."

We swim toward shore, and I wait for her past the small break, not wanting to get too close and be rolled onto the sand, naked. I feel the water on me, in me—it's funny how such a little amount of fabric completely changes the sensation. It's how guys must feel, the water brushing them, the swath of fabric not constantly pressed to them. I float on my back, keeping my pelvis down, my legs kicking, and after looking around to make sure no one's near me, I press my hips up, for the fun of it, the silliness of it, and to see myself fully, a small, naked thing floating in a big bay.

After getting my shorts on, after telling the story to the other girls, we jump over and over again, my lost bottoms somehow empowering us. Her friends look at me differently, it seems, like something happened to me that they wished had happened to them. It's a good story, and I'm sure they'll borrow it somehow, star themselves in it. Who knows—they could make me look dumb in their version, though it's hard to be cast that way when you continue to leap off the black, glimmering rock. The girls with the coolers look at me differently too, I think. I'm jumping with shorts on, a local, just like them.

29

WHEN WE GET BACK TO THE MAIN HOUSE, INSTEAD OF dropping Whitney off and parting awkwardly, I go in. I'm grounded and can't go out at night, but technically, I haven't left the property. And I don't even want to drink or anything. I just want to hang out, to not be alone. I don't want to miss anything.

"What should we do?" Whitney says. We stand on the lanai. "Should I see what's going on?"

I shrug, and she mimics my indifference. I wonder if she's okay with being alone, or not doing whatever her friends are doing. I don't want her to text and make calls, make plans where we'll have to wait until ten, then scout the island for parties. The pressure to have fun, to have the best night, can be so tiring.

For her sake, I answer, "I'm grounded, but you can give your friends a call."

She shrugs. "They're your friends too."

"Not quite," I say, not wanting to sound defensive, but wanting to keep things truthful. Actually, I want her to be truthful, not patronizing like her mother.

"They can be, I mean," she says.

I nod. That's better.

"That is, if you even want them to be. Mari's such a pussy, right?"

I spurt out laughter, which makes her preen. "Yeah, she kind of is."

"I mean, not just the rock thing, but everything. When I see her, I just want to shake her. All hunched and shit—always, always looking at Brooke after she says something, like she's waiting for knighthood or to get her head chopped off."

"That's a good way to put it," I say. Did she feel left out by her friends who showed up at Waimea without telling her, and then with that awful greeting—*What are you doing here?*—like a buffer?

"I like Brooke, though," I say. "Who's your closest friend?" I hang on to the wooden post on the lanai and swing around it. Whitney stands on the edge of the lanai on one foot and moves the other so it looks like she's pushing herself on a scooter.

"I don't know. It used to be Mari—we were really close, but then Brooke came freshman year, and she was just, like, this big deal, you know? Like, she modeled in Japan and shit. So Mari went thataway."

"That's lame," I say.

"Yeah, but maybe we were so close because Mari made it that way, you know? Like how she is with Brooke—she was like that with me, but I didn't recognize it. Her agreeableness, or whatever . . . shape-shifter," Whitney says. "That's what she is."

"Sucks," I say, then worry she might think that about me, too, because of Will.

The wind carries a faint spray of ocean.

"It wasn't an even friendship," Whitney says. "I realize that now. She did all the work, and part of me probably wanted it that way. So I was a crappy friend too."

"Friends need to be on even turf," I say.

"Right," she says. "No one should be better, even if . . ."

She doesn't finish her sentence, and I'm not sure how she's finished it in her head, but in mine, I am thinking, *Even if one is actually better.*

Prettier, richer, more popular. Even if one has a hotel and guys pine for her and girls mimic her. Though she says none of this, I appreciate that what she has said has made me draw these conclusions for myself.

"I'm glad you guys are staying here," she says.

"Totally," I say. "Me too."

"Like, we probably wouldn't have even known one another."

"I know."

I hop on and off the step for something to do, and she mimics me.

"I'd have no friends," I say in a comically sad way.

"Oh, please," she says. "You're pretty, and your body's banging. Girls like you always make friends."

"Shaddup a hundred times," I say and shake my head.

"You have no idea, either," she says. "That's what's so cool about you. You look like you don't need anyone and don't care."

I look down, proud and embarrassed. "Anyway, let's get off this topic right now. Because then I'll say how pretty you are, and you'll say 'oh, stop'—"

"No, I won't," she says. "I'm waiting. I want to hear." We both laugh, then she jumps with a silly enthusiasm. "Want to make a big dinner and just grind and watch movies?"

"'Totally,' I say, and I execute a ninja-like kick, and we both run toward the kitchen.

She thinks I look like I don't need anything, anyone. Meanwhile every cell of my body seems to be on hyperalert, always assessing, interpreting. I guess I'm communicating what I've strived for, but is it truly what I want? I feel that part of the reason I like Whitney is because she makes it seem okay to be myself. She turns the music up, and we gather our ingredients. I'm relieved that I don't have to sit in silence while she coordinates with friends. I don't have to watch headlights come and go from my perch in the cottage. This friendship is pure comfort.

We decide that we've eaten a shitload. We went to town in the kitchen, making burritos stuffed to the gills with the things that spoke to us—mushrooms, ground turkey, white beans, Andy's Salsa, avocado, lime tortilla chips, and Irish cheddar. It all worked, and so did our dessert burritos—peanut butter, bananas, maple syrup—baked, like ourselves. We didn't drink, but we did smoke just a bit of pot, taken from Eddie's drawer. It's something I never do at parties, only with close friends, so if I get weird or paranoid or have caveman rants, it's okay.

We go back outside with the hems of our shirts tucked into our bikini tops, which we still haven't changed out of. We are forcing ourselves to not lie around and watch TV just yet. It would be hard to get back up again.

Whitney looks down and tries to make her stomach ripple. "'Roll your body and move your feet,'" she says, and I join in, recognizing the cheer.

"'Stand up, everybody—get that buff and blue beat!'" We

repeat the song and then Whitney claps and kicks like the Punahou cheerleaders, teasing them, but maybe envying them as well, their lives of staggered splits, rolling pom-poms, and spirit hands. They seem so happy all the time. I can't imagine smiling that much.

"'I need another hit, hurry, quick, hurry, quick,'" I rap.

"What is that?" she asks, giving in a bit by sitting down and leaning back on the coral-stamped pillows.

"Song with weed reference," I say, thinking of Danny, my teacher in old-school rap. "But I think they're talking about crack. And crack is wack." I laugh.

"'My oven's on high when I roast the quail,'" she says. "'Tell Bill Clinton to go and inhale.'"

I cover my mouth and laugh. "Whoa, excellent citation! Ho snap, Whitney from the block! How did you know that?"

She laughs crudely. "Summer camp."

"That was off the charts," I say, which makes her try to rap again—we both do—from "Rapper's Delight," but can't remember enough of the words to make it really go. We settle back into the quiet, which isn't that quiet at all. There's the constant whoosh and crash of the ocean, the sound of the palms like cards being shuffled.

"What do you want to be when you grow up?" she asks.

"God, I don't know. I'm just trying to figure out where I want to apply to college. I only know what I don't want to be."

"And what is that?" she asks.

"I don't know. A clown . . . or a pilot."

She laughs. "I don't know if I can even go to college, I'm so stupid."

"You need to stop saying that," I say. "Do you think you'll work for your dad one day?"

She looks at me and is about to say something, then stops herself. Her eyes water.

"Oh my gosh, what did I say?"

"Nothing," she says. "Sorry." She laughs away her emotion. "I have such an old dad," she says. "I don't know what's happening to him."

"That's so sad," I say. "At least you have one," I joke, but she looks at me like I just hurt myself or like I'm trying to hide the hurt. Not having him has probably defined who I am more than I care to admit.

"I want to write children's books," she says.

"Really?" For some reason, I figured Whitney would do what her mom does—be someone's wife, which is lame of me to think. Why shouldn't she do what her brother will probably do? Run a company, be a boss. It's sad, but I know it's because she hasn't been raised to think she can.

"I'll show you sometime," she says. "The stories are about girls who play dress-up, and the things they choose to wear transport them to that time. Sort of like Jack and Annie—I have little lessons about the era, but it's for younger kids. Picture books."

"Yeah, real stupid," I say. "Are you kidding me? You're going to be, like, a hotelier slash writer slash socialite ruler."

"Oh, please," she says. "You won't catch me in Hawaii Luxury."

"They'll catch you," I say.

I look out at our view, our ocean, thinking of the ways we are working and will work ourselves out. It's like we're here on the brink of our lives, strategizing the best way to cross the channel. It's a good sensation, to feel youth, to be aware of it, electrified by it. We will become one day. We are becoming.

"I wonder what our moms wanted," I say, imagining them on the lanai on a night like this. "What their conversations were like."

The thought lifts me up, seeing us all in solidarity, but then it brings me down. I don't see Melanie being silly or joyful, weird or sullen. I don't see my mom as a bundle of nerve endings set off by a remark or a touch or the proximity of another body. They seem so old. We are almost like toddlers. We can have fun anywhere. We can always find something to play with. My mom and Melanie—women—they need an event, an elaborate premise, costumes and props. When did they become? What happens to you?

"Let's go swimming," I say.

"Okay," she says. Easy. Like a three-year-old. I want to take this with us, cross the channel armed with this easiness, this willingness. Me and Whit at fifty, night swimming, rapping, looking out at the ocean, still wondering how to cross.

The pool lights are a muted gold, the shadows in the water like grooves and knots in wood. We are treading and side-swimming and lying on our backs. This time I've got bottoms on. We rehash the event, laughing, adding on—it will become a highlight of spring break, and my embarrassment will be feigned, my insistence not to tell meaning *yes, do tell,* something that will be understood in our reenactment for others. I know this already.

"It felt cool, though," I say. "Skinny-dipping. Down there."

"Yeah," she says. "It feels sexy. So does lying in the sun sometimes."

"Yeah," I say. "Or walking out of the ocean."

"Or now."

She sinks a little, tilting her head up to the sky, then straightens back up and tosses her bottoms to the edge of the pool. I do the same with the bottoms I borrowed from her.

"Will better not come home," I say, hoping for the opposite.

"He'd think we're lezzing out. God, Will would love that. I mean, not if I were here, but if I were someone else."

"And I were someone else," I say, testing.

"No, you'd be just fine," she says. "Obviously."

I touch the bottom of the pool and bounce from foot to foot, trying to read her expression.

"Will likes anything that moves," she says. "Or doesn't move."

She seems to be sending me a message, and it hurts me. She wants to make me feel bad, like I could have been anyone. I want to believe that it happened because it was me. I want Whitney to be okay with it. Maybe it's the pool water lapping at me, the mysterious, flattering light, the way I can look at us from above, the sensuality of us in this pool by the ocean, under a clear night sky. The tall palms seem bent toward us, listening. I want to talk about him more, but this just creates a weird vibe, and I hadn't been thinking about him in the first place. It's like I have to choose sides.

"It must feel different for you than it does for me." I laugh.

"What does?" she asks, looking like she's clocked out. I want to pull her back into her good mood. I bounce from foot to foot, then do a kind of twist.

"Your thing," I say. "Your parts. Since you wax it all off."

She tucks her chin. "Oh yeah," she says. "You must have . . . tugging."

We both laugh.

"I do have tugging! It's weird."

"You should take it off. Get waxed." She bounces closer to me.

"No way," I say. "It would be . . . I don't know. Lonely."

"Lonely? My vagina is not lonely." She splashes some water at me.

I splash back. "It's cold! It wants its blanket back!"

We both crack up and go into variations, riffs on the absurd topic, until she says, "I'm cold," and I say, "Told you so."

We go to her room to change back into our clothes and watch TV from her bed. It's only nine thirty, but I feel like I could fall asleep after the beach day and the food and pot. Whitney yawns so big her jaw cracks, and we both say, "Ouch."

We watch reruns of *Downton Abbey*, and when my eyes keep falling shut, I sit up to go, but then I hear footsteps from the pool side of the room. My heart beats as though we're doing something wrong.

"Did you hear that?" I ask.

We listen, and then there's a light tapping.

She doesn't seem concerned or afraid. "Go see," she says. "It's locked."

I go to her door and look through the blinds, and there stands Mike, using his hands as binoculars to look in.

"Mike?" she asks, without having seen him.

I turn, nod. Yes, Mike Matson is at the door.

She makes an expression of annoyance and familiarity—this is something that has happened before, and I think of the other morning, how I thought she was hiding Danny.

"Should I let him in or make him stand there?"

"I don't know," she says, rocking up to sit. "I'll deal with it. Pothead booty call. He's like a kid, asking if my body can come out to play."

I cringe. It's too crude. I know girls in my grade have sex, but usually they're the ones with boyfriends. I wonder if she's just being provocative, like how we've been with one another—using words to entertain. I'm annoyed and left with a juvenile sense of unfairness, an urge to tattle, as if I've drawn what I see as a complete, wonderful picture, and she's marking it up with her Crayolas.

Still, I play along, going for an expression that connotes conspiracy, maturity versus bewilderment. If she's a friend, this is part of the package, then. More knocking. Her other life wanting in.

"Well?" I say.

She's still on the bed, holding the edge of her blanket. I don't feel like my emotions are so weird after all. She looks a bit confused, not ready for the change of scenery. "I just want to go to bed," she says.

"Then go to bed," I say. "Do you want me to tell him?"

But then her face lights up. "You want to see him naked?"

"What?" I say. "No."

"Come on." She swings her legs off the bed. "I'm going to mess with him. Get in the closet."

I look at the closet door on the other side of her room by the TV.

"Just leave it slightly ajar."

For some reason, I'm more shocked by her using the word *ajar* in this moment than I am by the actual situation. I go to the closet, my heart beating as though I'm about to hide from a serial killer. I leave the door slightly ajar.

I hear her letting him in—the clank of the blinds, the suction and swoop of the sliding door. I can see a slice of her in her long T-shirt.

"What's up, playa?" I hear Mike say, and I cringe for him, for her, for me, for girls everywhere.

"What's going on?" she says.

I hear the slap of slippers, and even back here with her clothes and shoes and what looks like school stuff, I get a whiff of the salty outdoors.

"What are you up to?" he asks.

"Just chilling," she says. "About to go to bed."

"To bed? You can't go to bed."

"I can do whatever I want," she says, and I immediately think of the script, how it's as though I'm watching a really shitty show that I can't keep my eyes off of.

"I was thinking of you," he says, and I roll my eyes.

"Okay," Whitney says.

"My parents are at that thing tonight, with your parents, so . . . just making sure you weren't too lonely."

Whitney walks across the room, briefly glancing in my direction. I see a flash of her smirking face and then Mike trailing behind, looking up and rolling his neck.

"My back is killing," he says. "South swell's on fire. What did you do today?"

"Nothing," she says, and even though I know she is coaxing out a little sitcom for me, I can't help but be offended. I want to jump out of the closet and say, *We did a lot today! We took risks, cooked dinner, swam naked!* I almost crack myself up. When I put it that way, we sound like a couple. I look around the closet, the boxes of papers, and I wonder if she keeps her children's stories in here. I wonder if the idea for them came from a longing to be transported, the urge to try on different personalities, seeing what fit best.

"Want to go out?" Mike asks.

"What?" she says. "No."

"Or mess around or something?"

I can't see them and don't know where they are in the room, so I'm left to envision her reaction, or his face after he has boldly, nakedly, expressed why he's here.

I am left to imagine their faces and gestures, and then I see her—she walks in front of her bed, to its center, and it's like I've gone from book to film. I don't need to imagine the characters anymore. There's her face—coy, seductive. There's his stance, strong, slightly twitching with impatience.

"I'll mess around," she says. "Take your clothes off."

He makes a clucking sound, and normally, I think he's super

cute, powerful even, one of these *big guys,* but now he seems reduced, shriveled in a way, which I guess is what she has intended. I can't help but think, though, that if I weren't here, this wouldn't be how it played out at all. She would be the small one.

He leans down and tries to kiss her, and I automatically close my eyes, a blink, as though feeling it for myself. She pulls back. "No," she says. "Just stand there and take everything off."

"Why?" he asks.

"Because I like it."

"Yeah?" he says. "So frisky."

Mike crosses his arms and pulls his shirt over his head, but the collar gets stuck on his chin, and he has to tug and push, and I feel like I'm watching him being born. I stifle a laugh, and so does Whitney.

"Okay, you take something off too," he says after getting his shirt off.

"No," she says, and I'm relieved, knowing I'd feel like a pervert if she did, because I'd keep watching the bad show. I'm filled with a churning kind of sickness and thrill, like being on a ride at the carnival. Mike pushes his thicket of bangs to the side.

"Can we turn off the lights at least?" Mike is olive-colored from the sun. His back muscles, defined, ebb down into his jeans.

"We need tunes." She leans back on her bed and reaches for her phone. A song plays, one that's on constant rotation on 102.7, catchy and upbeat, something you love now but know you're going to hate in a month.

Mike slides his jeans down his legs, revealing blue boxers stamped with something yellow. I step closer to the door: Labs.

Yellow Labradors. I want to joke with her about his toddler-like undergarments and the goose bumps on his arms. Now, this is fun. The music has made it better—the song's scratches, the cyclic strokes of keyboard notes, the ethereal refrain. Another air enters the room, and we're just kids with a soundtrack, but then Mike, as if tearing off a bandage, sheds his blue boxers, taking away the puppies and revealing a white ass, almost like its own entity, since the shade is so different from his legs, which sprout curled brown hairs. The good air dissolves, making way for something else.

On Mike, only a thin gold necklace remains. *Oh my God,* I keep saying and thinking to myself. *Oh my god, oh my god, oh my god.* And then: *I hate when guys wear jewelry. Gode jewry.*

Mike shrugs his shoulders, a sign of sportsmanship. Whitney tells him to turn around. He turns to face me and laughs, flexes and poses, his boxers still cuffing his ankles. I've never really looked at a penis before, and it's only now that I realize I haven't seen this thing that's everywhere I go. I touch my neck, thinking of Will, feeling him through his boxers. And there were times during make-out sessions with my boyfriend in San Francisco, but I never really studied it or anything. I trace back and confirm that, yes, this is my first penis, past the age of say, eight, when Bobbie Schmidt flashed the row of us at a field trip to the symphony. Mike's is off duty, and it seems as if there's a puppet peeking out between his legs, Gonzo, perhaps. Gonzo's nose begins to point at my feet, then wavers like a temperature gauge. Shit, that thing's ugly.

He turns back to her, moves in, puts his hands on her thighs. I look down, put my hand on the doorknob.

"Happy?" he asks. "Can we do this now?"

From this angle I think he briefly touches what I've come to think of his puppet and then he moves his face toward Whitney's. She moves back, and I don't know whether it's to get away or to lie down. I feel like I'm watching myself and Will, but it's not the same. Mike doesn't even care who she is right now. She's just a body that is willing to have him. And then he will go. Whitney knows he has a girlfriend. What is she doing?

I step back and almost trip on her shoes and then I intentionally hit a hanger, which makes a meager noise, but hopefully enough to alert her, like a faint SOS.

"Time's up," Whitney says. "I think my parents are home. My dad's going to feed you to the sharks."

"Shit," Mike says, and he hops back into his boxers and jeans, moving in tiny circles like a chicken. I cover my mouth from my front row seat. He slips on his slippers, then walks to the door, his shirt balled in his hand.

"Bye," Whitney says.

"Late," he says. "You owe me. See you at the hotel. I'll bring weed."

I can't see her expression, if she's joking or angry, happy or hurt.

After hearing the outside door slide closed, I open mine slowly and walk out.

"Wow," I say. "That was crazy."

"Hilarious, right?" she says. She searches my face as if for clues on how she did, like it was all for me, and maybe it was. Maybe this thing with Mike isn't known by her other friends—this habitual booty call—and she wants to see my reaction, how

I receive this parcel of truth.

"Right," I say. I lower my gaze. I just want to go.

"Say something," Whitney says, her face falling a notch. Her smile has become nervous and slightly defensive, as if she's expecting me to say something she'll have to refute.

I sigh and smile at the same time. "That was funny."

She looks down. I don't think I was very convincing.

"Are you okay?" I ask.

"Of course I'm okay. Jeez, lighten up."

"What about Maile?" I ask, trying to keep a light smile.

"I didn't do anything," she says.

"But you would have. He would have."

"Life is short," she says. "I'm just trying to have fun."

"I know," I say. *But you don't even like him,* I want to say. *So how is it fun?* Life is long, I think. "I'm going to go, okay?"

There's no point in my being here right now. We're both pretending. She knows that I'm judging her, that we had a great night, but now it's like a hinge is moving in the wrong direction.

Something hardens in her face, a look I remember from when we did the truth walk across the gym—she sees me, but doesn't know me, doesn't care. Her eyes flicker resentment. I don't know what to say. The only thing I want to say is too cheesy. *If you're happy, then this is all okay.* But I can't imagine being happy this way—as someone's secret. Someone's last resort.

I turn to walk out the front door.

"What about Lissa?" she asks. I stop walking but don't turn around. "They're still together and will probably always be together. It's like an arranged marriage, practically."

I think of Vicky and Melanie cooing at the two.

"Guess that makes two of us," Whitney says.

I hold it all in—words and reactions.

That makes two of us. What, exactly, does that make us? I don't want to fill in the blanks, but I know what she's thinking: that I have no right being disappointed in her if I'm not going to include myself. I was someone's secret, someone's last resort. I turn back to her, wanting to deny everything, but I can't lie to her.

"You're just like everyone else," she says. She looks disgusted, and she fidgets, as if surging with anger and irritation. "Using me to get to my brother, using me for this house, the hotel—"

"What? Oh my God, that's not true at all. I could care less about your house or the hotel." But as I say this, I can't hold eye contact. I totally care. I knew way more about her than anyone else at the school because of these things she has. I've already admitted to myself that it's part of the package that makes everyone rank her so highly. But that's not why I'm here now. "We're friends," I say. It's all I can think of to say.

"Have you hooked up with Will?" she asks.

She watches me, and I feel I can't escape. "Yes," I say.

She shakes her head.

"But I didn't *use you* to get to him." Did I? Did I want to spend time with her just on the off chance Will would be around too? What about her? Did she use me to have Danny around?

"I didn't ask to come here," I say. I relax my shoulders, stepping into myself. "You seemed to like it when I had Danny over. And your mom wants us here because of what my mom can give her. It goes both ways. At least I don't buy friends."

She shakes her head and rolls her eyes, but I can tell this

stung. She doesn't have a comeback, and this makes me feel kind of sick with myself.

"I don't even know what we're fighting about," I say.

"I do," she says.

"What, then?" I unintentionally make a huge gesture with my hands as if holding a great weight. I let my arms fall to my side. "Why didn't you invite me to the hotel? I don't care about you having a hotel, okay, I'm just curious why we seem to get along and then—"

"I knew you hooked up with Will. I've been waiting for you to tell me, and you didn't say a word. My dad has some crush on your mom and gives her money so you can go to Punahou."

"That's *not* true," I say.

"Whatever," she says. "Don't talk about not caring about what I have. Maybe that's why I didn't invite you. I've been waiting for you to be a friend that's different."

"I am different," I say lamely. "And why is this all coming out now? Why didn't you say anything?"

She closes her eyes for a moment. "I don't know," she says. "I don't know what I was waiting for." She opens her eyes, and they are unfocused and hard. "Anyway," she says. "You're just a guest we're all supposed to be nice to. You can go now."

I don't know what to say. She has her arms crossed, and she's looking away, tapping her foot in annoyance. She clears her throat, and on that note, I walk away.

30

I WALK ACROSS THE YARD, CRYING, THE PALMS ABOVE rubbing their leaves together like hands. *Fuck you, palms. Fuck you, Kahala.* I have a sudden and intense longing for our old place, our old town, the Ko'olaus, set back and minding their own business. Thirty minutes away, same island, but the soil is different, and that affects everything—what we taste like, how we grow. I roar into the sky. It's more like an *arf,* nothing fearless or powerful about it.

I walk into our cottage, our nanny's quarters, with the same feeling as a hangover, parched and hungry, the things in my head—neurons, electricity, all misfiring. I'm hating my body, and it's hating me right back. When I see my mother in the kitchen, it's like I'm looking at myself. She's sitting at the counter, gripping her forehead like it's a bat. She straightens when I come in.

"Where were you?" she says, then registers my face. "Honey, what is it?"

"I got in a fight with Whitney," I say and walk to the kitchen, wanting to hide my tears. I get a banana from the fruit basket, which has been replenished, probably by Melanie. I find myself glowering, hating Melanie's kindness, her selfish selflessness. Charity can be so greedy. Paying for Punahou? I want to die.

"Lei?" she asks.

I zero in on the small, whisker-like lines around her eyes, how something that should age her merely makes her look punctuated.

"What did Whitney mean by her dad paying for Punahou? He has a crush on you still, so he pays for—oh God! And everyone knows this?" I bite the banana and don't taste a thing.

She places her hands on the counter, tucking her chin so that her hair covers her face. I chew until my heart simmers down.

"I want to know everything everyone else knows," I say.

My mom takes a deep breath. "Whitney shouldn't have known that."

"What the—? Is he in love with you?"

"No," she says. "He's just confused. He's trying to say good-bye—being with people who meant something to him once. I don't know . . . sometimes that's the only way he knows how to show friendship." Like Whitney, I think. My mom looks off toward the window with true confusion.

"What does spending time with you have to do with paying for us? Are we that poor? How can that be possible? Your friends from *Law and Order* don't have to do this shit, do they?"

"No," she says, frustrated. "Let me begin at the beginning, okay?"

"Go ahead," I say, shoving my hand up. I stand at the counter, too riled to sit.

She shakes out her hands like she's drying them off and then she launches in.

“This starts with your dad.”

“My dad?” I get a sense of vertigo. My eyes feel tired, my head heavy.

“Just listen,” she says. “After the summer I told him I was pregnant, he left and never talked to me again. No phone calls. Nothing.” She faces me. “But then letters came. Very brief notes with no explanations, no return address. *Sending love,* they’d say. And they’d have money in them. Once a year, I’d get a note with money.”

“How much?” I ask. I face away from her and just listen.

“A very helpful amount,” she says. “It covered rent. When I added it up, it basically covered it all. When you were four, he wrote that he would start paying for school. I just had to tell him which school you went to and bills would go to him. I sent a letter back to him at some PO box, and when he didn’t respond, I figured he just didn’t want me to find him and bother him. It was the only time I wrote. From then on, he contacted the schools directly. It changed where I applied you. He has done that for every year of your schooling. Sort of,” she adds.

I’ve never known what to think of this. I’ve felt like someone out of a Dickens novel—a child with a wealthy patriarch investing in me. I’m grateful, but why not talk to me instead? Why not fly me out to meet him or take me to lunch? No words, no love, just direct deposits. My eyes water.

“Will you make popcorn?” I ask, sitting down next to her.

She puts her hand on my back and must be wondering why I’d ask for popcorn at a time like this, but then she seems to understand that I need to be a little bit alone in my sadness. She gets up to make the popcorn.

"It was incredibly generous," she says, her back to me. She pours the seeds into the paper bag, then adds the olive oil. "It changed our lives. I had no work in the beginning. I would have been able to afford private school eventually, but then I wouldn't have been able to put as much toward college, the classes, the trips, and . . . and you got this amazing education." Her voice rises. She puts the bag in the microwave, then turns to face me.

"It allowed us so much," she says. "It was something I could give you—we could give you—without stress, without stipulations, and I've seen you become this wonderful young lady—"

She cries then, and my eyes start to water. The popcorn fires like a machine gun. She waits, then opens the microwave, always trying to time it so there are no burns and no remnants.

She pours it into a bowl, brings it back to the counter, and rubs my back. I wait for my throat to unclench, and she seems to be doing the same. She kisses my head, then pinches the place between her eyes.

I've been so absorbed in her storytelling that I haven't been thinking about what she's saying. Then the horrible thought occurs to me: "Oh my God, is Eddie my father?"

"No!" she says. She smiles slightly. "No."

"So why does he pay now?"

"Let me finish," she says. She lifts her shoulders, then relaxes them, as if easing in for a long ride.

She sits back down, grabs a handful of popcorn, and takes her time eating it. I wait it out, expecting the worst. My father decided he wants to be paid back in full, so Eddie is helping, or he's going to sue her or file for full custody, or he's dead and can't pay.

"Did he die?" I ask.

"What? No." She looks over at me again, as if making sure I have everything I need to understand her. "When I was making plans for our move here, I talked to Joanne in the office to tell her to stop payments on Ray's account. I wanted to handle the rest of the school year on my own. I could have written him or found him somehow, but I was at your school anyway and needed to sign the waivers so they could transfer your forms. I felt a little bad, not telling him. Paying was his way of keeping in touch, sort of, seeing you in a way. But I could handle Punahou for two years, and I guess the switch made me wonder why I kept any connection to him at all. Maybe part of me was hoping he'd reach out to you in other ways. I know how much you've wanted that."

"I haven't wanted that," I say, my head in my hands.

"Lea, yes you have, and it's okay."

I don't protest. I give in. I close my eyes and listen.

"Turns out they couldn't stop payment," my mom says. "Ray would need to call them himself, and I knew that once he found out you transferred, he'd follow up with the other school. I still tried to let it go. Forty-four grand. So I told her to contact Ray, and if he insisted on keeping it coming for Punahou, fine. If not, I'd be okay." She looks at me guiltily, as though she shouldn't have told me what my tuition is for the rest of high school.

"And then what?" I ask, imagining Ray in his Ray-Bans, taking care of me from a distance. I tuck my hair behind my ear, foolishly envisioning him watching us from a satellite feed.

My mom continues: "And then Joanne asked, 'Who's Ray?' So I said his full name, Ray Piston, and she had no idea who I was talking about. So I said, 'Lea's father, who pays the tuition,' and she looked at me like I was senile. She scanned the computer, pressing keys, and I was getting impatient and a little embarrassed, so I just told her to stop payments from the person paying your tuition.

My mom seems to harken back to the state she was in, physically changing—becoming flustered, bewildered.

"Joanne looked at her computer, looked at me and said, 'You mean Edward West?'"

I stop breathing and imagine she must have back then too.

"I could have won a damn Oscar for my performance, Lei. I did a full-on monologue explaining away my mistake and confusion, blamed it on an actor I was in the middle of a scene with, who looked just like Eddie, blah, blah, blah."

"This is crazy," I say.

"I know," she says. "Believe me I know. It took practically, what, twelve years for me to find out it had been Eddie this whole time?"

"But why?" The faceless image of Ray Piston gets usurped by Eddie. I see him on the lanai, shaking his cocktail glass, basking in a moment of peace. What was his reasoning? What's the investment? A crush?

"He introduced me to Ray," my mom says. "He felt guilty."

"He felt guilty?" I'm holding my handful of popcorn like it's a stress ball. "That's expensive guilt."

"I know." Making herself explain this to me is either confusing Mom more or forcing her to reconsider or rearrange the facts. "He felt guilty about Melanie. Then he felt guilty because he really thought Ray liked me, that he was changing, even though he wasn't. Ray was seeing Melanie's best friend at the time, and other girls too, apparently."

My mom slumps her shoulders. Everything about her seems to cave in. "God, it was such a mess. So much drama." She shakes her head. "This was when Melanie did not like me one bit. I was nobody. Some wannabe actress from Kailua. I was teaching step aerobics." She laughs. I wait while she sorts it all out, letting her ramble to see where it leads.

"Eddie tried to take me under his wing after Ray left," she says. "I wouldn't accept his money, I thought that was absurd—I mean, he wasn't the one who did anything wrong, but I took him up on his friendship. He was there when you were born." I see her going somewhere else in her head, remembering something nice, but then her face hardens.

"Friendship didn't work, though," she says, and looks my way for a moment, then chews her popcorn thoughtfully, as if reflecting on something so simple. "Melanie banned him from me. Her friends too—it was like I didn't exist. I didn't even deal with it. I got out. I just did what I was going to do anyway, continued on my course. But with you."

I can't believe she went back to LA with me, no job, no inkling that her desires and work would pay off. I see her vividly as a young adult, how she felt like I probably did with Will, out of her league, yet liking it there. She probably felt used even before she knew she was getting used. Still liking it there. Then: desertion, shame. The feeling of being plundered.

And then me, a reminder, the result of it all.

“You okay?” she asks.

I consider the spread she has laid out before me, sorting the pieces by intensity, but it’s all intense. It all pops. I guess the shiniest thing out here is the fact that Eddie’s been with us all these years. My dad has settled back on his old shelf where I had him, and Eddie is spotlit on a podium.

“Does Melanie know?” I ask. “About the tuition?”

“No,” she says. “Not that I know of, at least. If she knew, the world would know. I don’t think Whitney really knows for sure, either. I’ll work it out so that she thinks he’s confused or . . . I don’t know. I’ll do something.”

“It’s okay,” I say. “Let her think it. It’s the truth. This is just so crazy.” I lean forward on my chair, making it balance on two legs. “God, Mom. Don’t you think he’s loved you all this time?”

She shakes her head, truly bewildered. That’s how I feel too—mystified, stunned into silence—as if I’m an observer of something happening to someone else. I bring my chair back down.

“No,” she says. “I don’t think so. I think he did when he first started paying and then it just became a habit.”

“I need a drink,” I say.

My mom looks at me sharply.

“What? I’m just kidding.”

“Good,” she says. “I could use one, though.”

“So hypocritical.” I bonk her on the leg with my fist.

“No, no, no,” she says. “Adults appreciate the flavor of wine, its nuances and such. And we have major problems and stress. You don’t know how good you have it.”

“Yeah, real good. This hasn’t been stressful at all.”

She gets up, kisses me on my temple, then pours herself a glass of wine. I'm relieved for a bit of a break, an intermission before the rest of the show.

We talk into the night. Mainly I let my mom talk. We have moved to the couch, put the TV on to provide some other noise, and I watch her reflect and remember, unraveling herself.

"Why are we here?" I ask, such a simple question.

"Honestly," she says, "I thought it would be nice. It makes Eddie happy. Melanie has been great, too, bringing me to things. She's all into her Housewives clips, and it's hard to pay people like the Wests back. So I've gotten permission for her to film at the premiere. It's just something I could do."

I understand, yet it's not anything I don't already know, really. I can't help but feel that we're working for them, they're working for us, and this isn't how friendships are supposed to be.

"Why did you keep it a secret once you found out?" I ask. I feel I've given my mom a shakedown and everything's clanging to the floor as if she'd stuffed it all up her skirt.

She lies down, her eyes heavy. "Because I knew you'd go to school with Whitney and Will and I didn't want you to feel ashamed."

She was right to tell me and right about the way I'd feel if I knew.

"Whitney doesn't know about the other schools, though," she says.

This doesn't make me feel any better. I want to ask her if we can make it stop, but don't want to know the answer. I have an urge to tell Danny—nothing seems real until I tell him. I lie down, resting my feet in her lap and imagining our conversation, how Danny will make it right. Thinking of him seems to lay a kind of foundation for me—like no matter what, here is the ground, here is this thing I can stand upon.

I look at my mom's hands rubbing my feet, her veins and pores, her sand-colored nails, her turquoise ring, the thin wrinkles at her wrist, the small scratch on the knuckle of her thumb.

We fall asleep on opposite sides of the couch.

31

EVERYTHING SEEMS SO SMALL TODAY. IT'S WEDNESDAY, another day in paradise. It shouldn't be this hard. I look out my bedroom window toward Whitney's house, and my mind races with comebacks and insults. Why couldn't she just tell me what was on her mind instead of putting me through a test? Why does she care about me and Will, anyway? We can all be together.

Then there's me—the things I've kept from her. Do I tell her about her dad, the entirety of his help? Do I tell her I'm hurt when I'm left out? Do I make her admit that I *am* different from her other friends and she and I both know it? New problems keep popping up like the heads in Whac-A-Mole at Chuck E. Cheese's. I need to talk to her.

I see Melanie walk out the front door, gabbing on the phone, dressed to go somewhere, probably a club. What's with the clubs—the events? Camping clubs, beach clubs, golf clubs, always something to sequester themselves from whatever they think they need protection from. Ugliness? Chance? Things unforeseen? People not from their club?

"Mom!" I call and walk to the kitchen.

"Yeah?" she calls back from her room.

"I'm going to go to Whitney's."

She walks out of her room, brushing her wet hair. "Are you okay with everything?"

"Yeah," I say.

"I'm going to run to the mall with Melanie. She needs a dress for Monday night. I'll look for one for you too, all right?"

It's my mom's premiere, and she needs to help Melanie?

"Whatever," I say. "Thanks."

I knock on Whitney's door, but she doesn't answer, so I go around back. I stop and want to run when I see Will and Lissa on the daybed, but it's too late. They see me. Will's face is close to hers, and he looks at me over her head.

"Hi," Will says.

"Hi," I say.

Lissa grins—a flash of teeth, her eyes lit from within, then her face falls back into its prior state of gloom. She's wearing a translucent dress with a bikini underneath. She looks like she's vacationing in Morocco, or like a model in a fashion magazine, in a jaw-dropping place, but still glowering at the camera. She holds her phone up and starts scrolling while sipping a smoothie with a little umbrella in it.

"Do you know Lea?" Will asks.

"I don't think so," she says, not looking at me.

"I'm in your creative writing class," I say. "And I paddled."

"Oh, right," she says, still focused on the phone.

"This is Ali Lane's daughter," Will says. "They're staying in the—"

“Oh!” she says, looking up. “I didn’t put that together.”

She becomes a different person right before my eyes. I never know what to make of this. When someone doesn’t respond to my mom’s job, I don’t like it, and when someone lights up, I don’t like it, either. It’s how I feel with name-dropping—I hate when people do it, and yet sometimes, saying my mom is an actress and naming some of the people she’s worked with who have gone on to be huge stars gives me a voice, makes people want to talk back. It’s not about wanting to be known, to be seen as important, or to be admired. It’s just to join a conversation, to be visible, to make people put down their damn phones. Plus, what’s worse? The dropper or the person who picks up?

“I am so excited for the premiere Monday!” Lissa says. It’s weird to hear that her voice has a range. “I just think it’s so good for the economy, and fun to see all the places you know, you know?”

I glance at Will, who’s twisting his mouth as if hearing an unpleasant noise.

“And to see the real Hawaii,” she says. “Not all fake and touristy. It’s gritty, you know? Real. Like, this is how we live.”

Says the girl drinking from a glass with an umbrella in it, the sun spotlighting her mollusk-colored hair, the surf behind us crashing into the wall of a tropical estate. I don’t tell her that the show isn’t even depicting Hawaii. Hawaii is a stand-in for some generic island. I imagine the state of Hawaii waiting in the corner until they’re ready to shoot the star that’s dressed in the exact same clothes.

“Willy, you should ask Ali if we could be extras,” she says, in a decided voice.

"Right, okay, on it." He looks at me and rolls his eyes. "How's your day going so far?" he asks, then clears his throat because his question came out of the gates as if it's the first thing he's said all day. Whether it's from nervousness or just natural causes, I'm immediately empowered by his voice. I realize I can say anything. I could change this scenery in a snap.

"Great," I say. "Yours?"

I look at him directly, and he smiles slightly at my confidence, which he may be seeing as flirtation. Maybe it is.

He turns his head to Lissa. "Wonderful," he says and takes a sip of water. Ice crashes onto his face.

"I can't wait to meet Alex Crane," Lissa says. She bats her lashes at Will. "Don't worry. I vow to never cheat on you with Alex Crane or anyone else."

Will and I lock eyes. "Maybe Will should promise the same thing," I say. He makes a sound—I'm not sure if it's a cough or a laugh—then holds his gaze on me while taking a sip of his drink and chewing the ice. His confidence makes me feel stupidly out of my league, like I am that ice cube, and I could easily be crushed. I add, "He should vow that he'll never cheat on you with Alex Crane." He sits back, his arm brushing Lissa's.

"You're so funny," she says, in that horrid way that so many girls say words. *Funny,* I want to say, not *funnay.* She puts her hand on Will's leg. "Hey, did you reserve a cabana?" she asks. "Some of the girls are coming by."

Though I don't know what she's talking about, I assume she's talking about a cabana by a pool, which makes me think of Melanie—everything has to be paid for—she can't just go the normal route and sit by a pool. Of course this is who she wants her future daughter to be.

"You want to come with?" Lissa asks me, her face animated. Eyes blinking and expectant.

"Where?" I ask.

"The Wests' coast. Will's hotel. We're not staying the night, but Whitney and her friends have a room."

The Wests' coast? That is so cheesy.

"Weren't you going anyway?" Will asks.

And there's my heart and my pride, getting into the elevator and hitting the lobby button. Down, down, down they go, descending even farther to underground parking. Whitney told me Friday, but has obviously changed the plan, and I can't help but think it's to spite me.

"I was," I say.

Lissa gets up and walks toward the living room. "Let's leave in five," she calls, then goes in.

I walk closer to Will.

"Sorry," he says. "She came over with her mom and stayed. I didn't know."

I pretend that I don't need an explanation, but am relieved he doesn't seem to want her here.

"I talked to my mom last night about your dad helping out," I say. "You don't need to hide it from me anymore. I know you know. I'm sorry for . . . for us. I feel like a burden."

"You're not," he says then laughs. "Don't worry. I've been reared for this."

I sit at the edge of the bed.

"What about Lissa?" I ask. "Are you reared for her too?"

He shakes his head.

"I know you're with her. Just tell me," I say. "I don't want to look stupid."

"I miss you," he says. "Come to the hotel." He hits my leg with his foot, and I try to hide a smile. My heart gets back in that elevator and goes up. I tell myself to be strong, to not care about him, but as soon as I see him, I'm always a goner.

"Where's Whitney? She's not very happy about us."

"Don't worry about her," he says. "Come with me. Have fun." He looks toward the house. "Lissa won't be there the whole time."

I pretend to hesitate, but I know I will go.

32

I SIT BY THE POOL UNDER THE SHADE OF THE CABANA, a part of me excited by Lissa's company and effort to be friends and a part of me guilty. Will gets out of the pool in front of us. It's the first time I've seen him without his shirt. He has a bit of a farmer's tan from golf, and his shorts are pulled up a little high, not like Danny's, whose shorts always ride so low I have to tell him I can see his crack.

Lissa hands him a towel, and I'm glad I didn't do the same. I keep forgetting that she's the girlfriend, or at least thinks she is. Will puts the towel around his neck. "Hey!" he calls.

Nick Sopuch, Ross Love, and Gabby Chun walk toward us on the pathway. Seniors. I'm kind of relieved it's all guys, but then Celeste Baldwin runs up between them, putting her keys in her purse and squealing, "Willy!", which somehow harkens back to the old days when people would go to the hop. They gather around, loud with greetings.

"How was your trip?" Will says.

"Very nice," Nick says. "Powpow, sun, all good."

"Pull up some chairs," Lissa says.

"How you doing, Lea?" Nick says, and it's strange to hear my name coming from his mouth.

"Good, thanks," I say.

Gabby tilts his head hello, and Ross leans down for a brief hug, a gesture that makes me feel older and part of it all. Celeste starts chatting with Lissa, and I overhear talk of graduation. I don't know where Whitney is, but I want her to see me, see that I'm here and okay without her. If we're not going to get over it, then I guess I'll show her that I'm moving on.

It ends up being fun by the pool in the seniors' company, maybe more fun than it would have been with just me and Will. I feel like his friends' presence is a thickening agent, helping us form something that will set. He's being seen with me, or around me.

I also like the big group camaraderie, having never really felt it while I've lived here. Dishes keep being brought out by waiters, and our jokes and laughter make our spot the place to be. Every now and then, Will and I look at each other, or our feet will touch.

Will walks me up to the hotel room. Now it's just us since all his friends, including Lissa, have gone.

"What if Whitney really doesn't want me here?" I ask.

"She'll be fine," he says. We get out of the elevator and walk down the hall of the twenty-fourth floor.

"I think she was mad that you and I are hanging out," I say.

"I don't see why she'd care."

"I know, right? Did you tell her?" I ask, my voice coy, like I've caught him talking about me.

"No," he says. "What would I tell?"

"Just kidding," I say, so lamely.

We walk down the hall, and every time we pass someone who works here, they say, "Aloha."

"That gets old real quick," he tells me, and I imagine him running this place one day.

"You don't want to stay here tonight?" I ask.

"God, no," Will says. "People just get hammered and stupid. I mean, I don't mind that, but it's like . . . this is going to sound pretentious, but it feels like it's at my house, you know?"

"Yeah, I get that," I say. Your house. Your coast.

"So I don't want a bunch of my sister's friends at my house. I don't want to see random people taking advantage either."

"But Whitney likes it?" I'm having trouble piecing her together.

"Whitney," Will says, mulling something over. "Whitney doesn't want to be alone. She always has to be in something. She's expected to throw these parties. Before you came along, she always had to be going at full speed."

Before I came along. Why does this make me feel like I've abandoned her? Like I've given her the chance to move at a slower speed, to be herself, and without me, she's thoughtless. Will takes my hand and stops in front of suite 2440. He knocks on the door.

"If you want to stay and have fun, that's great," he says. "Otherwise I'll take you home with me."

I love the way that sounds. I move to kiss him, lightly, but then the door starts to open, and he drops my hand.

"Oh, hey," Danny says. The calm I felt disappears, along with last night's thoughts on Danny—how he is this solid thing in my life. Him being here makes an angry heat shoot through my chest.

Will looks at him coolly. "Hey. Excuse me," he says, and walks in, where he's greeted by all the girls in the room.

"Guess you forgot to give me the change of date," I say to Danny.

"I thought Whitney told you," he says.

"Nope," I say. "She's apparently done with me."

"Don't fight with Whitney," he says, glancing behind him.

"What? Why? Because she'd turn the island against me or something? Turn my best friend against me?" I feel exposed just then, admitting that's who I consider him to be.

"I mean, don't fight," he says and shrugs. "She does enough of that with her other friends." I think of Lissa and Mari, using her to get someplace else. I take in the action behind him—Mike Matson is here, along with the usual group of girls and guys. There are seniors here, too, but not Will's friends. More of Danny's crowd.

"Should I try to talk to her?" I ask.

I see her now, head thrown back, laughing at something Mike's saying.

"You should," he says.

"'Kay," I say. "I'm not staying, but I'll say hi."

"Are you going back with Will?" Danny asks. He looks over my head and flexes his jaw.

I shrug and smile.

"He's a player, you know," Danny says. His eyes look red from salt water.

"Takes one to know one," I say, but Danny just looks like he feels sorry for me, and I guess it's an insult that doesn't really ring true.

I go out to the balcony where Whitney is pouring herself a drink from a pitcher. The ocean glimmers beyond, a bright turquoise, so vivid it almost looks unnatural.

"Oh, hey!" Whitney says in a fake voice. "Nice stalking." She's wearing a crop top and short shorts, and I see her registering the fact that we dressed so similarly today.

"Stop it," I say with a firm voice that takes us both by surprise. I close the sliding door behind me.

"Stop what?" she asks, her eyes wide and innocent.

"It," I say. "All of it."

She lowers herself onto a recliner, and I sit down right next to her, the sides of our bodies smashed into each other. She scoots away. I move closer, hoping she'll give in and laugh, but instead she stands and leans against the railing.

"Whitney," I say. "Come on."

"What?" she says and turns her head. "You think everything is just okay now?"

I look behind me at the scene of the party. Some of the girls are filming one another on their phones. "Yes," I say. "I think everything is okay. What isn't okay?"

"We've talked about it already. You and Will are not okay."

"Why not?" I ask.

She doesn't answer, just looks back at me, raising her eyebrows like I should know.

When I came out here, I wanted to resolve this, bury it, but I can't help but defend myself.

"Well, it's not okay that you stuffed me in a closet, where I had to watch some seriously sick shit." I get up and go to the railing, yet not right next to her.

"Oh, please," she says. "You just waltz in here and take advantage of me and mess with all of us—"

"Oh my God," I say, truly appalled and desperate for her to address this seriously. I feel like screaming, *Take it back!* and while I have never uttered these words, even as a kid, I understand why they're said. You're desperate for logic, for sense, and the first step is getting those wrong words erased from the atmosphere.

"How have I *messed* with any of you?" I ask, facing her even though she's still looking out to the sea. "I didn't ask to come here."

"No," she says. "Your mother did. And she's taking advantage of my dad because he doesn't know what's going on."

"Can we stop talking about our parents?"

"What else is there?" she says, with a desperate look on her face. "That's what's happening right now. Who's going to be here or there, or where I need to go, or who Will needs to be seen with. It's like a reality show, and I don't care about you, okay?"

She looks unconvinced, not quite at home with her words but still committed to them.

When I'm sad, I know it. When I'm confused, angry, envious, left out, I know it. Whitney doesn't seem to know how to identify her emotions. They're like foreign objects she can't digest.

Voices carry from the pool below, and beyond that the breaks roll in, carrying surfers and canoes.

"Are you sad?" I ask her.

She nods, quickly, and I think this nod got away from her. She wasn't planning on admitting that, but her body had a reflex.

I hear the music from inside.

"I just want to get fucked up," she says.

"You already are," I say, angry that she's not working with me. I tried.

I turn to the room and see Will inside, slapping hands with Mike. I walk out, toward her better half.

I close the sliding door behind me, then give Will a look, telling him I'm ready. He reads it perfectly and comes to me. I feel so good leaving with him. I look back and catch Danny's eye as Will and I leave. His face is slack, sad almost, as though he has given up on something he loved.

33

WILL AND I SIT ON THE BEACH IN FRONT OF HIS HOUSE, away from the lights cast from the coconut trees. We've been here for a long time, drinking cold beer and talking. I lean against him for warmth. The lights illuminate part of the ocean in front of us. He kisses the top of my head and puts his arm around me.

"Hey, Samantha," he says, then holds my neck just under my chin and kisses me. I kiss back, and my head spins. This kiss is working like a seal or a pact, something like love, even though we aren't—how could we possibly be?—there yet. I look at his mouth when we pull away.

His phone cheeps again—it's been doing that all night—clanging with texts or rings. I don't care about Lissa or Whitney or Danny. I'm with Will now. He glances down and says, "My mom needs to relax."

"Maybe you should just get it," I say.

"We'll go up soon."

But we won't, and that's the whole point of coming out here. To drag things out a little longer.

"Are you tired?" he asks, running his fingers down my leg.

"A little," I say.

"Rest right here," he says, pointing to his lips. I lean in and rest.

"Let's go up to my room," he says, while kissing me.

"Okay," I say.

The big house is lit up like a fire. We try to walk softly, except outside it seems wherever you walk, a light comes on, making you feel like you're wearing those light-up children's shoes. I wish this was our own home.

"Oh, shit," Will says and lets go of my hand.

Melanie walks out of the house to the lanai, her hands on her hips, her nostrils flaring a bit. Her face looks tighter than ever.

"Where were you?" she asks Will, not looking at me.

"We just went for a walk," he says, his expression reminding me of Whitney's, her wide, innocent eyes.

"I have been trying to call and text all night." She looks past us as if we might be hiding something.

Now my mom comes out. I can't read the look she's giving me, but it's loaded with exhaustion, as if they'd been in some kind of emotional triathlon.

"Sorry," Will says. He shrugs, then laughs. Down on the beach, he moved like he owned the world; now he seems hesitant about every step. "Hi," he says to his mom. "Here I am."

"Will I am," I blurt, and he looks at me and quickly smiles, but in a way that tells me he doesn't get the joke.

"Your sister went to the hospital," Melanie says.

"What?" we both say at the same time. "Why?" Again at the same time.

"Because someone"—and Melanie briefly glances at me—

"someone drugged her. That boy. Your friend, Lea, who you've brought to our home."

"Melanie," my mom says, "come on. We've—"

"Danny?" I say.

"Yes," Melanie says.

The thought is laughable. First that he would drug anyone, second that he would have the kind of drugs that could send someone to the hospital.

My mom looks like she's praying that everything implodes. She keeps biting her lip and jiggling her leg.

"Is she there now?" Will asks. "At Queen's?"

"No, she's here now," Melanie says. "Asleep. It has been a terrible, terrible night."

I always feel that when people say something twice in a row, they're weakening their own argument.

"How do you know he drugged her?" Will asks. "What do you mean?"

"We don't know—" my mom says.

"Because I know—" Melanie says.

"But what happened?" I ask. "What was it? How was she drugged?" Melanie looks at me as if I'd interrupted the president.

"As I was saying"—she trains her eyes back on Will—"*someone* gave her a brownie drugged with marijuana—"

Will laughs. "'Someone'?"

"Who, her hand?" I say while looking at Melanie, the grand house behind her, the dark sea behind me. I don't look away, expecting an answer.

"Lea," my mom says, and I try to plead with my eyes, *Let me speak. Let me talk back.* I'm tired of being polite. "What?" I say. "I mean, come on."

"Your sister could have been killed," Melanie says, "and I seriously doubt she would have volunteered herself to be in the state she was found in."

My mom looks away from me quickly. I swear I saw a flash of amusement. Now the face of impatience settles back in.

"Mom," Will says, as if she were a child, "it sounds like Whitney ate a pot brownie and tripped out. Did *you* send her to the hospital?"

"Yes!" Melanie says, and oh God, I want to laugh.

"So what happened?" Will says, his voice rising a bit with controlled hysteria. I accidentally let out a whimper of a laugh, and my mom won't meet my eyes.

"The hotel staff found her curled in a ball in a lounge chair by the pool," Melanie says. "I guess they were watching a movie in the suite and wouldn't change it, and the movie was scaring her so badly that she had to get away."

Will and I are both trembling a bit, and we keep looking over at each other, desperate for some release.

"The woman who found her said she had a big scrape on her knee and might have hit her head or something. Clearly, *clearly*, she had been drugged. And you say it was a pot brownie, but who knows? There are kids everywhere dying of molly—"

That's it. I have to turn around. I can't take it, and neither can Will. He has his hands on his knees, and he's bending down trying to get it together. When he comes back up, he is actually wiping his eyes.

"Mom," Will says again, as if she were the one who'd been

drugged and needs to be brought down, "I'm sure it wasn't molly."

"Drugs don't take themselves," I say.

"Lea," my mom says again.

Melanie's shoulders fall, as if, deep down, she knows this to be true, but almost immediately, she reassumes her fighter's stance.

"All I know is you kids have been using the hotel for years, and not until your friend shows up does something like this happen. I could alert the school about this."

My hysteria dies. I want to shake her. Everyone gets fucked up at that party and Mike Matson is known for making brownies. Why Danny? There must be countless others Melanie doesn't even know about. It's not like there's a guest book. It's not like her kids are ever supervised. But I know no matter what I say, she will deflect it, sending it out into the surf. My mom's look also tells me that she's been through this all night, probably said—nicely, carefully—all the things I want to scream.

I won't scream. I'll try to say this as politely as I can. "But you don't know if Danny did anything, right?" I say. I glance at Will, expecting him to chime in. When he doesn't, I prompt, "And, Will, you *know* that things like that happen every year. It just happened to Whitney this time."

I wait, and inside, I'm rooting for him to come on and resolve this.

"I have no idea what's going on," he says.

I realize I've been holding my breath. I wait for more. This can't be all he has to say. "Danny wouldn't bring pot brownies," I say. I don't say he's against them in principle or anything, but

I know he wouldn't take the time to bake them. He'd rather slow-cook a pork loin all day and come up with some crazy marinade. He is such a cooking dork. He'd rather surf all day or listen to music with me, play the uke or hike. I wish he were here to take a stand.

"Whitney told me it was Danny," Melanie says. She looks like someone on the news, giving me a verified report with a composed face.

My mom takes a deep breath with her eyes closed.

"Well, then, she must be out of her mind," I say, my heart beating fast, my hands in fists.

My words are being deflected, zinged to a coconut tree.

"Sweetheart," Melanie says, and looks at me like I've said something endearing. She walks closer, a smile on her face, but behind it, I can see she's organizing a circus act. She blinks rapidly, and she has those lash extensions that everyone her age seems to get. They make her look like a camel.

"I'm going to let you and your mom get some rest." She places her hand on my shoulder, and I try to stay still. "Will and I need to talk a little more. And so do you and your mother."

"Let's go," my mom says, and Melanie takes her hand off of me.

"I think Whitney was a bit upset," Melanie says. "Which may have caused the bad reaction? I'm not sure how these drug things work, but . . . I didn't realize you'd had a falling-out."

So now it's my fault that she tripped out on a brownie? She could have possibly died *of molly* because of me?

My mom takes my hand, and her grip feels both odd and necessary at this moment.

"We'll let you have your own talk, but, Lea?" Melanie says.

My mom squeezes my hand.

"Yes?" The wind moves my hair to the side, cooling my neck.

"Maybe give Whitney some space," she says kindly and with the lilt of a question. She laughs and makes the laugh infuse the rest of her speech. "Maybe Will too."

She walks over to him, as if to retrieve him, and pats him on the back. He looks down.

"Lissa is like a daughter to us. I'm sure Will would like to be your friend, but not if it's going to confuse you. Ah, puppy love," she says to my mom.

My mom's grip is unrelenting. I want to run away. Will won't look at me. He's not telling his mother she's crazy. He's not telling her that he's been puppy loving me right back. He should be the one taking my hand right now. He should say something, anything, right now.

"Will?" I say, but he doesn't respond.

I can't look at him then—I'm pissed, wounded, and plain appalled. How weak he is.

"Will," I say, taking a step toward him, shaking my mom's hand off, wanting so badly for him to redeem himself, to show his mother he's not like her. "Mike Matson was there," I say. "Tell your mom he brought the brownies."

"Sweetie, Mikey would never hurt Whitney," Melanie says.

"Will?" I say. My mom takes my hand again and pulls me back.

"I'm staying out of it," he says. He meets my eyes then, but they're glazed over, distant and decided.

I look at their house, wanting to throw a rock at the glass, but they'd just get new glass. I want them to be faced with something they can't replace so easily. I shake my head, not quite believing how cowardly he's being and how he'll probably always be this way. He'll end up marrying Lissa, or some family friend whose name is also on all the buildings. They'll go to fund-raisers and the Outrigger and sip cocktails and spike one another's volleyballs.

"Unfortunately your actions led to a lot of drama tonight," Melanie says, still with that touch of forced cheer. "We're just glad Whitney's safe." She places her hands in front of her as if smoothing a tablecloth. "It will all work out. Will, come on inside."

They walk toward the house.

"My actions?" I say, to their backs. "Is she crazy?"

"Just walk," my mom says, pushing my back, leading me toward the edge of the house where the garbage cans are kept. "I got you," she says. "Walk away."

I think about that truth walk across the gym floor, how different it would be now, even though it's only one month later. I've hurt people, been hurt, felt ashamed, have regrets, done something illegal, check, check, check.

We cross the lawn, then reach the cottage, and my legs burn walking up the steps. I just want to sit down and cry. I don't want to talk about Will with my mother. I'm so tired of being in trouble.

She holds the door open for me and then does something that surprises me. She closes the door, tells me to have a seat on the couch, and when I'm settled, asks, "Are you okay?"

The question hurts more than an insult would. Her concern is sincere, intense. She's got love for me written all over her face.

My shoulders shake, and I give in and cry, weak yet relieved with this relenting.

"I'm so sorry," she says.

I'm not sure what she's apologizing for, but I apply it like an ointment to everything—to my embarrassment, to Will, to my broken friendship with Whitney and her betrayal, to my father and his rejection of us, to my ignorance, to Danny being blamed, to my fear about what's going to happen next, and to this seismic shift that seems to be happening with my mom and me—her seeing things about me I don't want her to see, and me seeing things about her, and all of this happening in a goddamn beautiful place.

"Do you want to tell me what happened?" She sits up straight, looking serious, ready to work.

I want to cling to her as if she were a buoy and I a castaway, starved and wrecked. I try to get it together. It's not that hard. It's like the tears are a passing squall.

"Which part?" I hold the arm of the couch, pressing my fingers into the fabric.

"At the hotel," my mom says, "could Danny have—"

"No! Mike Matson brought them. Whitney even told me he was bringing them."

"Oh, great. His mom's another friend of Melanie's." My mom shakes her head, annoyed.

"And I wasn't even there," I say. "How can I be responsible?" I wipe the skin under my eyes, checking my hands for mascara marks.

"So you were here with Will this whole time?" my mom asks.

This is so humiliating. I can't look at her. Nothing's mine anymore. Before, these problems—Will, Whitney, my lack of a father—these topics were mine to ruminate over, to let burn holes into my chest. They were my loose teeth that I couldn't help but bother. Now I'm open. I'm like a cut apple—the bright, clean fruit browning from exposure.

"Yes, I was with Will," I say.

"Are you okay?"

"I'm fine." I think she's holding her breath, not wanting me to talk about this but knowing we need to.

"Did he take advantage of you?" she asks, her face tense like she's ready to pounce.

"No," I say. "I don't know. What do you mean?" God, this is so awkward.

"Did he try to have sex with you?"

"Oh my God, no, I don't know," I say, my voice rising, even though I'm trying to control it.

"I am so angry right now!" she says.

"Mom," I say, "no . . . it's just . . . he didn't do anything I didn't want him to do," I say quietly and look at my lap.

"What?" she says.

"It's not like he forced me to like him. He wanted to do . . . some things, and I went with it. Just kissing, though—"

"He's dating Lissa," my mom says. She moves closer to me. "They were at the event the other night together. Her mom is always talking about Will. They're going to Stanford together and everything, honey," she says and looks at me with so much sympathy.

"Okay," I say. "Stop. It doesn't matter." It matters more than she'll ever know. I was so willing to be lied to, and it was so easy for him to lie because I had been so willing. I remember thinking of *Sabrina* when we first moved here. I was thinking of it in the voyeur sense, poor me gazing across at the fabulousness. I wasn't thinking of the brothers—and in my movie, there is no nice brother and no love at the end.

Why did Will even bother with me? Because he could, because I was there and so convenient? Because I was new.

"I'm sorry," she says. "I had no idea you liked him." She looks stricken and guilty.

"He told me they were done," I say. "I'm not a bad person." My voice quivers at the sound of this, half statement, half fear. I wonder what I would have done if we had gone up to his room. I imagine Mike and Whitney. That would have been me.

"He reminds me of your dad," she says. "I didn't want to see anything else when I was with him. I didn't have a lot of respect for myself."

She hesitates—maybe she worries that she's revealing too much.

I think of my grandmother, loving her when I was little—baking cookies, playing Hanafuda, making Rorschach's inkblots while listening to my grandpa play guitar. She was never an actual person, though. She was Grandma—there and existing for me.

After she died, I learned that she had gone through a period of depression.

She went to some kind of rehab facility in California. She also smoked cigarettes and was engaged to two men before my grandpa—one, a descendant of Thoreau who now owns a cattle ranch in Wyoming that sells the sperm of black Angus, and the other, an East Coast banker she met while backpacking in France.

Whoa there, Tutu! I thought when I first heard all of this. It's something you don't tell the grandchildren, of course, and yet it was wonderful to have her colored in. I wish I could have known those things about her when she was alive, when I was her granddaughter. To see that version of her. I guess things don't happen that way, and maybe they can't. It's like time zones, people existing at different hours. When someone else is thriving and living, you're fast asleep.

"Maybe we don't need them anymore," I say. "The Wests."

"We just need to get through this," my mom says. "Melanie has this party planned for the premiere—"

"So what?" I say.

She looks like she has an answer, but is holding back. I want to say, *You think I was duped by Will? What about you? Melanie's using you, and Eddie's basically buying your companionship.* But I think my mom knows all this—it doesn't need to be said.

"If she's going to blame Danny and me for what Whitney did to herself, then how could we possibly stay here? What if she tells the school about Danny?"

"That's not going to happen," she says.

"I wanted to punch her when she brought Danny into this," I say. "Like, something came over me."

She laughs at me popping my fist into the air. "Of course," she says. "You love him, sweetie. You guys would do anything for each other." She places her hand over my fist. I close my eyes. We will be so small when it goes back to just the two of us, which it will. This has to come to an end.

34

I WAKE TO A BRIGHT, HIGH SUN, THE SMELL OF GARLIC, and the noise of a blender. I walk out while the blender's going and am startled by the sight of my mom and Danny working in the kitchen. He's using the blender, his back to me. My mom has a light step as she moves around the kitchen, as if everything were normal.

"What are you doing here?" I ask when the blender has stopped.

He turns his head, scans me in my pajama shorts and T-shirt. "I don't know."

"What are you making?" I put my hair up in a high ponytail.

He turns again, this time fully facing me. "I don't know."

"You know," my mom says, elbowing him. "Snap out of it."

"I forgot," he says. His eyes are vacant, as well as his voice. He also looks paler than usual. I don't want Melanie to see him. She'll think he's on drugs. I wonder what's in store for Whitney today, if she'll be grounded or totally exonerated, the blame thrown over the Ko'olaus to the boy from Waimanalo.

"Sichuan," my mom says.

"Sichuan eggplant," Danny says. "For the roasted ono."

"Our roasted ono," she says. "Danny is staying for dinner."

"Dinner's kind of a long ways away," I say.

In his eyes there's a little anger, like I've betrayed him. It's a wrong thing for him to be feeling. Ever since I brought him here that first day and he bonded with Whitney, he's been cold toward me, and I think I handled it well. I let him go.

"I thought we could hang out," he says.

"Okay," I say. I look down, aware I'm not wearing a bra.

"I'll let things marinate," my mom says. "You guys go play. I'm going to talk to Melanie. I'll take care of everything."

Danny looks both contemptuous and afraid.

"I'll go change," I say.

We drive down the avenue toward Diamond Head. It's good to be in his truck, on the warm, salty seats, listening to hip-hop. I love riding in his truck, the way it makes me feel like I've lived here all my life.

"You've been to to Doris Duke's, right?" I remember Will's forced tour and how he never went to the beach below it because it was so local. "To the beach below the mansion?"

"Cromwell's. Of course." Danny nods his head to the beat.

"Let's go there," I say.

We park and walk down a hill to the coast, the breeze carrying a scent of hot mock orange, fish, and that distinct smell of a garbage can at the end of a beach access. We reach the sand, and it's very nice, but there's hardly a beach at all—just reef and a slab of sand near the garbage can. I walk to the right, but when I look back, he isn't following.

"This way," he says. He nods toward the rocks. Houses are

perched above, clinging to the wall as if trying to escape a shark. He takes his backpack off his shoulders. "I'll hold your slippers," he says.

"Thanks," I say, putting them on top of his towel.

I follow him, walking on crags of rock. It hurts my feet, but I kind of like having to think about every step.

"Have you talked to Whitney yet?" I ask.

"No," he says. "But her mom called my dad. To let him know there was *an incident.*" He uses a mocking voice.

I have to walk faster to keep up so I can hear. The sharp rocks don't seem to bother him at all. I have haole feet.

"What did your dad say?"

"'Yes, ma'am, uh-huh? Is that right? I think you may be mistaken.' Then he hung up and worked in the garden. He knows I wouldn't do that and isn't going to argue unless he has to."

"I can't believe Whitney said you gave it to her in the first place. Why don't you just say it was Mike? Nothing will happen to him. His dad's a trustee. And isn't the middle school named after him?"

"No," Danny says. "Steve Case."

"Well, something! Matson Language Lab, I don't know."

Waves begin to come in faster sets, splashing against the wall. A black crab skitters up and then into a crack. I use the wall for support, my hand running across opihi shells suctioned to the rocks.

"Let's wait out this set," he says.

We watch the set of waves crash against the reef. There's no wall now, just a slope of rocks. The ocean spray is cold. I lick the salt on my lips.

"Your mom said she'd take care of everything," he says. "I'm not going to rat out Mike for a stupid pot brownie like some narc spank."

"So what happened last night?"

He runs his hand through his hair and, for the first time, grins.

"You and ill Will left," he says, and something catches in his voice. "On your little date, and Whitney's mood changed. She got all bitchy, and she was kind of getting on my nerves, then Mike busted out the brownies. Not to me, selfish knob. I think he just had one for her and one for himself. He probably thought he'd get her all loose, but the dude couldn't even move. Looked like he was wearing a straitjacket. He was watching the movie—"

"What movie?"

"Just some movie," he says, but by his expression, I can tell that something's up.

"What movie?" I ask again.

He says something, but a wave crashes, splashing water all over us and drowning his voice.

"What?" I ask, watching for waves.

"*Grease*," he says. "So then—"

"*Grease*? You guys were watching *Grease*?"

"Yes, okay?" He is trying not to smile.

"Like a porn version or—"

"No, not a—what's wrong with you?" He grins, the dimple appearing, and pushes my shoulder. We're both on the same rock, so I have to grab him for balance. His skin is hot.

"Well, I heard she was freaking out." I laugh. "How do you

freak out about *Grease*? I mean, the ending doesn't make much sense. There's no magic whatsoever, and all of a sudden, the car flies—I mean, what's up with that? But other than that, what was she tripping on?"

"Brownies, evidently," he says. "The girls were all singing along. *Tell me more, tell me more.*"

He sings these lines, which is hilarious, and now I can see them all watching this movie—it's something Whitney and I would have done alone, and now I feel like that's all gone.

"You guys are so hard-core," I say. "Meanwhile I thought you'd be getting shit-faced and having twerking orgies or something."

"You are a sad, sad teenager," he says, taking a step up to the next rock.

"Um, you spent a night in a hotel room without parents and with unlimited funds watching *Grease*, so don't be calling me a sad teenager."

He looks back and scratches his head and twists his mouth, that gesture he makes when caught. He extends his hand. I hold it, then jump onto his rock, bumping into his warm body. He wipes his eyes, using our hands. I think of a time when we were kids. Danny has beautiful long lashes, and one time our babysitter put mascara on them. His mom was so pissed when she got home. I let go of his hand, realizing I'm still holding it.

"Where is this place?" I ask.

"Almost there," he says. A huge wave slams against our rock, soaking us, and he puts his hand on my back.

"After this one," he says and bounces a bit as if to usher in the wave. After it crashes, he moves off the rock and I follow, my heart beating fast, trying to keep up and liking the way it feels to be close to him. I trail his steps, wary of what seem to be more waves about to hit us. He looks back at me and waits.

"What set her off about the movie?" I ask. "I thought you were watching a horror movie or something. I was prepared for chainsaws or creepy dolls."

"Rizzo was freaking her out," Danny says.

"Rizzo?"

"Yeah, the slutty, tough, pregnant chick. She kept saying, 'I'm going to end up like Rizzo. I'm Rizzo,'" and she finally ran off, and no one went to find her for a while. We figured she was being dramatic since we wouldn't change it. And that's it. It was only, like, seven at night."

"Then a worker found her?"

"Yup. The worker found her, called her mom, who sent her to the hospital." He laughs. "We all thought it was small kine hilarious, but then her mom . . . you know the rest. She flipped out, thinking Whitney OD'd on heroin or spice or something."

We scamper across the next set of rocks. Up ahead, it just seems to end.

I follow him, trusting his steps, and we round the point I mistook for a dead end. And then . . . it's like we've walked through a portal and into another world.

Danny looks back at me, prepared for and sweetly satisfied with my awe-filled response. It's as though someone took a tablecloth, flicked their wrist, and—voilà—magic and light unfolds. I look up at Doris Duke's house, Shangri La, and what appears to be a magnificent pool house with intricate tiles and earthy hues. I don't know where to look—the estate above or this ocean pool below, a rock-walled cove filled with water clear as glass. It doesn't even seem like ocean water, more like a clear cold lake, something you'd find on a hike in the mountains of Yosemite, bordered with a rock wall. Beyond the wall is the ocean wild.

And then Danny, beside me, jumps into this ocean lake, and I laugh, startled, touch my face, then bring my hand back down again. He surfaces, then immediately looks up at me. He wanted to make sure I was watching. He climbs back up the seemingly flat wall, then stands and shakes his body and head to get the water off him. I remember when I saw Will's body at the hotel pool yesterday I tried to shoo away the thought that he looked like those mainland guys on Waimea rock—not very tan, not very sculpted. He looked perfectly suited to a hotel in Waikiki.

"Nice form," I say.

"Your turn," he says, taking quick breaths.

I look at the other side of the cove for an exit. "I don't know if I could get out like that," I say. "How did you even get a hold?" The wall seems so flat.

"I'll help you," he says.

He turns away when I start to take off my clothes. I remember my suit, what happened the last time I decided to jump off a rock, and I'm nervous, mortified by something that hasn't even happened.

"Ready?" he says. "I'll go with you."

"It's deep, right? Should I—"

"Just go," he says. "You know how."

He counts to three, and I jump into the chilling, breathtaking water.

• • •

We do it over and over again, at first swimming across the way so I can climb the rocky embankment, but then I give the flat wall a shot and find that I can do it. Danny shows me how to wait for a push from the ocean, which gets sucked in and out by a tunnel in the rocks. When the ocean comes in, you move with it as it rises and reach for a hold. A few kids are playing in this tunnel. They crouch, then wait for a wave to spit them out.

When I reach the top, I see that Danny has put a towel out and containers of food. There are more people here now. Locals with coolers and music and beer.

"So cute," I say, sitting down next to him. "You packed a picnic."

"I grabbed things from your fridge," he says. "Forgot forks, though."

He opens the containers—pasta salad, crackers, and slices of roast chicken. Perfect. We lean back against the rocks, watch the guys do flips off the wall, and eat with our hands.

"How's my picnic?" he says.

"Super," I say.

"You cold?" He places his hand on my leg for a moment.

"I'm fine."

"I'm popping this pasta like it's candy," he says. I look over at him, his body so different from Will's. Water glistens on his stomach.

"Why did Whitney blame you in the first place?" I ask.

He looks ahead and squints. "I kept asking about you," he says. "You and Will. I think she thought I was thinking about you too much. She tried to kiss me. I kind of shut it down."

I don't say anything. I'm still feeling his hand on my leg, and I'm nervous in a way, but it's a nervousness charged with something else. We look like boyfriend and girlfriend sitting here in this idyllic place, and the anonymity makes it even more real, like this is a scene on a canvas we have magically walked into. We have an audience above, a group touring Shangri La, their presence making me feel in the know, as if we're doing something we always do.

"I guess I was worried about you," he says.

"Thank you," I say, bumping my shoulder against him. "I've learned my lesson." I remember thinking wealth was like an artificial additive for girls—making them prettier or more interesting—but I did the same thing with Will, gave someone not nearly as attractive as Danny a boost.

"I'm not with Will," I say.

"And I'm not with Whitney," Danny says.

"And here we are," I say.

"Friends," he says. He has a shy smile and questioning eyes.

A man walks up from the other side of the rocks, carrying a spear that's skewering an octopus over his shoulder.

"Whoa," Danny says.

"That's awesome," I say. "I want that for dinner. Grilled—"

"A little butter, miso—"

"Or Greek style, with olive oil, basil."

"Figs," he says. "That would be nice."

We pop the pasta into our mouths, our hands brushing against each other's in the bowl.

"Maybe we should try to make it sometime," I say.

"We should," he says.

The dreaded "we should."

"Or we could go out to find it one night," he says. "A restaurant would do a better job than us."

Now it's in my court. I almost say, "We should."

"Let's," I say instead, and we sit there against the hot rocks, our eyes heavy, watching the man with a spear, carrying the catch over his shoulder like a bandana bindle sack.

"Poor little octopus," Danny says. "Tickled out of his hole just for us."

"Sucks," I say, and he laughs, and it is and it isn't like old times. Something has changed, and he's treating me like a girl he wants to know more about, not like a girl he's known forever.

I tell him about Eddie and how my dad is back to square one—a person who may not even know I exist. Strange this is conceivable for men—that there could be remnants and versions of themselves walking the earth without their knowledge. It seems to me a very sad thing.

"You're having a hell of a time in Kahala," he says. I look at his profile, strong as though chiseled from rock.

"I know. But I'm handling it pretty well. I don't have daddy issues. Too bad for you," I add.

"What does that mean?"

"You know—people with daddy issues sleep around a lot. They're kind of wild."

"So why too bad for me?" He looks over at my legs, then up at my face with those same questioning, flirtatious eyes.

Really. He's going to force this out of me. I need to somehow reconfigure it all—make myself into an everygirl and him an everyboy.

"Well," I say, finding a grip, "rumor has it that boys like girls, and so when girls offer themselves up easily, this makes boys happy."

"Now, that's crazy talk," he says. He squints and sniffles.

"I'm going to talk to Eddie," I say. "I guess I do have daddy issues after all. Sugar daddy issues."

"Lucky me," he says, and the flirtation is almost too much to bear. I remember when he was in the outdoor shower, my urge to kiss him, an urge that peeked out suddenly, only to quickly retract.

"What's going on?" I say, looking straight ahead, a slight smile on my face.

"I don't know," he says.

I trace back to when I moved here, the amount of time we spent surfing and hanging out at Kalama's, or hiking to the top of the Pali or the Lanikai pillboxes, making fun of tourists below as they struggled with big yellow kayaks. We'd go to Habachi to get poke and boiled peanuts, the farmers' market to get pho at the Pig and the Lady, then listen to the kids' rock band, the Random Weirdos, playing the White Stripes and Heart in the parking lot. It was always just the two of us—it's like you need other people around to show you what you are.

"Food coma," Danny says, then gets up, standing over me and extending his hand. I take it, and he pulls me up. We stand close now, whereas we wouldn't have done this before; we stand so that the sides of us are touching.

"Should we jump?" he asks. "To wake up?"

"Yes," I say.

We walk to the edge, and before we jump, I look up at colorful Shangri La, the beautiful whites, blues, and ochers, how the ocean pool below seems to absorb these pigments. I imagine Doris Duke in this house, basking in the beauty or maybe saddened by the task of loving something alone. Danny takes my hand. I don't want to be anywhere else.

A few tourists stand at the railing, their cameras trained on us, and when we jump at the same time, I wonder what we look like, what they've captured, and how magic it seems, that we—that all of this—is in their tiny machines.

35

AFTER OUR LONG GETAWAY, WE GO BACK TO THE cottage so Danny can help my mom in the kitchen. I walk over to the big house. It's cool out, a nice trade wind, which seems to make the clouds march across the sky. When I go around back, I hear music coming from the house, and it transforms the familiar setting, elevating it to something momentous. I love the way Hawaiian music can outfit something or act like an undercurrent, carrying us all along, making me feel like I've been here before and will be here again.

I don't see Eddie at first, but then I see him by the gate, looking out at the ocean where a low froth of cloud has settled on the horizon. Bright orange sunlight shoots up and down.

He turns then and nods his head when he sees me, an approving, observant look, as if I were walking down a runway. When I get to his side, he says, "Your mom said you wanted to talk to me. I'm told you've been brought up to speed."

"Yes," I say. "She told me everything."

"About what now?" he asks. "I've forgotten."

My mouth is open. I need to fill it with words somehow. After being with Danny today, I was prepared to go in strong with my shoulders back. Instead I stand, hunched.

"I'm kidding with you," he says. "I'm still here. Still got it. I'm like a vampire. It comes at night mostly. As of now."

"I'm sorry," I say.

"Don't say you're sorry."

"I'm not sorry," I say, meeting his eyes.

"There you go," he says. "Now, that's refreshing."

But I am sorry. My mom told me that it could happen so quickly. I imagine him being swept off in a flood, but managing to stay afloat in its rapids for years, barely thinking, just grasping for air and solid ground.

"Thank you for taking care of me all these years." I'm losing control of my voice, and he looks at me quickly, detecting it.

"What have I done?" he asks, then I grin. He's kidding again.

"Thank you," I say, "for helping my mom."

"She deserved to be helped." He clears his throat, then takes a sip of his clear drink. "I'd like to keep helping if it would be of use to you."

Of course it would be of use.

"We don't need your help anymore," I say and hope it's true. "And then you won't have anything to hide. Why did you do it?"

He sighs, as if I were his own incorrigible child. A slice of his hair lifts in the wind, then falls like a wing.

"Because I could," he says.

I let that sink in, see if it satisfies. It does, mainly because of its simplicity and directness. Maybe it wasn't so complicated—just habit, like paying the electric bill.

"Are you in love with my mom?"

He laughs in a quiet and resigned way. "No," he says. "Maybe. When you're this old, you're in love with everything that happened a long time ago." He makes a diamond shape with his hands as if capturing a shot. "That's all set in amber. Easy to be nostalgic about old shit."

"Right," I say. "You don't have to be old to know that."

He looks my way as if someone new had appeared beside him and points his finger at my nose.

"I don't want Melanie to know that you've helped," I say, thinking that the information will make it onto her show if she ever makes the cut. How *wouldn't* she be able to make the cut? She's a perfect housewife. She's like a robot, looking at people and expertly scanning them for their worth and capabilities, their potential and their roots. She should really have a job. She'd be so good at it, anything from interior designer to venture capitalist. But she has taken this role as mother and wife and social entertainer like someone out of the past. She belongs in a different era.

"I don't want her to know either," he says, out to the ocean, a blue canvas, brushstrokes of whitecaps. "But sometimes I can't shut up."

Because she blamed me, blamed Danny, because she snared my mom like a bluefin tuna, because she basically casts her children's friendships and love lives, I boldly ask, "What does Melanie want?" I don't know how to say, *Why is she the way she is?* I truly want to know: how does one start out as a girl and become a woman like Melanie? Or a woman like Vicky, or the countless types who never seem to have sand between their toes. And why do their children seem to replicate them exactly?

I'm about to add to this when Eddie faces me with a hard look in his eyes. "We're who we are because of each other."

His tone is stern and unforgiving. It reminds me that I'm talking about his wife, the mother of his children, the woman he fell in love with. It also reveals that her faults, whatever I see them to be, are partly due to him. She became the woman she is while being married to him. At least I think that's what he's telling me. He seems done with the conversation now. Something has dulled in his gaze. He turns to the house and scans the yard lazily, contentedly, surveying a place he knows deeply. I do the same, for the first time realizing that I can be comfortable anywhere.

"We're moving out," I say.

"I know," he says. "But have your mother remind me," he winks. "And go find Whitney. She's lucky to have you."

He doesn't know a thing, I realize. About our falling-out, about Will, about dramas at the hotel, or dramas in his own backyard, and not because of his health but because it's not his job. Melanie does it all. Men like him are off the hook.

I walk with him back toward the house, but slowly make my way apart from him. "Thank you," I say again.

"You don't owe me anything," he says. We're at a distance now where we have to raise our voices. "Unless you want to," he says. "Make you work harder."

Something in his face kindly dismisses me, letting me go. He raises his hand in farewell.

36

I MAY BE THE ONLY PERSON ON CAMPUS RELIEVED THAT spring break's over. I watch Will walk out of money management and stop myself from going to him. He has yet to say anything, do anything. He's staying the course: money management to Jazz Age and the Lost Generation, home to change, then Waialae to golf. He will keep going in life; he'll keep staying out of it. Get into it! I want to yell to him and to everyone. What's the point of us otherwise?

My mom and I packed on Friday, were out by Sunday and back to our old place in Kailua. We drove out of Kahala in silence. The sky was bright and cheerful on the other side of the Pali tunnels, the ocean so vast yet familiar, like a backyard pool. It felt so weird to leave—a kind of sadness, and yet there was a sense of accomplishment. She felt it too, I think, a sweet fulfillment from not needing something anymore, from cutting off ties. There's something satisfying about leaving things behind, something invigorating about hard endings—the way they make you feel like you're growing or something. It's kind of like hiking to the top of the Pali with Danny. When I get to the top, it's difficult to move because of the strong wind, and yet I hike there to feel just that.

Whitney should be getting out of Geology of Hawaii and then I know she has Bollywood Dance for her ASPE credit. I walk toward the track to wait for her. I'll force her to talk to me, even though I don't know what will come of it.

I walk past the groups—the lacrosse boys heading to the field, the manga/anime club kids crowding over something on the bench by the art studio. This year is going by so quickly. When I think of myself as I first started out, I seem like another girl. So quiet and cautious. I acted like I didn't need or want anything, and now I want it all.

I have time to kill so I walk by the lily pond and watch the little kids squatting to see the tadpoles. After school, the campus takes on a second life with soccer and dance, volleyball and theater, all these things to make us well-rounded or tire us out.

Mike and Maile are strolling down from the chapel steps, and I wonder where they're coming from, or if they're just doing the same thing I'm doing. I walk back to the gym, far enough behind them, but close enough to note the way he is with her, deferential, soft, entirely different from the way he was with Whitney. You want to be the chill, cool girl, yet you don't. You'd rather someone just hold your hand.

I veer off at the end of the pool and wait at the bottom of the steps to the studio. I can hear the seniors practicing their graduation song—a song about unity and aloha, the bonds that will remain in their hearts. They harmonize, they project, and it brings tears to my eyes, as a live song will, the way when words are sung, they sound like a beautiful truth that can be lived.

About fifteen minutes later, they file out, and I feel like I'm watching graduation. Soon they'll be at the Blaisdell Arena, singing their songs, the girls in their white holoku dresses and haku leis, the boys in their suits and long maile leis draped around their necks. Ninety-nine percent of them off to college, off the rock of Oahu.

After they leave I'm alone with the sounds of clanking steel from the weight room next door, shouts and whistles from the track above, and then I hear doors from Forrest Hall open upstairs. A few girls walk down the steps and then there's Whitney walking by herself. She seems to be pondering something, or maybe she's just still in a zone. When she gets toward the bottom, I say, "Namaste," with a shrug, a smile, a look that says, *Can't we just get this over with?*

The lightness isn't returned. What's returned is a look that's hard and cold and, sadly, indifferent. She walks past me, leaving the scent of sweat and Lycra and that ubiquitous shampoo. I want to point out that I can see the bottom of her butt in those shorts, that if she fears becoming Rizzo, she better cover that ass.

"Whitney," I say, "come on."

She quickens her pace, and I do too, but then she ducks into the gym and I run to catch up. When I get there, she has stopped midway across the gym floor. There's a boys' volleyball game on the other side of the partition, so she has nowhere to go.

She looks to the other door, but maybe realizes how stupid this is. We're not going to play chase.

"What's up," she says, but doesn't pose it as a question. It's a demand: *tell me what you want.*

Her outfit makes me feel like I'm at an advantage. In her quick head-to-toe glance I see her approval of my gray skinny jeans and yellow, off-the shoulder tee. I've developed a bit of style, not from imitation, but by gathering things as I go. I look like I live here now. *I am who I am because of you,* I want to say, but never will.

"Talk if you're going to talk," she says. "I've got shit not to do."

She looks away, twisting her mouth to hide a smile.

The last time I was in this gym was for our walking exercise with the peer counselors. That feels like ages ago, different versions of us. The sound of sneakers screeching on the floor makes me want to play ball and eat candy.

"So much has happened," I say. "Let's . . . I don't know. Let's dissect."

I always hear the expression *That is so high school,* meaning that it's small or silly. I know that what is big now will be *so high school* later, but I'd like to think that it all matters, that it all adds up to something.

She looks at me warily.

"What happened?" I ask. "What did I do wrong? I'm sorry about Will, okay? But I wasn't using you to get to him."

She shrugs, widens her eyes, and I can tell she's decided to not relent.

"Come on," I say. "We don't have to be like this."

Sneakers screech on the floor next door. Whistles blow. I can hear grunting.

"Be like what?" she says. "I'm not doing anything. I don't want anything. What is it that you want?" She opens her arms, making me want to tackle her.

I take a deep breath. "Why didn't you tell your mom Danny didn't do anything?"

She looks away, guilty. "It's over already."

"I know, but it's lame you let your mom think that about him. Why him?"

"Don't worry," she says. "I've already told her I made it up. I told her it was Mike."

I didn't think she'd ever do that.

Whitney laughs. "But she says I don't have to make things up, and she's now convinced that room service gave me bad fish—all the radiation these days. You can't trust room service."

"No way," I say.

She absentmindedly kicks the gym floor. "*Oui,* way," she says. "She wouldn't dare blame Mike."

"Why'd you say it was Danny in the first place?" I ask.

She shrugs. "I don't know. It was an answer, and I guess I liked him and felt like shit when he dissed me. And then Maile came and Mike ditched me and . . . I just . . . did . . . and I was off the chain stoned. I thought my mom was a skinny walrus."

"Oh my God." I laugh, and she tucks her lips in and looks away.

"Well, thanks for telling her," I say.

"I was being like you," she says, finally looking at me. "Always doing the right thing."

"Obviously not," I say.

"My brother and Lissa go together like ham and cheese. He was totally using you."

"Maybe I was using him right back," I say, believing it. A kind of recognition shows in her expression. We're not pitiful. We have a say in all of this. Stupid but aware. Or not stupid at all. Just testing the waters. All of this can be used. Head to tail, the whole lot of it. Love, deception, pettiness, pain. Lust, mistakes, regret, triumph. We get to decide how to season and cook it.

"That's not very cool to Lissa," she says.

"I know," I say. "Or Maile."

"I know," she says softly.

"Well, there. We owned up to it," I say.

She imitates the peer counselors. "Own it," she says. "Make your mistakes your rocks. Stand on your rocks."

I can't help but smile a bit, and she does too, betraying herself.

I use her same tone. "Okay, peeps," I say. "Walk if you've sold someone out."

I feel like we're in a duel. I don't look away. I hear the noise of boys, spiking balls, making calls, a whistle, a cheer. I can smell sweat. I want so badly for her to play along.

"Come on," I say. Whitney looks ahead. "Walk."

She takes a step, then smiles in a contemptuous way that she can't maintain. She doesn't look at me when she says, "Sorry about Danny, okay? And sorry my parents are . . . whatever. What they are. Just—I know you moved out, and . . . sorry." She shakes her head, then begins to walk away.

"Walk if you're not your parents," I say. She stops, her back to me.

"Walk if you feel they're always going to be bigger than you." I take five steps. "I'm walking, by the way. Just so you know. Now walk if you know they love you and you don't need to live your life like it's your last and you can make your own path."

"That was a bit much," she says.

"So what?" I say. "I'm going to get all touchy-feely. Deal with it."

She leans onto one leg and crosses her arms.

"I don't know who my dad is," I say. "I do know that he had the Outrigger waitresses bring him his lunch while he sat in an anchored canoe. He made them wade out to him with his pork chops and Blue Hawaiian. He slept with tons of women while he was with my mom. He was like frickin' King Kamehameha, conquering a chain. But a total mainland haole. So King Cam-mie-ha-mee-ha."

She turns. It looks like she's biting the inside of her cheek.

"He doesn't know I exist," I say, and saying it out loud is hard. For the first time, I see this as being sadder for him than it is for me, and this makes me feel stronger.

"Sometimes I feel mine doesn't know I exist either," Whitney says. "I don't think he expects anything from me."

She plays with the end of her ponytail. It's so loud next door. Voices boom and echo, and we just stand here, quiet.

"Walk if you're ashamed sometimes," she says. "Just totally ashamed. Totally used. By boys, girls, everyone." She lifts her shirt to wipe her eyes, then walks, and I do too.

"Walk if you're a virgin," she says.

I walk. She doesn't.

"Walk if you don't necessarily want to be," I say, and I take five steps so that I'm closer to her. I continue, "Walk if you're so hot and a super-cute boy couldn't resist you."

She looks ahead again, walks, then says, "And expected you to keep doing it, and could hardly look at you after, and would always call his girlfriend from your room." She walks.

"And now you move on," I say. "Onto something new."

We're side by side now. I turn to face the same way she's facing.

"Walk if you miss your friend," she says. I could barely hear her, but I did.

We both take five steps.

"This is so cheesy," she says.

"I know. Go with it. Eat the *fromage.* Spread it on a cracker."

"Oh my God," she says. "You are so odd."

"Okay, my turn," I say. "Walk if you want to have a real friendship. No manipulation or lies or trying too hard. No being fake. No giving too much, no taking too much. Just be. We'll root for each other instead of bringing down."

We walk.

"And we'll never be on Hawaii Housewives," I add. "Unless you really want to. Then I'll support you. And watch you and make fun of you in the privacy of my own home."

We look over at each other, laugh, and wipe tears from our eyes.

"Walk if you'll be so embarrassed if someone is watching us right now," she says. We both jump forward. "And walk if you promise not to be one of those girls who blow kisses in photos. Or post daily bikini Instas."

"That's so seventh grade," I say. "Or take legsies by the pool—"

"That's the worst!"

"Or wait for guys," I say. "Promise we won't be one of those girls."

"Or be with guys who are with other girls," she says. "Mike is cut off."

"Good," I say. "He had an ugly penis anyway. Not that I've seen a pretty one or anything."

"Once again, you are a ball of oddness," she says.

We don't walk anymore—it feels like we're in a ceremony, saying our vows. Vows to ourselves and to friendship.

"Walk if you've OD'd on Betty Crocker," I say.

She grabs my hand and laughs. "Oh my God, that was seriously bad. I thought the pool was a big mouth. I was freaking the fuck out. Then mama walrus came, and that was the limit."

I laugh, watching her reenact her freaked-out face, and begin to sing "Summer Nights."

"Oh my God," she says. "Stop!"

We link elbows. "Okay, walk if you're bare . . . down there," I say.

"Whatever," she says, hitting me with her hip. "Walk if you're rockin' an Afro down there or if you lost your bathing suit bottoms jumping off a rock, rookie."

"Whatever," I say right back. "Walk if you scarf five tacos, then have seriously the worst gas I've ever smelled in my life."

She drags me toward the volleyball side.

"Walk if you've made out with your friend's brother!" she says. "Right in the open, like, moaning and shit!"

"Oh my God," I say and look down, unlink my arm from hers, and walk the walk of shame.

"So gross," she says. I feel the grossness, and yet it seems like a long time ago. Totally insignificant.

"His loss," she says, walking up next to me. "Love him, but he is so me, myself, and I." We're both quiet for a second.

"Okay, walk if once upon a time your mom and my dad probably did it!" she says.

We both squeal and groan. It's crazy that they were ever young.

"Walk if you're with Danny now," she says, raising her eyebrows.

I walk, so that she's behind me. "I saw you guys going up to the cottage. You looked so cute. So happy."

Sabrina comes to mind—the poor girl watching all the action from afar. But it's Whitney watching me. Sabrina's mistake was choosing the wrong brother. It's still like that, but this time it's a brother and a sister. I've made my mistake, and now I know which one deserves my loyalty and love.

"Does he have a pretty penis?" she asks, and I push her back and bite my lip.

"Walk if you want to go grind at Andy's," I say, walking back to her.

"Nom nom," she says.

"And surf."

"Or just mush." She slouches.

"Or go to the premiere with me tonight," I say.

"Really?" she says, her eyes lighting up. "I'd love to do that."

We face each other. "Are we done?" she asks.

"I think so," I say. "Should we group hug?"

"Okay," she says. We approach shyly, and then she clobbers me, and we do a kind of hugging wrestling move.

"I'm sorry," she says.

"Me too."

• • •

The campus is still busy. It's like everyone's training for the Olympics or something. We walk the length of the pool filled with swimmers and water polo players. Up ahead by the bench that circles the tree are some seniors, the eager type, voluntarily practicing their songs.

As a junior, I've always felt we were on the cusp of something so much better, but maybe this is the stronger state. Juniors are observant. We see how the leaders act and note what we'll do differently. We watch our so-called superiors, then do it better. It's kind of a good thing to take away—keeping yourself always on the verge of something, ready to reign while knowing that not everything gets left behind.

"I can't believe it's almost graduation," Whitney says.

"I was just thinking that," I say. "Are you nervous?"

"Yeah," she says. "Nervous I won't get into college anywhere and I'll have to work at 7-Eleven."

"So. Free Slurpees. You'll get in somewhere."

We get quiet, maybe both thinking of the future: our summer—the jumps and risks we'll take, the books we'll read, the friends we'll see, the meals we'll make. My time with Danny before he goes to college, her time with her family, then the year after that. Juniors to seniors, confident and afraid. On the edge and ready to jump across the ocean to college. I can see it, and I can't see it at all. Who knows what will happen?

We get to the end of the pool, then pass the ramp that leads up to the track. I remember my first day here, walking on the zigzag ramp, trying to find my Children's Studies class by the gymnastics room. I went up and down, passing people who knew exactly where they were going and pretending I did too. It's so much better not having to pretend.

We walk past the gate and out to the street, then wait at the light, cars speeding by, moving my hair and shirt.

"You could have taken Danny tonight," she says.

"He wouldn't have liked it as much." I smile to myself. "We're going out tomorrow night."

"So sweet," she says. "You should oof him."

"Shaddup."

I look back at the rock wall lined with the night-blooming cereus that Will told me about.

"I need to come here at night to see."

She follows my gaze to the wall of cacti and closed petals. "It's really nice," she says and keeps looking at them. "Cute how they tuck themselves in during the day. We can come back later tonight. After the premiere?"

"Perfect," I say.

I see us from a distance then, and everything becomes so simple: two girls going home, waiting for the light to change, then tonight: two girls in a car, driving by their school to see flowers bloom. We'll be two girls on a small island in the Pacific Ocean, listening to music, moving forward, moving on, so happy in the moment, wanting to stay in it, and yet ever ready to become.

ACKNOWLEDGMENTS

THANK YOU TO MY TEACHERS AT PUNAHOU, MY SCHOOL from kindergarten to graduation. I recall being semi-disruptive and argumentative, attention-seeking, and sassy. Yet for some reason you interpreted my antics as creative, funny, and unique. Thank you—those words are so much better. Your support was palpable and motivational—it made me want to prove you were right.

Asha Appel, Brad Yates, Dr. Kerwin, Mr. Earle, Mr. Tsujimoto, Mr. Woody, Paul Hamamoto, Ms. Kulp, Flo Van Dyke, Steve Wagenseller, Ms. Sakbun, Ken Smith, Mr. Luckenbach and Ms. Vincent-Lum, Mrs. Yap, Mr. Georgi, Mr. Tuttle, Mr. Torrey, Mrs. Byrne, Ms. McKibbin, Ms. Patton, and the list goes on . . . Mahalo.